W9-AML-740

Praise for national bestselling author
Anne Calhoun

"Entertaining [and] entirely satisfying."
—*Publishers Weekly*

"Anne Calhoun delivers a steamy, intense story
that tugs at your heart."
—Jill Shalvis, *New York Times* bestselling author

"Anne Calhoun's writing offers emotional
intensity, wicked hot sex scenes, and characters
that pull at your heart strings."
—Beth Kery, *New York Times* bestselling author

"Scintillating sexual chemistry, wonderfully
drawn characters—a total winner."
—Lauren Dane, *New York Times* bestselling author

"One of the best."
—Sarah Wendell, *Kirkus Reviews*

Also by Anne Calhoun

Going Deep
Under the Surface

The SEAL's Secret Lover
The SEAL's Rebel Librarian
The SEAL's Second Chance

TURN ME LOOSE

Anne Calhoun

St. Martin's Paperbacks

To Jeffe, for her friendship.

To Sassy, for her courage.

As always, to Mark, for love.

ACKNOWLEDGMENTS

With gratitude to Sassy Outwater for her generous and frank insights into the mind-set of a young man diagnosed with cancer, and to Cynthia for explaining the consequences faced by a student with a serious illness while enrolled at a military academy. I've adapted both situations to fit the story; any mistakes are mine. Jeffe Kennedy provided a much-needed late read on a tight timetable and came up with gold. Thank you.

CHAPTER ONE

Seven years earlier . . .

Past midnight, but Kaffiend Coffee House hummed like a train station at rush hour, packed with students studying and socializing in equal measures. Riva held her hand over her coffee cup when the waitress came by. Rereading her econ assignment pushed her past the point of diminishing returns. Another half an hour to review her American History reading response paper, and then she'd call it a night. "Just the check, please," she said.

Without a word the waitress moved off, refilling cups as she worked her way back to the counter. The bell over the door dinged, and Riva looked up.

The man standing in the doorway wore a Lancaster College T-shirt, faded jeans, ankle-high brown motorcycle boots, and a really nice jacket, a leather moto deal she knew was expensive because the thin leather

clung to his shoulders. Long fingers wrapped around
the strap of his backpack slung over his shoulder, his
helmet dangling from his thumb as he scanned the
tables, looking for an empty seat. Riva watched him
for a moment. He was tall, a little thin, older than the
rest of the crowd. Her brain jumped through under-
classman to senior before settling on grad student, one
she hadn't seen here before.

His gaze caught hers. Electric shock, a spark of
something that made her aware of her heartbeat, its
newly irregular rhythm. His gaze lingered just a second
before moving on, and she was grateful she'd done the
full hair and makeup routine before leaving her room.
Despite the late hour, the wood-paneled room was
packed with nervous students cramming for midterms,
some of them looking for a little something to keep them
going, others looking for a little something to calm them
down so they could sleep. Two months into her college
career and she already had a reputation for providing
quality product: pills to sleep or stay awake, a little
weed, something for the pain. She'd made four sales
tonight, quick deals either in the ladies room or in the
alley behind Kaffiend, where people stepped outside to
smoke. She'd have good news to report when she
checked in.

Another heart-skittering moment of eye contact,
this time with a heated glint in his eye that threw his
motivations into question. Was he looking to score
from her, or with her? The seat across from her was
open, and the owner encouraged table sharing. Maybe
he just wanted a place to sit. Maybe he'd want to sit
next to her.

She glanced down at her open textbook, counted to

ten, then looked again. Wham, this time a full-body electric jolt, and he looked away first. Maybe it wasn't her product he wanted, but her.

The thought made her heart pound.

A moment later he found a table being vacated by a guy Riva recognized from her Principles of Marketing class and sat down. The process of settling himself involved textbooks—Analytical Philosophy, something by Kant—a laptop, an order for coffee, and another glance Riva's way. A little thrill skittered over her nerves; this time she offered a smile. For a second he didn't smile back, and Riva wondered if she'd misunderstood his intention. But then the corners of his mouth curved up, revealing a deep, long crease on either side of his mouth. Mentally she revised his age upward a couple of years, to PhD student, and she couldn't look away if her life depended on it.

His gaze darkened. He shifted in his chair. Maybe he was shy. He had the unassuming demeanor hot nerds usually had, like their good looks didn't factor into their self-awareness at all. Feeling bold, she got up and paid her bill at the counter, then walked back to his table, where he was hunched over the textbook.

"Hi."

"Hi," she said. Up close he looked even more vulnerable, a little pale, his hair tumbling over his forehead. Her heart was flicking against her throat. "I saw you watching me."

He flushed. The skin over his cheekbones actually turned pink. "Yeah. I guess I was pretty obvious."

"I guess I was pretty flattered," she replied.

His gaze sharpened, snared hers. "Yeah?"

"Yeah. Riva Henneman."

"Ian Fallon." He held out his hand, which made her laugh even as she shook it. "Have a seat."

She sat, letting her bag slump to the floor at her feet. "Interesting reading you've got there."

He looked down at the textbook, smeared with blue highlighter, notes in pencil along the margins. "It's okay. You?"

"Intro to Econ and American History," she said, hardly knowing whether she was making sense. The chemistry between them was sparking, making her skin hypersensitive, her cheeks flush. "I'm a first year. I'll probably major in business but the history fulfills a requirement."

He nodded, like he knew all about that. "You have Kessler?"

"No, Rosenberg."

"She's good."

"I like the class."

Another searing look brought the conversation to a halt. Ian glanced at the door as it opened, then said, "I heard you could get me something I need."

Her smile disappeared under a wave of disappointment. "Did you?" she said, striving for a light tone.

"Yeah."

"Like what?"

"E."

"Not today," she said.

"Pot?"

"Those are two drastically different chemical results in your body, Ian."

"I like to cover all my bases. Help me out here. I've tried a couple of other guys, Brian Deluca and what's his name, Sammy from Hamilton, but they were out."

Sammy and Brian were the two other go-to guys on campus, and her competition, such as it was. Brian was set to graduate, and Sammy was lazy as hell, buying product mostly to be sure he had a constant supply for himself. Ian obviously knew his way around Lancaster College's drug scene. "Okay. Meet me out back in five."

Riva sidled past the line of people waiting for the restroom, opened the door into the alley, and stepped out into the cool October night. She leaned against the brick wall and inhaled deeply. The dumpster reeked of coffee grounds but the cool air kept the worst of the trash stench to a minimum.

The door opened again, and Ian stepped through. The light above the door cast stark shadows, hiding his face and eyes. Riva's nerves jerked into high alert. He had angled himself so he stood between her and the doorway as well as the opening at the end of the alley.

"How much?"

She named her price, just wanting this over so she could get back to the business of asking him out.

"No problem," he said, reaching into his front pocket.

She unzipped her backpack and pulled out a baggie containing an ounce of marijuana, waited while he thumbed through the cash in his wallet, then handed it over. She gave him the bag.

Without letting go, she reached into her messenger bag pocket and pulled out a pen, then turned his hand palm up and wrote her number on his palm.

"To save you the trouble of asking," she said, looking up at him through her lashes. This could still go either way, but either way, he'd need her number.

"That'll come in handy," he said.

Delighted, she grinned. He was gorgeous, all man, and obviously smart. The books lacked the used sticker, so the creases and scuffs were all his. No one read that stuff that frequently, for fun. "Call me anytime."

He shoved the wallet into his jeans pocket, then reached behind his back. Steel glinted in the light over the door, and for a terrified split second she thought he'd pulled a knife on her.

A click echoed off the watching brick as he flipped the curved pieces of metal apart. It wasn't a knife. It was a pair of handcuffs. "Riva Henneman, you're under arrest."

CHAPTER TWO

Present day . . .

"Okay, team, huddle up."

The evening birdsong trilled through the screen door as servers, chefs, sous chefs, and the night's hostess gathered around Riva. She leaned against the prep table and scanned their faces, checking in with each kid. They were enrolled in the East Side Community Center's Teen Cuisine program, getting training on all aspects of a restaurant's operations. Kiara, the night's hostess, came in last, pen and paper poised to write down the night's menu before transferring it to the chalkboard intended for the front porch.

"Run it down for me, Chef Isaiah," Riva said.

Proud of his lead role in the kitchen, Isaiah straightened. "We have three mains today: the usual rib eye and chicken, and the special, salmon seared in a sauce of shallots and grapefruit, accompanied by asparagus and potatoes roasted in garlic, rosemary, and olive oil. Appetizers are the usual bruschetta, plus mussels, and we have brussels sprouts roasted in olive oil with bacon and onions."

Riva nodded approvingly. He'd come a long way from the kid who couldn't tell a brussels sprout from a stalk of asparagus. "Anyone have any questions about preparation? All of the greens are from the early plantings at the farm, so they're nice and tender. We'll substitute ingredients from the other farm-to-table suppliers when we run out of our own stuff."

Her dream was to eventually quadruple her greenhouse space, enabling her to start planting earlier in the season and supply not just her restaurant but others in the area. One step at a time. Take it slow, grow organically, and, most important, without drawing any attention to herself.

"Where's the salmon from?" Amber asked.

"Alaska. Wild caught and flown in yesterday," Isaiah said without prompting. Amber made a note on her server's pad. "It's as fresh as you're gonna get in landlocked Lancaster."

"What do you recommend?" Kiara asked.

"It's all good," Isaiah said, "but if anyone asks, go with the salmon."

"What are we gonna eighty-six first?"

"The salmon," Isaiah said. He extended his hand over the large cast-iron pan heating on the eight-burner stove, the movement automatic, practiced. "Early bird gets the worm tonight. Dessert is ice cream from Blackstone Creamery. Chocolate, vanilla, mint chocolate chip."

"Thanks, Isaiah," Riva said. "I'll come around one

last time to check your stations. I'm working the front tonight, so you guys are on your own."

Subtle signs of tension rippled through the group. "You've got this. It's a Tuesday night, so we won't be very busy, but even if we were, even if we got slammed by Maud Ward and her entire entourage, you'd still have this," Riva said. "Work your station, and work together."

Kimmy-Jean, a newer addition to the program, worried at her lower lip. "What if no one comes?"

In the spring Oasis operated on a pop-up basis, opening on selected evenings and promoted through social media only. "They'll come," Isaiah said. "You just worry about getting your mise done, yo."

She walked through the kitchen, swiping up a bit of spilled parmesan, adding extra bowls to Carlos's station, making sure the bus boy/dishwasher, Blake, had his trays lined up and ready to go. She ran through another checklist out front. The tables were all neatly set, silverware wrapped in linen, bud vases with a single bloom and small votive candles centered between the settings. She'd learned how to set a beautiful table from her mother on the rare occasions when she surfaced from a fog of Xanax or Cymbalta to host one of the social events her father insisted would strengthen and expand his network of business contacts. Lately during their phone calls her mother had been nervous, speaking in a whisper when her father was in the room, unable to maintain a train of thought even when he wasn't. Riva was worried; her mother had always been high-strung, nervous, talkative, and always moving, never quiet.

She set aside her worries about her mother and focused on the people she could help right now. "Let's not light the candles just yet," she said to Kiara.

The front was designed to look like a large, screened-in porch, the glass windows folded back to open the room to the breezes drifting in from the eastern fields, carrying a scent of warm earth and tender, growing things. The walls were covered in weathered barn boards, the tables made from smaller pieces reclaimed when she'd torn down the outbuildings that were ruined beyond repair. The server's station was just outside the kitchen, making it easy for the staff to grab a pitcher of water or a damp rag as they passed through.

Looking around, Riva couldn't believe she'd made this herself, supervised the renovation, done most of the interior work and decorating herself, scavenged and bargain shopped, painted walls and built tables. She'd come a long way in the last seven years, and the farm and restaurant were only stage one of her business plan.

When the first customers arrived, a couple of minutes before the restaurant officially opened, Kiara guided them to a table near the west windows, overlooking the back fields rolling down to the river. Riva lit their candle and offered them the menu. "Do you want the windows shut?" the man asked his date. He was obviously anxious, taking out his phone and silencing the ringer, setting it on the table, then putting it in a pocket.

"I'm good," she said, giving him a pleased smile. "The air's still pretty warm. Maybe later."

"I'll be back in a minute with your drinks," Riva said, then looked up as the door opened again.

The evening progressed smoothly, just as Riva predicted. Tuesday nights weren't big evenings in the restaurant business, so she used them to give the kids a chance to get used to running both the front and back of the house before giving them charge over a busy summer Saturday night.

The program was a simple one, developed in conjunction with the East Side Community Center run by Pastor Webber. Get kids who'd grown up in the impoverished, blighted neighborhoods so common to food deserts access to fresh air, sunshine, and the earth. Teach them to grow their own food, and cook it, which enabled Riva to teach them about healthy eating. It also meant Riva could give back, pay for the mistakes she'd made, help other kids avoid the same mistakes.

Working in the front let things develop organically, for better or worse, in the kitchen. She liked waiting tables. Most of the recipes were her own, and getting feedback directly from customers enabled her to fine tune accordingly. It meant she was close if the kids really needed her, but not watching like one of the hawks circling over a field, ready to pounce on every single mistake.

The sun hung heavy over the tops of the cottonwood trees when Riva started lighting the candles on the unoccupied tables. She automatically looked up when the door opened and saw a single man standing there, his face hidden by the shadows. Tall and lean, he was nothing but a silhouette of a male figure in a suit, nothing that should have made her heart *thunk* hard against her chest and adrenaline dump into her nervous system. All her muscles screamed at her to drop the box of matches and bolt.

Don't be ridiculous, her brain told her body.

Then he took another step forward, far enough into the light for Riva to see his face. She knew she should have trusted her body, but by then it was too late.

Officer Hawthorn stood in her restaurant.

Kiara approached him, menu in hand. Riva couldn't hear their conversation over her blood thrumming in her ears, but she could decipher it well enough based on the way he looked around, then the way Kiara extended her arm.

She'd seated him in Riva's section. A two top, in the corner. He always sat with his back to the wall. Riva remembered that well enough from seven years earlier. The table gave him a view of all entrances, doors, and the parking lot.

"Blaze on table fourteen," Kiara said to Riva, using the kitchen's slang for a hot customer.

Riva stifled a hysterical laugh. Ian Hawthorn was a blaze in every sense of the word, hot, and so dangerous she should turn and run. She could ask someone else to take the table. It wasn't a practice she encouraged, as it led to confusion in the restaurant, and there was no advantage to it for the kids. All tips were pooled and split among the kitchen staff and servers at the end of the night. They worked for one another, not just for themselves.

Worse, if she asked another server to take the table, the kids would wonder why. In milliseconds, they'd peg Hawthorn for a cop and start asking questions that would lead them to her past, to the mistakes she'd made, to the girl she'd left behind. Right now her goal was to serve him and get him out of the restaurant before anything happened to jeopardize the life she'd built.

Besides, it had to happen sometime, meeting him again. She'd been dreading this for the last seven years. Might as well get it over with, so she could move on. He was her past; this was her future.

Shoulders squared, she took a deep breath and let it out slowly, then plucked her notebook from her apron as she walked to the table. "Welcome to Oasis. My name's Riva and I'll be taking care of you tonight."

The look on his face when she started talking was almost worth what it cost her to walk across the floor and talk to him. His jaw literally dropped open.

Priceless.

Then his gaze skimmed her from her ponytail to the tips of her clogs. She knew how it looked, wearing the same uniform as the other servers, black pants and blouse buttoned to her collarbone, her makeup subdued to the point of pale and nondescript. In every way she was conscious of setting an example for the kids from the ESCC. His reaction time, always quick, hadn't dulled. A split second to look her over, the sharp flick of his gaze striking sparks she felt from her earlobes to her nipples to deep in her belly. That's what it had been like, his gaze flint against the tinder of her young, impetuous desire.

Then he shut his mouth, and the laptop bag. "Hi, Riva."

She ignored that. "Can I get you something to drink while you look at the menu? We have craft beers from several of the local breweries."

He looked at the menu, then back at her. "Water. Thanks."

She nodded, then spun on her heel and walked away. The look in his eyes before he adopted the all-too-familiar expressionless demeanor had been shock, then pity. When she'd met him she'd been a college student. Now, to his eyes, she was a waitress. Worse, her standard greeting—*I'll be taking care of you today*—sounded like an innuendo. God knew she'd thrown enough of them at him, desperate, angry, pushing back the only way she could. He'd held all the cards, and she'd hated him for it.

"It was your fault," she muttered as she poured ice water into a glass. "You were the stupid one. He just did his job."

"What?" Kiara said.

A second wash of fear coursed over Riva, because the only thing worse than Ian showing up in her restaurant would be the kids she helped now learning why she reacted to him the way she did. "Nothing," she said quickly. "Just talking to myself. It's a sign of old age."

"You're not that old," Kiara said.

Twenty-five. Twenty-five years old. Seven years older than when she met him, old enough now . . .

She forced herself to smile. "How are you doing?"

"It's a little boring tonight," Kiara said.

"You could top off the sugars and stock silverware early and close the windows. It's getting a little chilly in here. We don't want food getting cold so quickly the guests can't enjoy it."

"Yes, ma'am," Kiara said. Riva snagged a warm bread basket from the kitchen and used the trip to ensure everything was running smoothly. "We still have the salmon?"

"Got plenty," Isaiah called from the stove.

When she came back out, Hawthorn was staring at his laptop screen. She set the bread basket on the table. "Are you waiting for someone?" He had to be waiting for someone.

"No. Just me."

He's alone. Why is he alone? Her heart did a traitorous little skip in her chest. She gathered the silverware and bread plate from the spot across from him. "Do you have any questions about the menu? We're a farm-to-table restaurant," she started, taking refuge in the standard patter. "The origins for the ingredients are noted on the menu. With the exception of the salmon, they're all from Rolling Hill Farm, or other farms around Lancaster. The rib eye comes from a ranch up the road. We harvested the asparagus this afternoon, and the brussels sprouts this morning."

His gaze was no less piercing, seven years later. "What do you recommend, Riva?"

He used her first name like he always had, like he had a right. That option was never available to her.

Assuming his tastes hadn't changed in the last seven years, she knew what he liked well enough to answer that question. Nights sitting next to him in an unmarked police car often included a run through a drive-thru window, so she knew he preferred grilled chicken to burgers, salads to fries. She'd spent enough time with cops to know their diets were frequently atrocious; the Eastern Precinct smelled of sweat, gun oil, coffee, and fast-food grease. "The steak is our specialty, and very good, but tonight I'd recommend the salmon. Chef Isaiah developed the sauce. It's a grapefruit-and-shallot sauce, very light, and it's delicious."

"Does it come with the asparagus?"

"Yes."

"I'll have that."

"Wine with the meal? Beer?"

He scanned the wines listed on the back. "A glass of the Shale white," he said.

Dismissed. She hurried to the kitchen and put in the

order, then poured a glass of wine. Shale was a local winery, and he obviously knew their reputation. Trying not to think about Ian taking a date on a local winery tour, she left the glass with him, touched base with her other tables, and brought more bread and a second beer to the first-date couple, who had both set aside their phones and were leaning over the table, actively engaged in conversation. She watched them from the safety of the server's station. It was an experience she hadn't allowed herself in seven years, and the reason why was sitting at table fourteen. Any relationship more serious than a casual hookup would require her to either tell the truth about what she'd done or to found a relationship on lies. She couldn't bring herself to do either.

With no appetizer, his meal should be ready in under twelve minutes. At the ten-minute mark she ducked into the kitchen. Isaiah meticulously wiped a dab of sauce from the edge of the plate, then presented it to her with a flourish. She gave the kitchen staff a thumbs-up, took the plate from him, and carried it through the door.

On the way to the table she ran through the ways she could tell him he was wrong about her, that she wasn't just a waitress—except there was nothing wrong with being a waitress—that she owned this building, the farm it sat on, and the tiny house hidden in the folds of the valley, too, that she'd been able to get loans, pay them back on time, help others. But in the end, she couldn't change the past, and she knew perfectly well that of all people, Officer Ian Hawthorn had no reason to give her the benefit of the doubt.

She set the plate in front of him without comment. "Can I get you anything else?"

"No. Thanks." He picked up his knife and fork.

"I'll be back to check on you in a few minutes."

The first-date couple ordered two bowls of ice cream drizzled with hot, dark chocolate and topped with raspberries. Head held high, she walked to the first-date couple's table and set out their desserts. "Enjoy," she said with a smile.

As she walked away from the table, determinedly not looking at Ian, her phone buzzed with an incoming call. *Mom Home* lit up the screen, along with a picture of her mother holding Sugar, her teacup Yorkie. As always, Riva's heart gave a glad little leap when she saw the picture. As always, she shunted the delight aside, and the regrets, too. They would return in the middle of the night, when she was alone, and, for the thousandth time, trying to figure out a way to have any kind of relationship with her mom.

Setting a good example for her staff, she silenced the call. Except the phone rang again. Immediately. The universal signal for bad news.

"Hi, Mom," Riva said. "What's up?"

"Hi, dear. Are you busy?" her mother asked in a high, tremulous voice.

"We're in the middle of the dinner shift," Riva said, looking around the front. No new customers, everyone else served. She plastered a smile on her face, knowing it would come through in her voice. "I've got a minute, though."

"Of course you're busy with the restaurant. I was going to ask . . . but I should have thought of that. Never mind."

"Ask me what?"

"You know the auxiliary is raising funds for the drug treatment center at the hospital?"

"Yes," she said. Her mother had mentioned it on one of their infrequent calls a few months earlier.

"I'm not on the steering committee, only the leadership committee, but I was asked to host a thank-you luncheon for all the committee members. It's a big honor, so much responsibility, and would be so helpful to your father's business. I was going to ask you if you'd come home and help me plan it, but you're too busy. Stupid me should have thought of that," she said, scolding herself in a way that was all too familiar to Riva.

This definitely wasn't the sort of emergency Riva had in mind. Her father's reputation could indeed benefit from the connections a successful luncheon would bring, but Riva couldn't be less interested in making tarragon chicken salad and tea sandwiches for the Memorial Hospital Women's Guild. Riva tucked the phone between her cheek and her shoulder, and went to lower the blinds on the west windows. "You're not stupid. When's the luncheon?" she asked automatically.

"A few days from now. It's not much notice. I'm sorry."

Riva rubbed her forehead. Of the three members of their family, her mother had the least to be sorry for, and yet every other sentence out of her mouth was an apology. "Mom, I wish I could, but we're gearing up for the busy season at the farm, and I've got a new group of kids learning the kitchen."

"I know. Your life is in Lancaster, not Chicago. I wasn't going to call, but you haven't been home in so long . . ."

Seven years, to be exact. A fist closed around Riva's heart and squeezed just enough to let her know she wasn't as unfeeling as she'd hoped to be. "I know, Mom. I'll get home. Just not right now."

"I wish I understood why."

And Riva wished her mother would never, ever know why. "It's no big deal," she lied. "I just got busy here."

A stifled sob came through the line. "Mom? What's wrong?"

"It's Sugar. She's not doing well."

This was definitely an emergency. Since the day they brought the teacup Yorkie home from the breeder, Sugar was never more than a few feet from her mother, and more often than not, in her purse or her lap. Fussing over Sugar was one of the few good memories Riva had with her mother, but her father thought Sugar was worse than useless. "Oh, no," she said.

"Your father says I need to start thinking about . . . you know . . . but I can't. I can't think about that!" she ended with a hiccupping sob.

"Mom, I'm so sorry," she started, when a couple of short yelps from the kitchen were followed by an "Oh fuck!" audible throughout the dining room. The swinging door to the kitchen slammed against the wall, Kiara flying through it. Riva's nose knew first, the stench of acrid smoke already filtering into the room. Her body was already turning for the kitchen by the time her mouth caught up to say "I'll call you back" to her mother.

"Fire!" Kiara gasped.

Three strides and Riva was through the door. A grease fire roared on the stove, spattering everyone in the vicinity with burning oil. Isaiah was on his knees in front of the big stainless-steel stove. Beside him, Jake swatted at it with his dishtowel, the surest way to injure himself.

"Stop!" Riva barked.

He stopped.

"It's a grease fire," she said. A small one, at that, but fire was fire. Her voice was calm, only slightly louder than normal, but it got the attention of every kid in the room. "Work the plan. Step one."

Galvanized, Jake scrabbled at the knob controlling the gas heat and first turned it up. "Shit," he said when the flames spurted for the range hood. He twisted the knob the other direction and the gas died.

Kimmy-Jean had a big water pitcher filled. Arm extended, Riva stepped in front of her. "Step two."

"I'm on it." Isaiah came up with the right lid and slammed it down on the pan, effectively throttling the flames. Oily black smoke hung around the now-silenced stove.

"Good job. It was a small fire, so what else would have worked?" Riva said.

"Baking soda. Lots of it," Jake said.

"Kimmy-Jean, get some, please."

Kimmy-Jean flung the pitcher into the sink and leaped for the shelf of baking ingredients. Brandishing a large box, she turned and looked at the ominous pan.

"Isaiah, lift the lid. Kimmy-Jean, be ready." The fire, as she expected, was entirely smothered. "If the lid hadn't smothered the flames, dump lots and lots and lots of baking soda on it. But that only works for small fires. What don't you do?"

"Pick up the pot." Three of the kids responded. She had them now, back in their brains and bodies, connected to themselves, one another, her. "You'll burn yourself," Kiara added.

"Good. What else don't you do?"

"Throw water on it."

"Why?"

"Because water won't put it out, and the splatter can spread the flames or burn someone."

"Sorry," Kimmy-Jean whispered, her pale face flaming almost as brightly as the fire had. "I didn't know."

"Now you do," Riva said gently. "This one didn't spread. What if it had?"

"Fire extinguisher," Kiara said.

As one, everyone in the kitchen turned to look at the brand-new extinguisher, hanging on the wall beside the door to the dining room.

Where Ian Hawthorn stood, just inside the door, his laptop clasped loosely in his hand.

All the air sucked back out of the room, like he was the still center of a black hole. "Po-po in the house," someone murmured.

Riva turned her back on him, ignored him in favor of the important teaching moment. "Jake, will you please demonstrate how to use the fire extinguisher?"

Giving Hawthorn the side-eye, Jake pulled the extinguisher from the bracket. "Pull the pin, aim at the fire, using sweeping motions," he said, demonstrating like a cabin attendant, ending with a flourish. The rest of the kids giggled nervously.

Isaiah poked at the pan's contents. "These brussels sprouts are, like, bricks." He held the pan out, showing the room the burnt husks in what was left of the grease.

"Clean the pan out, Isaiah, and start again. Where are we with the orders?"

"One more salmon and a rib eye to go out."

"On the fly," she said, but Isaiah was already in motion. "Whose table is it?"

"Mine," Lucy said.

"Go back, explain the delay, tell them we're comping their meals, and offer a glass of wine or dessert on the house. Quick in," she said, waving her hands to draw everyone in. "Nobody got hurt. We're all ok. You've got this."

She gave Isaiah an extra pat on the back and Kimmy-Jean a hug. After inspecting the stove for spilled grease, she directed Jake to wipe it down carefully while Isaiah scoured clean the pan. Hopefully, if she ignored him, he would get the message that everything was under control.

But when she turned around, he was still standing there, like he had every right to be in her kitchen without permission. The front staff had sidled past him, returning to their work. Riva walked right up to him. She'd fooled herself into thinking she'd forgotten what he looked like, that time had faded her memories of his face. But here, in the kitchen's bright light, she saw him like it was the first time and like they'd been apart for seven years.

His hair was dark brown, no hint of red or blond to the fine strands, and cut shorter than when she'd first met him. His eyes were too dark to be green, too light to be brown, and as shuttered as ever. The twin grooves bracketing his mouth were deeper, better suited to his face. Back then he'd been too youthful for the lines—and the eyes—to make sense. Now, it was as if the rest of him had aged to catch up, a web of fine lines visible by his eyes.

All this she saw in the blink of an eye, enough time for her animal brain to register impressions and send another bolt of desire along her nerves.

She covered with belligerence bordering on rudeness, keeping her voice down for the sake of the kids. "What are you doing here?"

"I smelled smoke and came to help."

She almost laughed. Almost. "We don't need help," she enunciated. "Please return to your table."

He didn't have to move. She knew that. He pointed, she walked. He insisted, she gave in. He judged, she swallowed her pride. Seven years ago, he'd held all the power in his hand, because helping him was the only thing that stood between her and prison. She'd resented him with every cell in her body, and wanted him just as badly.

And all the while a red-hot tension simmered inside her.

His gaze searched her face, unflinching, as if he were unaware of everything she'd thought and felt. Of course he was. He'd used her to get what he wanted, seen her as nothing more than a college student looking to make a few extra bucks dealing pot and pills from her dorm room.

Heart pounding in her chest, she extended her arm, indicating he should go back to the dining room. It was bravado, a last ditch effort to impose her will on him. To her utter shock, he turned and went. She gave him a moment to settle himself back at his table, then approached.

"Can I get you anything else tonight? Some dessert?"

"No, thanks. Just the bill."

"Your meal is on the house," she said.

He paused in the act of angling his laptop into the protective slot in his bag. "That's not necessary."

"I appreciate your willingness to help," she said.

"That's my job." He meant running toward fire, gunshots, people in trouble. Or people making trouble. Like she had. "Most people panic, or freeze. You did well in there."

She took a deep breath, because times had changed, but no good ever came from snapping at a cop. "Again, I appreciate your willingness to help and would like to thank you by comping your meal. I'd also appreciate it if this was your last visit to Oasis."

His gaze flickered over her face, then down while he finished zipping the laptop bag. "That's a shame. The food was really good."

He stood up, shouldered the bag, and walked out. She picked up his plate and found two twenties tucked under the edge.

Damn him.

She slid the folded bills into her apron pocket and cleared the table. In the kitchen she put the money into the tip jar to be shared equally among the staff at the end of the night. In the middle of the comforting, familiar noise and smells, she inhaled, hoping to catch the scent of fresh greens, seared salmon, or even freshly scooped ice cream.

Instead she caught only the acrid stench of scorched possibilities.

CHAPTER THREE

Seven years ago . . .

Riva Henneman shifted in her seat, the handcuffs obviously biting into her wrists. She'd been in the interview room alone for less than ten minutes, but without a clock to gauge time, it could feel like moments, or hours. The room was featureless, no clock, no windows except the one looking out into a squad room. Ian watched her through the interview room's one-way glass and tried to gauge her emotional and mental state. The bright-eyed, pink-cheeked coed from Kaffiend had disappeared, leaving behind a pale, silent girl who looked far too young for Ian to feel what he'd felt when he'd walked through the coffee shop's door and made eye contact with her.

"How did a girl like that end up one of the biggest dealers on campus?"

Jo's tone made the question rhetorical, but in the

end, Ian didn't give a damn. Riva was nothing more than a stepping stone to the bigger fish he intended to fry in court.

"Are you sure she's old enough she doesn't need a parent or guardian?" Jo asked.

He'd run her Illinois license through the database. No priors, no tickets, birthday the preceding June. "She's eighteen," he said.

"She made her phone call," Jo said. "Whoever she called, the conversation was short."

Great. Now he needed to convince the girl and her lawyer to take his deal. He needed an informant to wear a wire and record evidence against the suppliers distributing drugs to the college ring he was going to bust to add some shine to his record before the next round of promotions came up. His best bet sat in the interview room, the florescent lights unable to dull the reddish gleam in her hair.

"Let me know when the lawyer shows up," Ian said, and walked out of the observation room.

Riva looked up when he opened the door and set the folder he was carrying on the table. He'd shucked his leather moto jacket but still wore the Lancaster College T-shirt, adding the symbols of his job: badge, gun, handcuff case on the back of his jeans. Empty, because Riva was wearing them. Her gaze flicked at his forearms and wrists, then his chest. Anything to avoid looking at the gun, or his face.

"How are you doing?"

At that her gaze met his without flinching. "Fine."

"Want something to drink?"

"No. Thank you," she added, a reluctant courtesy.

Jo had underestimated her. Anger simmered under the fear.

"Let's take off those cuffs."

He couldn't help but touch her as he did, noting automatically the way she leaned away from him, the rigid set to her muscles when his fingers brushed her wrists. He'd tried to stay dispassionate, but there was an unavoidable intimacy to all of this. He folded them and tucked them back into the case at the small of his back, all the while watching Riva. Small talk wasn't getting him anywhere, so he kept silent as he took the seat across from her, opened the file folder, made a couple of notes. "How long until your lawyer arrives?" he asked, keeping his tone offhand and casual to downplay the offer.

"I didn't call a lawyer."

"Do you want a public defender?" he asked, doing the right thing against his better judgment.

"No."

Her voice was oddly tight. When he looked up, she was staring at his left hand. He turned it over and saw in the curve of his palm her phone number, written on his skin.

By the time he glanced at her face she was staring fixedly at the wall a couple of inches to the left of his head, color high in her cheeks.

His heart did a funny little lurch, and the nerve endings in his fingertips flared, sending up a sense memory of her soft skin. For a brief moment he wished he could smooth that over somehow, but he needed her cooperation. "It's late, Riva, so I'm going to make this short. We have you on possession with intent to deliver.

That's a felony that carries some serious prison time, even for a first offender."

She stared at him.

"But because your record prior to this is completely clean, I'm going to offer you a deal. Help us out."

Her face was as white as the paper in front of him. "By doing what?"

"Make some buys for us."

"How many buys?"

"A few."

"Where?"

"On campus. In return we'll drop the charges and make this go away."

She looked at him. Something flashed in her eyes, but disappeared with a blink of her thick lashes before Ian could do more than note it, much less identify it. Relief? Shock? "How did you find me?"

"A couple of other kids we've picked up since school started mentioned a female dealer. We've been watching activity around the school for a couple of months."

"Watching me."

He nodded.

"Why?"

"We thought you'd be the easiest to turn. Young, female, new to the business. Why did you do it?"

She thought about that for a moment. "I needed the money," she said. "What do I have to do?"

She looked so young, so innocent, and very small, curled in on herself in the interview-room chair. For a moment his concern got the better of his drive. "I'll walk you through what you have to do. Are you sure you don't want a lawyer?"

"No. No lawyer."

Present day . . .

Ian Hawthorn pulled into a parking space at the back of
Eye Candy's parking lot and killed the engine on his
city-issued Ford Taurus. A line of oak trees separating
the lot from the street arced overhead, and the shade kept
the car's interior temperature cool as he scanned his sur-
roundings. Behind Eye Candy a crane swiveled to hoist
another panel of reflective glass to the top floor of Mobile Media's building. Ian scrolled through his contacts,
then watched the workers guide the panel into place
while he waited for the call to connect.

"HealthNorth Oncology."

He recognized the receptionist's voice. "Hi, Nancy.
It's Ian Hawthorn. I need to cancel my appointment."

"Again?" Sounds of clicking and tapping came
through the line as she worked away at her computer.
"When was the last time we saw you?" she said, almost
to herself.

Ian knew the answer to that question. Nancy probably
did too, but she never said anything without confirma-
tion. Oncology appointments were tricky, and the last
thing a staff member wanted to do was put her foot in
her mouth.

"It's been two years," she said. "Dr. Ripley attached
a note to your file. It says *don't let Ian reschedule again*."

Dr. Ripley was exactly what he wanted in a cancer
doctor: brisk, efficient, no-nonsense. "Tell her I'm busy
at work right now," Ian said. "I'll call back in a couple
of weeks and schedule the appointment."

"It's a simple blood draw," Nancy said. "We can do
the draw at your convenience, and schedule an appointment to discuss the results."

"I really can't right now," he said.

"Just come in, Ian," Nancy said almost desperately. "Anytime. Lunch hour, after work, before work. You show up and we'll fit you in."

Now he felt like an asshole asking for special treatment. "Thanks. I appreciate that," he said. "I'll see what I can work out in the next week or so."

He hung up, then clicked off his phone and tucked it in his jacket pocket. Eve Webber's efforts were paying off, with increased traffic on the city's east side, new restaurants and shops opening their doors in a neighborhood once considered risky. The spaces were filling up fast, people eager to shed what remained of winter's hold on the city and celebrate a beautiful spring Friday night on the patio of the city's hottest nightclub. It should have been tempting. But nightclubs made him think of the bad decisions he'd made in the wake of a diagnosis of non-Hodgkin's lymphoma he'd gotten at twenty-one.

"You're still making bad decisions," he muttered as he snagged his laptop bag and slid out of the Taurus. Like postponing his blood draws. It wasn't the needles; he'd preferred the constant sticks to the alien feel of the port inserted into his chest during his chemotherapy, the small plastic lump a constant reminder of his body's weakness and everything he'd lost as a result.

But he was ten years NEC—no evidence of cancer— and busy. The blood draw would wait. He was in the middle of the case of his career, involving drugs, corrupt cops, and a chance to put a huge dent in the drug supply coming into Lancaster. He was up for captain, earned the top score on the exam, and was only waiting for a spot to open up. His life was humming along, impossible to derail.

Or so he had thought, until Riva Henneman walked up to his table.

Ian had always been in control of his life, so no one was surprised when, after his older brother Jamie became a SEAL, Ian won a spot at Annapolis, or when, at the end of his plebe year, he was ranked near the top of his class, on track to graduate with his choice of assignments: to go through BUD/S and lead a SEAL team. The only surprise was the tiredness, weight loss, then the high white blood cell count, and then the cancer diagnosis.

The doctors used the word "diagnosis," keeping it technical, medical, clinical. In the journal the psychologist insisted he keep, Ian wrote not of diagnosis, but of betrayal, of his disloyal cells and duplicitous immune system. He was just telling the truth. Keeping it real.

Fifteen months of treatment got him a clean bill of health and the news that he could graduate from the academy, but with a medical board that ended his military career before it began. No commission in the navy. No chance at the SEALs. He'd beaten the cancer, but in the process, Ian had gone from being a warrior to being a miracle.

He'd loved being a winner, a warrior, a competitor. Someone to reckon with, someone who cleared all the bars and set new records, new standards. He'd really loved being a plebe.

He hated being a miracle.

For the first time in his life, his circumstances dictated his options, not the other way around. Miracles were grateful for a second chance, a new lease on life. Ian wouldn't have taken it on a silver platter. He didn't want a second chance. He didn't want a trip to Disney

World or a chance to race the Indy track with a Formula One driver, or any of the other stupid wishes other cancer victims got. He wanted the life he'd built for himself before he got sick.

No one could give him that. In that frame of mind, angry and frustrated and resentful, he'd met Riva Henneman.

At first all he'd seen was a girl he could use as bait to hook a bigger fish. Then he'd spent hours and hours in cars with her, wiring her up for conversations. He'd smelled her skin, felt her hair against his hands and wrists, once against his face when the wind caught loose strands and tossed them against his neck, his cheek.

His brain said, *suspect*, then *confidential informant*. His body said, *female. Desirable, sexy woman*.

But cops had ruined careers with infatuations with pretty girls of any age, and he had no intention of losing what he had left. When he'd gotten what he needed from her, he'd turned her loose, knowing he had no right and no business staying in touch with her without being the worst kind of creeper. He'd had power and authority over her; there was no way to initiate a relationship not founded on that imbalance. So he'd put her out of his mind as best he could, except for fever dreams hot enough to drive him crazy.

He'd thought she was gone. Forever.

Cesar, the big bouncer at the front door, looked up as Ian approached. "What are you reading now?" Ian asked. Cesar's big hands made the book look small, but Ian could tell it was about four inches thick.

Cesar, a man of few words, flipped the cover closed. *War and Peace.*

"Like it?"

"Liked *Anna Karenina* better." Cesar shrugged, like reading the Russian greats outside a club on the city's embattled east side was commonplace.

"This for fun?"

"Sort of." Cesar tried to stifle a proud smile, and failed. "I'm in the Upward Bound program at Lancaster College. This was on the reading list for the core curriculum."

Ian managed to control his eyebrows. Even after a decade as a cop, people still surprised him. Usually this was a bad thing. Tonight, it was a good thing. "Cool," he said, and opened the door.

He made his way along the hip-high wall enclosing the dance floor and started up the spiraling staircase to the office overlooking the bar. A quick double rap on the door and it opened from the inside. Joanna Sorenson, one of his detectives, peered through the gap.

"You're late." She gave him the naughty-naughty finger shake, which made him laugh. He'd known Jo since they were kids on the same T-ball team, part of a small cadre of second-and third-generation cops with the Lancaster Police Department. Technically, he outranked her; in formal situations Jo followed the chain of command with a punctilious officiousness that amused him. In private, she gave him hell like the sister he'd never had.

"Yeah, yeah." Ian looked over the group and saw that the most important person wasn't yet there. "I beat the mayor up here, so I'm ok."

Jo huffed a laugh and closed the door behind Ian. He sidestepped the sofa lining the wall and hunkered down beside Eve's desk to pull out his laptop and power it up.

The small office was crowded, even more so when the door opened to admit Eve Webber and the small, silver-haired mayor of Lancaster.

"Thanks for your time, Mayor," she said, setting a couple of pitchers of ice water with sliced lemons and a tower of stacked glasses on the opposite end of her desk. "Let me know if you need anything else."

There was a moment of silence after the door closed behind her as everyone in the room tried to figure out who was running this show. There was enough brass in the room to start a band: Ian, a lieutenant; Swarthmore, the captain of the Eastern Precinct; and the mayor of Lancaster, plus Dorchester, Jo, and McCormick.

"I'll do the introductions," Sorenson said brightly. "Mayor, you know Captain Swarthmore. Detective Dorchester. Officer McCormick."

The mayor shook Matt's hand, then said, "Good to meet you, McCormick. How are you holding up?"

"Fine, sir," McCormick said, trying not to look like he towered over the mayor and failing. McCormick made professional football players look small.

"Undercover work is tough; going deep to investigate crooked cops is tougher. You have what you need?"

"Yes, sir," McCormick repeated, clearly surprised by the mayor's blunt statement.

"He's just waiting for us to wrap this up so he can take off and be famous," Dorchester said from his position against the wall. He had one foot braced against the cinderblocks and a grin on his face. The only thing he liked better than a chance to check up on Eve Webber, Eye Candy's owner and his girlfriend of nearly a year, was a chance to needle McCormick.

The mayor's eyebrow lifted.

Dorchester said, "As soon as we're done with him, he's off to head up Maud Ward's security detail."

"Congratulations. That's quite a coup."

"I'm dating her, sir."

Both of the mayor's eyebrows shot up. "It's a long story, mayor," Jo said. "Eventually you'll see it on a behind-the-music special. You know me—"

"—and trust me, I regret it—"

"—and I believe you've met Lieutenant Hawthorn before."

"I believe I have, Jo. Ian."

"Dad," Ian said.

His father didn't take his eyes off Ian's face; when it came down to a battle of wills, his dad would win every time. He knew Ian was due for an appointment with Ripley. "In a couple of weeks, Dad," he said.

A quick narrowing of his eyes, a downward tilt to his eyebrows, and Ian was a recruit at the academy again, standing at attention before older cops he'd known his whole life. "We're a little busy right now."

"I'll let your mother know you're too busy to go to your appointment," his dad said in a silky voice.

And that was his dad, chucking him under the bus. "I'll call her and explain."

His dad all but snorted. "Might want to text. She's looking for someone to clean out the greenhouse before the garden club meeting."

He wasn't totally in the doghouse yet. "Thanks for the warning."

"Keep that appointment or I'll offer you up to get the beds ready for planting."

Motivating, but not enough. He loved working with his mom in the garden. Always had. Who else in the room knew about his cancer diagnosis and treatment? Jo did, but she was as inscrutable and silent as the wall she leaned against. Swarthmore probably did; he'd been one of his father's shift lieutenants back in the day. Dorchester and McCormick didn't and wouldn't ask. The diagnosis had left his father shaken to the bone, something he showed to no one but his wife, Ian's mother, something Ian saw only because his parents thought he was asleep when his father started weeping. His parents, steadfast, supportive, and loving, had never lost the right to quiz him about his health.

"Explain to me why we're meeting here?" his father said, looking around the tiny office.

That was the former chief of police talking, not his dad. "Hidden in plain sight." Ian started laying pictures and files on Eve's big desk. He'd been here a couple of times when Matt Dorchester was protecting the star witness in a drug case, and more since Conn McCormick agreed to go undercover to infiltrate the Strykers. The group gathered around. "We've all been seen in this club for social reasons, and it's owned by a cop's girlfriend."

At the word "girlfriend," his dad perked right up. "You're dating Eve?"

"Not me," Ian said hastily. "Dorchester. Gather round."

His dad leafed through the report Ian had handed him, stopping at the organizational chart Ian and the team had pieced together. "Run it down for me."

"Eighteen months ago we started seeing a spike in crime we traced to cheap heroin, flowing in from Mexico. It was a new, more potent form, pure and cheap, and it flooded the market, driving prices down and spreading west, into the burbs. We also saw an increase in ODs, intakes at addiction treatment centers, and violence. We learned from Dorchester's encounter with Hector Santiago that the cartels were working with local gangs to gain new turf."

"That explains the spike in violence," his dad said.

"Exactly."

"How close are we to closing this down?"

And here was the reason for the meeting. This was his area. He'd gathered the data, traced it to the roots, and was close to shutting down the traffic. McCormick was undercover in plain sight, working his regular shift as a patrol officer with the city's Eastern Precinct. Only the people in this room knew he was also gathering data to arrest, prosecute, and convict the dirty cops who had swarmed in to take advantage of a vacuum in the city's gang leadership, created when Dorchester took out a vicious drug runner threatening Eve.

"We're close," Ian said. "Five months of work and McCormick has data on high-level distributors and their dealers."

McCormick cleared his throat and squared up. "Kenny knows where the meetings to deliver shipments will take place. He directs patrols away from that area and sends in one of his guys to make sure nothing goes down. Five minutes and everyone's gone, and the drugs are out for delivery."

Swarthmore added, "We've also got proof of cops taking money and drugs from crime scenes, coercion of suspects, and several instances of planting evidence to frame members of other gangs, illegal searches, false testimony."

"What do we know about the supplier?"

"Not much," McCormick admitted. "Kenny's playing his cards close to his chest. I'm in, but not the inner circle."

"Does it matter?" his father asked, switching to devil's advocate in the blink of an eye. "We can shut down the current distributors and clean house at the same time."

"According to Kenny, this guy's been trying to get into Lancaster for a while, opening new territory for a gang out of Mexico. If we don't shut him down, he'll try again."

Ian tapped the file with the question mark on a big blue sticky note on it. "I want this guy, Dad."

His father looked at him. Ian recognized the glint in his eye, having inherited his father's ruthless, relentless drive. He knew what Ian meant—*I want this bust, this clearance, our house cleaned from top to bottom. I want the captain's bars.* "How do we go about getting him?"

Swarthmore said, "Kenny's top distributor is a guy named Malik Hathaway. We've got enough on Malik to arrest him."

Ian shook his head. "If we go after any of them, the rest will run. I want to leave the top leadership in place." He flipped open Malik's file. "What about Malik's brother?"

"Isaiah?" McCormick blew out his breath. "We've picked him up for shoplifting, petty theft, but not in the last few months. He's not involved, as far as I can tell. His brother gets him to run packages every so often, but only as a last resort."

Ian studied the pictures in the file. Just another kid in a hoodie getting into another junker of a car with a brown sack in his hand. Just another means to an end. He pushed his memory of Riva, white-faced when she approached his table, then gorgeously furious with him when he dared broach the sanctity of her kitchen. "Do we have enough to arrest him?"

"Yeah," McCormick said.

"Bring him in. Let's see what means more to him, his family or his freedom."

The meeting broke up, Swarthmore and Dorchester catching up on another case, Jo checking her voice mail on her way down the stairs. McCormick took the back door through the empty apartment behind the office, protecting his cover.

Ian collected the folders and shut his laptop's lid. Looking at it brought back to mind standing by the kitchen door while Riva Henneman calmly directed a panicked group of kids through the procedure for dealing with a grease fire, and he clutched his laptop like a kid with a security blanket.

The memory hit him with all the unexpectedness of Jamie landing a punch Ian didn't see coming when they were sparring at Lancaster's boxing club. One minute he'd been getting his laptop out to work through his meal. The next Riva was standing there, drawing all the oxygen out of the room despite the wide-open windows and warm spring breeze. He'd looked up into her face, and all his brain could do was notice. Riva. Different.

All grown up. The slender body of an eighteen-year-old college student had filled out into a woman's curves. Her slouched posture was now ramrod straight, shoulders back, head held high, her pale blue eyes snapping. Finely arched brows. A wide, mobile mouth, alternately prim or carnal depending on the color of her lipstick and how heavily she applied it. She still wore her chestnut hair long but had stopped straightening it to that artificially sleek look. It was now pulled back in a ponytail, emphasizing the freckles spattered across her cheeks, nose, and forehead. They were a little darker but maybe that was because she was pale with shock at seeing him. He hoped it was shock. God knew his mouth was hanging open like an idiot's.

He'd chosen the restaurant because Eve had talked up the farm-to-table ethos and the owner's community involvement, and Matt had talked up the rib eye special. In the space of two racing heartbeats his day went from average, ordinary, data-driven metrics for breakfast, lunch, and dinner to the visceral, full-body memory of the erotic thrill he'd spent the last seven years trying to forget.

He couldn't have her. Ever. She'd been a suspect, a confidential informant he'd ruthlessly used to shut down a campus drug ring and earn his first commendation. He'd been ambitious, concerned with nothing other than proving himself as a Hawthorn, living up to his dad's reputation, and Jamie's. Everyone else acted like cancer gave him a pass, but he didn't want a pass and flatly refused to be the weak link in the Hawthorn family. He wanted to stand tall beside his brother and his father. Nothing more, nothing less.

Until he'd wanted Riva. He'd needed her cooperation, but been terrified the entire time, sending a slender, defiant, sexy girl into dangerous situations. Underneath all of that was the most dangerous thing in the world: the desire to throw it all away.

He'd taken all of that conflicted emotion out on her.

His father was waiting by Ian's truck. "What's up, Dad?"

"I'm a little disappointed. I thought maybe you and Eve had gotten together."

Ever since his brother, Jamie, finally convinced the love of his life to give a long distance relationship a shot, his parents were in full-on matchmaker mode.

"Eve's great." He clicked open the locks and tossed the laptop bag up on the seat. "I can't imagine holidays sitting across from Caleb Webber." Eve's brother was a hot-shot defense attorney who loved making cops' lives difficult.

"Dorchester seems all right with it."

"He's in love with her. I'm not."

"Is there anyone? Anyone at all?"

Just a tall, leggy, chestnut-haired former suspect turned organic farmer who hated him enough to refuse him service. He wasn't even sure what she did for a living. Was that farm hers? Just the restaurant? Or was she the liaison with the East Side Community Center? He'd given in and searched her name on social media. The farm had a page, but no clues about the owner. She had no social media profiles under her name.

"It's spring, so an old man's fancy lightly turns to thoughts of love?" he said.

"Who you calling old?"

"I don't want to steal Jamie's lovefest limelight."

"You think they'll get married soon?"

Jamie was an active duty SEAL stationed in Virginia Beach. He'd come home nearly a year ago and claimed the girl he'd never forgotten, Charlie Stannard, a former pro basketball player and now the girls' basketball coach at East High. They were still working out the long-distance-relationship details. "Ask Jamie."

"Jamie ignores the question."

A sure sign his brother was in stealth mode about something, probably the proposal. "Even when Mom asks?"

"Even when your mother asks."

"I'd prepare for a big announcement."

"So you don't know something we don't?"

"I know lots of things about Jamie you don't," Ian said. "But not that particular thing."

"Humph," his dad said. "You and your brother. Thick as thieves."

"You've got to renegotiate the city's contract with the sanitation service, and you're thinking about Jamie getting married?"

"Sometimes. Sometimes I think about you getting married."

"Give it a rest, Dad."

"Is it the cancer?"

No. Yes. Maybe. Ian didn't know how to answer that question, because sometimes, sure, a woman got a good look at the scar on his pectoral from the chemo port and bugged out. Sometimes she went all maternal and protective on him, and he bugged out. Sometimes she didn't ask, because talking wasn't part of the program.

"I'm not looking for someone right now. I'm busy at work, and this thing takes up most of my off-duty time."

"You want me to come with you?"

The last thing he wanted was company in the exam room. "No." He softened his tone. "I'll go. I promise."

His dad was more fine with Jamie joining the US Navy SEALs and going off on incredibly complicated, dangerous missions he knew almost nothing about than he was with Ian having cancer. It was the illusion of control. Jamie was highly trained, with his teammates, in control of his situations. Ian was alone with a ticking time bomb of a body that had deceived him once already. "I know, Dad. I'm fine. I'm sleeping, eating right, not drinking to excess, exercising. I'm fine. I'm just not dating, okay?"

His phone buzzed. He pulled it from his pocket and glanced at the screen. McCormick. *We got him*.

"I have to go, Dad. Work."

"Me, too."

"Have fun with the sanitation engineers."

His father snorted. "Stay out of trouble."

Ten minutes later he pulled into the parking lot behind the Eastern Precinct, known to the cops and most east side residents as the Block. To protect both the cruisers and cops' cars, the parking lot was fenced off with eight feet of chain link topped with barbed wire. He held the door for a cop bringing in a drugged-out homeless guy, then kept on holding it for two cops returning to their vehicle.

"Thanks, LT."

McCormick was waiting in the observation room, feet spread, arms folded, looking like he wouldn't move until doomsday. Through the reflective glass Ian saw a kid slumped over the table, face buried in the arm of a gray hoodie, nicked-up hands and a shock of blond hair the only visible identifying features.

"He asleep?"

"He's being eighteen," McCormick said.

"Any trouble?" McCormick was seven inches taller than Ian and had him by a good sixty pounds of muscle. Ian didn't expect him to say yes.

"Nothing beyond the standard."

"Charges?" They didn't need anything big, just enough to arrest him and scare him.

"He was named last week by a small-time corner kid as the guy who delivered his packages."

"Any truth to it?"

McCormick shrugged. "Probably. It's a Stryker corner. They don't usually use Isaiah for that, but he's done it a couple of times."

"Has he asked for a lawyer?"

"No. He made one phone call. I assume his aunt's gonna show up any minute." At Ian's raised eyebrow, McCormick added, "He and Malik live with their aunt."

Ian studied the top of Isaiah's head a moment longer. "Want some coffee?"

"Sure. He's not going anywhere."

Ian poured out two cups, added sugar to McCormick's, and shifted both cups to his right hand. On his way back to the interrogation room, he scanned the email on his phone.

Ian handed McCormick his coffee. "All yours," he said.

"His phone call's here," McCormick said, tipping his head at the glass.

Ian looked up to find Riva Henneman standing beside the table in the interrogation room.

"Shit," he said.

CHAPTER FOUR

Please don't let him be here.

Riva had chanted the mantra all way to the Block, switching from reciting it under her breath to mentally repeating it to herself while she asked at the front desk for Isaiah. She'd held her chin high the whole way back to a very familiar interview room, but Hawthorn was nowhere in sight.

To her relief, the room held only Isaiah and herself. Her heart was pounding, her stomach roiling like she'd eaten bad fish, but she held it together, reaching for skills she'd learned in this very precinct, in this very interrogation room. *Stay calm. Don't give anything away.* She dropped her purse to the floor and perched on the edge of the chair beside him.

"Isaiah, what's going on?"

"Got arrested," he said.

His blond hair fell forward, into his eyes. He was handcuffed to the table. The sullen look on his face, so different from the open excitement and delight she saw when she taught him a new recipe or approved an improvement he'd made to one of hers was gone, replaced by the kid who'd skulked into her kitchen back in February. All the progress she'd made was lost.

"So I see," she said lightly. "What happened?"

"Someone snitched."

Monosyllabic answers, closed-off expression. All too familiar. She waited.

"Little Ray said I delivered a package to him."

"Did you?"

"Yeah, but this was months ago. I've said no to Malik every time since I started working for you." His face closed off again, the expression of someone who didn't expect authority figures to believe him.

"I believe you," she said. But she also knew all about statute of limitations, and what cops would do to get an arrest, a conviction. "Did you call a lawyer?" He needed help, just as she'd needed one seven years ago. The conversation was seared into her memory.

Dad? I got arrested. Selling . . . you know. What you asked me to sell.

A few low, muttered words, "knew a girl would fuck this up . . . stupid bitch" among them. Then, *Did you tell them about me?*

No! Of course not!

Don't, if you know what's good for you. I'm not jeopardizing this relationship because you couldn't handle a job twelve-year-olds do without getting busted. Don't call me again.

Then he'd hung up on her.

"No money for a lawyer." At her glance, he added,

"Malik's the one with a good lawyer. I'm not taking his help with this."

She blew out her breath, then dug in her bag for her cell phone to text Eve.

I need your brother's work number.

You finally want to get a drink with him? I'll give you his mobile, but he's in Cleveland for a couple of weeks, doing depositions. I'll set the two of you up when he gets back!

"Dammit," she breathed.

Thanks, but I don't want to get a drink with him. I need a lawyer.

The response came almost immediately. *What's going on?*

It's not for me. For Isaiah.

Three dots appeared. While she waited, she said absently. "Where's your mom?"

"Gone."

She looked up. "Gone, gone?"

"Gone, gone."

"Your dad?"

"Where I'll be going."

Prison. Great. "Who's responsible for you?"

"I'm eighteen. I am."

"You turned eighteen six weeks ago," Riva said. "Who was responsible for you before then?"

"Malik, I guess. We live with my aunt."

"Tell me what happened. You said this wasn't recent."

"Cop rolls up a couple of hours ago and arrests me. Says I can have a second chance, if I roll on Malik. I'm not snitching on my brother."

A warning bell went off in her brain. "Tell me exactly

what happened." At his disbelieving snort, she added, "You can't shock me. Trust me on this one."

The story was all too familiar. He lived on the outskirts of all kinds of illegal activity; half of the east side made ends meet any way they could. Malik was up and coming in the Strykers. For the most part he kept his little brother out of things, but every so often, he asked Isaiah to do something he trusted no one else to do.

"Including delivering packages."

"Just the big ones," Isaiah said ironically.

Cops wouldn't hesitate to use family members to go after the biggest fish of them all, the suppliers.

"What did they want?"

"Malik's supplier."

"Do you know who supplies him?" Her heart was in her throat.

"Yeah. But I'm not giving up my brother."

"Let me guess." But it wasn't really a guess. Her past, her fate, was catching up with her. She leaned in close, keeping her voice down to a low murmur. "It's a guy out of Chicago, goes by the name of Rory."

The look on Isaiah's face was almost as priceless as the look on Ian's at the restaurant. Riva knew how shocking this must be to him, that his clean living, organic farming food arts and sciences mentor knew high-level drug dealers by name. "How do you know him?"

"Never mind," she said. "Just sit tight and keep your mouth shut until I get back."

Isaiah stared at her, eyes full of wild hope and total disbelief. "You can help me?"

"Yes," she said.

"How?"

Easy. All she had to do was give Ian Hawthorn what she'd withheld seven years ago. All she had to do was ask for help from the man she hated as much as she desired.

She opened the door and found herself staring at the bulging right biceps of a mountain of muscle standing outside. He wore jeans, a half-zip pullover, a gun on his hip, and a badge on his belt. "I'd like to speak to Ian Hawthorn, please."

He didn't blink an eye. "And you are?"

"Riva Henneman."

The door next to the interrogation room opened, and Ian stepped through. "Ms. Henneman," he said, unemotionally, like the encounter at the restaurant had never happened. This was the Ian she knew, cold, distant, walled off. "What can I do for you?"

"I'd like to speak to you in private." She chose her words carefully, striving for an even tone, working hard to give nothing away that would jeopardize Isaiah's future.

Without a word, he inclined his head. She followed him down the hallway.

"In here," he said, reaching past her to open a door with a glass window in it. His breath heated her ear, and she went still, electric tremors running over her nerves. To calm them, she focused on the sign next to the door.

LT. IAN HAWTHORN

He'd been promoted since she knew him. More authority. More power. More danger.

The thought carried her into the small office. Neatly stacked manila folders occupied the right-hand side of the desk, and cables trailed through an empty spot in front of two large monitors.

That must be where the laptop goes, she thought, nonsensically.

"What can I do for you?"

Was she really going to do this? Was she really going to risk her freedom and put herself in the hands of the man she feared and desired in equal measures?

Yes. For Isaiah.

But this time she held some of the cards. She lifted her chin. "I want to offer you a deal."

"That's not how this works. You're not his lawyer."

"I remember," she said, then glanced down at her phone. "I'm just waiting to hear back from Eve. Her brother, Caleb, might be able to take Isaiah's case. You know Caleb, right?"

Was that a flash of amused respect behind his facade? "I'm listening," he said.

"First, I want your assurance all charges against Isaiah will be dropped. He walks out of here today, and you never talk to him again."

"Depends on what you've got, but I'm listening."

That told her Isaiah wasn't the real target. She hesitated for just a second, holding on to the last moment in time when Ian respected the new person she'd become. "The name of Malik's supplier. The man behind the pipeline of drugs into Lancaster."

He blinked, and the light in his eyes disappeared. "You have that."

"Yes."

"How?"

"I'll tell you once I know you won't go after Isaiah."

His gaze narrowed. "Why risk yourself for him? He's in with a bad crowd. He's going to get in trouble again."

"No, he won't. Want to know why? Because the sauce

on your salmon last night was Isaiah's creation. He spent three weeks perfecting it, bought the ingredients with money I paid him to work in my greenhouse. The dirt under his fingernails is honest dirt. He wants to open a restaurant, and to do that he'll need money. Small business loans. Grants. All of which becomes impossible if he has a felony conviction. He knows that. He's committed to that dream, and he wants to get it the right way. The honest way. I'm willing to stake my life on it."

"It's not your life at stake," Ian pointed out.

"Isn't it? I have no guarantee you won't come after me. I just told you I know the name of a major drug supplier. I get involved in this and someone says I'm using my farm as a cover for drugs? You arrested me for distribution. You've got an easy conviction."

He looked at her, and she knew that once they struck this deal, any privacy she'd had, no matter how flimsy, was gone. The LPD would crawl all over her business, the farm, her records, her relationships. Ian would ask questions, better questions than he'd asked last time.

She waited for the next logical question. *How do you know the supplier? Are you selling drugs?*

"This sounds like it could get very serious, and dangerous for you. Do you want a lawyer present?"

"Thank you, but no. I don't need one."

"You're still fearless."

"You're still ruthless," she shot back. "Arresting Isaiah, threatening him with jail time unless he rolls on his brother. You think I don't know exactly what's going on here?"

"You think you do?"

Her smile wasn't a pretty, happy thing, and she knew it. "I do. Having any trouble with corruption, Lieutenant

Hawthorn? Cops helping dealers? Taking money for information, or to look the other way?"

His gaze sharpened. "Don't fuck with me on this, Riva."

"Let Isaiah go, and I promise you'll get everything I know."

"I could just arrest you, too."

"You could. But you won't."

"Because I know you won't say boo to a fucking ghost if I do."

"Precisely. Caleb Webber will make sure of that."

He hauled open his office door and beckoned. The mountain of muscle left his position by the interview room and walked over. "Uncuff him, get him a soda or a sandwich, but hold him for now."

"Yes, sir," the cop said.

Ian closed the door again, seated himself behind his desk, and opened the laptop. He sat back and reached for a pen, spinning it around his first knuckle, a nervous habit she remembered from seven years ago. "Start talking. Let's start with a name."

This was it. This was the moment she told the whole truth and lost any chance she had at Ian's respect.

"Rory Henneman," she said. "My father."

The pen flew up and over his knuckle, careening into the top level of his inbox/outbox tray. She remembered him spinning the pen seven years ago and never, ever missing the catch. "Your father," he repeated.

"Yes."

"Rory Henneman."

She must have shocked the hell out of him for him to repeat himself like this. Normally he remembered an astonishing degree of detail. Clearly he hadn't put together the obvious, which was that she'd known all about this seven years ago and not told him. "Yes."

"Is Rory short for anything?"

"No."

He typed something into his laptop. Silence reigned while he waited, then his gaze sharpened, eyes tracking back and forth as he skimmed the results. She'd done this dance before; cops started with plugging names into national crime databases and narrowed from there. But he wouldn't find Rory Henneman. He was too slick for that.

"A couple of speeding tickets, both paid, and bunch of unpaid parking tickets in Chicago. Nothing else," he said. He typed some more. "I'm getting hits for a Henneman Candy and Vending, out of Chicago."

"That's him."

"Chicago?" Hawthorn was scrolling and clicking, gaze flitting back and forth between the dual monitors. "He looks like a visible, respected businessman."

"And you looked like a grad student," she said. "While I looked like a first year. And Isaiah looks like a banger, not a budding chef. Let's agree that people are sometimes not what they seem."

Hawthorn pushed back from his desk, linked his hands behind his head, and fixed her with a look she recognized very well. It was his command-and-control glare. She gave him a little smile.

"Candy and vending businesses used to be fronts for the mob."

"Used to be," she said.

"How long has this been going on?"

Her stomach twisted into knots, the kind she couldn't easily untangle. "About a decade."

"So when I busted you, you were working for him?"

"Yes. My job was to check out the local suppliers, see how organized they were, get a feel for the market before he moved into it. I knew what his plan was. It included paying police to look the other way, if he could."

"You didn't tell me any of this."

He'd assumed she was a low-level dealer, a college girl looking to make easy money. His questions had been geared around getting evidence on the bigger dealers on campus, unaware of her father's mission. "I truthfully answered every question you asked."

"I just didn't ask the right questions."

A mistake he wouldn't make twice. Ian sat forward, fingers poised over the keyboard. The eager spring sunlight highlighted the slashes on his cheeks, the webbing of lines around his eyes, the muscle jumping in his jaw. "What evidence do you have?"

"Nothing right now."

He shoved back from his desk and strode to the door. He hauled it open and bellowed, "McCormick!" into the squad room.

"Sir."

McCormick was the giant of a man standing guard outside Isaiah's interrogation room. He moved quickly for someone the size of a small mountain, or maybe everyone was as terrified of Hawthorn as she was. "Charge him."

Riva scrambled out of her chair. "No, don't! I can get it. It's just going to take time."

"How."

It wasn't a question. It was a demand growled from the back of his throat. She looked at him, then at Mc-

Cormick. Hawthorn held up a hand. "Don't go far," he said.

When Hawthorn closed the door, Riva went on. "I can get you what you need to shut it all down. Just keep Isaiah out of jail while I'm doing it."

"You're doing this for Isaiah. Giving up your father for a kid you barely know."

"A kid with a future," she shot back.

"Bullshit."

She thought about her mother, about the long silences, her glazed eyes during their FaceTime chats, her nervous fingers picking at her cuticles during circular conversations about lunch menus and floral arrangements. This was about more than Isaiah, but Ian wouldn't care about her mother's nervous breakdowns or her father's role in them. "I should have done something about Dad a long time ago. I know that. I didn't. I am now."

Ian leaned forward, and the fury in his eyes froze her to her chair. "Or you took the deal so you could pass along what you learned when you were working for me, and now you're trying to get inside so you can help him slip away."

"No!" She met his gaze head-on, willing him to believe her. "I called Dad the night you arrested me, but Dad hung me out to dry. He said it would jeopardize his relationship with the supplier. That's why I took your deal."

No response. His fierce, intent eyes studied her face. She tried again. "Did you really expect me to give up my father, my family, if you didn't know about him? You set the terms of our arrangement, and I fulfilled them. You got exactly what you wanted from me. After you were done with me, I didn't want to have anything to do with drugs or cops ever again."

Tension thrummed in the room. Riva fought down her furious questions, because getting angry would get her nowhere. How could he understand what it was like to feel powerless, to face someone with an iron grip on your present, your future? When had he ever been truly powerless?

He glared at her, brows lowered. "If you quit working for your father, how are you going to get the information I need?"

She let herself exhale. That was the easy part. "I'll go back home and tell him I'm tired of working eighteen hours a day and being poor. That I miss him, and want another chance."

He sat down, typed something into the laptop. "Are you tired of long hours and poverty?"

"No," she said. "I love my life. I've worked hard for it."

"Why would he believe you?"

"Because he's a sociopath who believes the sun gets its heat and light from him."

"Why now? What's your cover story?"

"My mother's involved in a dinner-dance fundraiser for a hospital-wing renovation. She wants me to come home and help her with a luncheon for the organizing committee."

He stopped typing. "Come again."

"I'm going to make lunch for a group of my mother's society friends."

"I know what a dinner dance is," he said. "And a luncheon. This is your plan?"

"I'll go home, fool my dad into thinking I want into

the business, find his laptop, and get what you need. Do you have a better idea?"

Ian typed some more. "Do you ever bring home friends?"

"What?" she said, startled. "No. Why?"

"Never? Why not?"

"I don't go home much." Her heart started to pound. He couldn't be thinking what she thought he was thinking . . .

"Come up with a decent excuse, because I'm coming with you."

CHAPTER FIVE

Ian had learned the pen trick when he was eleven, racing Jamie to see who could learn it first, so the spin and catch were part of some really fundamental muscle memory. He couldn't remember the last time he missed the catch.

He'd been a cop too long, and through too much personally, to be that shocked.

But Riva had done just that, and he'd missed the catch.

It didn't take him long to put the pieces together: her father had been involved in the drug trade back when he'd arrested her. Through interrogations and stakeouts, through weeks of drug deals, she'd kept the whole truth from him. Protected her father.

The lie of omission stung more fiercely than it should, and not just because she'd withheld critical information about known illegal activities. She'd withheld a key piece of information about herself. All those nights sitting in a car together, waiting for a dealer to show, intimacy drifting into the air with the soft rock music, and she hadn't told him. He'd taken care of her, and she'd lied to him. But this time he would use Riva Henneman until he'd followed the pipeline of drugs back to the source and cut it off.

"Come with me," he said, using a curt tone to cover the emotional stew roiling inside him.

"Where are we going?"

Part of him wanted to ignore her question, throw her off-balance, but his better half won. "To see my captain."

She looked mutinously at his extended arm indicating she should precede him out of his office, but gathered up her purse and walked out. He kept one hand hovering at the small of her back, not quite touching as he guided her around the bullpen. As with everything about Riva, he was conflicted. The cop in him wanted to protect her as an asset.

The man in him wanted to feel the bare skin of her back against his palm, to protect her, because she was *his*. His CI, his asset, his in a way that went beyond labels and tidy relationships. She'd always been *his*, the power he had over her as close to owning another human being as possible, and therefore never his. Riva had never chosen him.

With a deftness born of long practice, he shut off his thoughts and rapped on the doorframe. "Got a minute, sir?"

Swarthmore looked up from his computer. His iron gray hair was neatly buzzed in the only haircut Ian could remember on him. He wore a tidy goatee, carefully trimmed to the department's regulations, and his brown eyes were sharp and guarded. He took in Riva with a glance, but paid more attention to the way Ian closed his office door. "What's up?" he asked, gesturing to the two chairs in front of his desk.

Ian sat down because he wanted Riva to be seated and comfortable. "We have an opportunity to get the supplier behind Kenny's bid to take over the drug trade in Lancaster."

Swarthmore's eyebrows shot up. "I'm listening."

Ian explained why Riva was at the station, her connection to Isaiah, what she was willing to give up in order to get Isaiah out of jail.

"You're going to go back to your father, infiltrate his business and his organization, and get the information?"

"Yes," Riva said. "It's going to take some work. Right now I can't hand you a laptop with all the financial details, names, places, dates in a spreadsheet. But I can get it."

Swarthmore studied her for a long moment, then transferred his unreadable gaze to Ian. "Ms. Henneman, thank you for coming in. I need to speak with Lieutenant Hawthorn. We'll be in touch."

"I'm taking Isaiah with me," she said, pushing her chair back.

"Fine," Ian said before Swarthmore could speak up. This was his op. He'd take that risk, and anyway, he knew where Riva would go. They could always pick up Isaiah again if they wanted him.

Ian pulled his phone from his pocket and texted McCormick. *She's coming for Isaiah. Let her take him and go.*

Got it.

Ian watched her walk away. Swarthmore raised an eyebrow when he finally returned his attention to his superior officer. "This is the stupidest stunt I've ever heard of, but if she wants to do it, we can't stop her."

It was about to get a whole lot stupider. "I'm going with her."

"No, you're not," Swarthmore said.

"Sir—"

"For a dozen reasons." Swarthmore overrode him and lifted a hand for good measure. "Starting with, you have no jurisdiction in Chicago."

"Sir," Ian started again. "With all due respect, it is my job to take down the cartel that's corrupted our department."

Swarthmore sat back and gave Ian a steely-eyed glint Ian knew far too well. "No. I know exactly what you're trying to do, Ian. You're trying to prove yourself. And you're angry with Riva Henneman because based on what I just heard, she withheld information from you seven years ago."

Ian went still.

"Did you think I wouldn't remember her name?"

Ian knew better than to answer that question. "I'm not angry with her, sir."

"You better be angry with her, son. If it's not anger in your eyes, it's something else that's much more likely to land you in a big, stinking pile of shit."

"Sir, for all I know the CPD has an investigation running on Rory Henneman. She's just my cover to get in there and see what's what."

"That's not what she said."

"I'm going to need her help," Ian admitted.

"She was a CI. She's aiding an investigation. Have you told your dad about this stupid stunt?"

The line between family and superior officer blurred

that fast. "She walked into the precinct an hour ago," Ian pointed out. "And you know I never take anything from the job to Dad."

"Don't start with this," Swarthmore said. "This isn't your area of expertise. You left the field as soon as you could. You're not McCormick or Dorchester. A few drug buys doesn't qualify you; anyone who's gone to college knows how to score drugs. You're not prepared for a long-term undercover operation. You're first in line for my job. You want a big arrest to boost your résumé?"

Everyone knew Ian didn't specialize in long-term undercover work. Swarthmore was pushing him now. Normally this kind of thing didn't get a rise out of Ian. He knew the tactics too well, heard them described at backyard barbecues and tailgating parties. But this mattered too much. "Yes, sir."

"You want my job?"

"Yes, sir."

"Your dad's?"

"Yes, sir. Eventually." He could control his career, even if he couldn't control anything else. His body. Riva.

"That's quite the little dynasty. You think this is your department?"

"It is," Ian said. "The department is only as good as the cops who wear the badge make it. Trust, integrity, respect are hard to earn and easy to lose. If we don't clean this up, stop it at the source, we're going to lose more than a few cops to prison."

"Save the sound bite for the cameras," Swarthmore said, but his voice lacked heat.

"I'd be good at the job," Ian said.

"You will be, if you don't lose your chance at it because you've got a big shit stain on your shiny reputation.

Getting to a captain's desk, or the chief's, is as much about avoiding the sewer as it is getting the commendations."

Ian didn't need a lecture about interdepartmental politics. "I know that, sir."

"My answer is still no. If Ms. Henneman wants to go back home and ingratiate herself into her father's confidence, then turn over the information, that's entirely up to her."

The thought of sending Riva into danger without him made his blood run cold. Ian leaned back in his chair and met Swarthmore's gaze head-on. "I'm taking a leave of absence."

"Now?"

"Now."

"You're in the middle of a major operation, Lieutenant."

It wasn't good when Swarthmore started using Ian's rank. "I'm aware of that, Captain. McCormick's undercover work is well established. He's got Dorchester, who is trained for UC work, and Sorenson, who knows more about policing than anyone else in this building. We've got warrants ready to go. What we don't have, sir, is the supplier. The man who's corrupted our department. I'm not taking the chance that he slips away. Again."

Swarthmore chucked his pen on his desk, where it skittered against his inbox. "Dammit, Ian, I can't deny you a leave. I also can't remember the last time you took a real vacation, and you've got the time banked. But if you do what you could hypothetically do, you've got no backup. No support if it all goes to hell. You are not going in there as LPD, but as Ian Hawthorn. A civilian. Got me? And if you go and shit goes south, best-case scenario you'll end up suspended, maybe up on disciplinary actions when you get back. No captain's bars. No stars."

"I'll take that chance." Because shit wasn't going to go south. He could do this, quiet and under the radar. The department would get the bust, he'd clean house and step into his mentor's job at the beginning of summer.

"Why?"

Good question. Because smoldering under his calm surface was a growing anger with Riva, blending into the desire they'd never satisfied. Because he'd gotten used to sending Riva Henneman into difficult situations and protecting her while she risked her life. "I can't let her go in there alone, sir. And she will."

"Not. Your. Problem. If anything, it's the CPD's problem."

"They have jurisdiction, but they'll make it a thing. An operation, with a code name and a hierarchy. They'll make noise. Lots of it. That kind of thing starts shaking the web, and Kenny will hear about it."

"How am I supposed to explain your leave?"

"Medical," Ian said without hesitating.

Swarthmore's eyebrows shot up. "Medical."

"Tests or something. There are just enough rumors about my medical history to say I've gone somewhere for tests."

"You've never used your history before."

Because it would make him look like he was playing for sympathy. Ian shrugged. "If it makes me look weak, or lets me hide something to my advantage, I'll use it."

"Riva Henneman needs to let that kid go. And you need to let her go."

"Not going to happen," Ian said.

"Since when do you break every rule in the book?"

Since Riva had showed up again. Since he'd gotten the second chance he never thought he'd have with her. But Swarthmore was right. It was out of character for him, taking him back to the kid he was after his first diagnosis and the angry young man he was when he first met Riva. He was going back to a dark place, when he'd been a man he didn't like very much.

He had no other choice. The roots of this had spread deep and dark seven years earlier. Time to finish what he'd started.

"Fine. Throw your career away. Fill out the paperwork. I'll sign it. But you are on your own, Ian." He paused for a moment. "Hypothetically speaking, if you were considering doing something this stupid, and if you were to go conduct something that smells like an investigation, I'd recommend paying a visit to your counterpart in that jurisdiction. Just in case shit goes south and you need backup. Which you won't need, because my advice is to use your time off to have a little staycation. Run yourself some bubble baths. Catch up on your Netflix watch list. This has nothing to do with the LPD."

"Unless it works," Ian said. "It might. If I learned anything from running Riva as a CI, it was to be careful about underestimating her. She might not look like much, but when push comes to shove, she's steel."

"Sounds like someone else I know," Swarthmore said. "Get out of my office."

Ian knew *dismissed* in all its various forms. He headed through the bullpen to McCormick, now sitting at a desk, filling out paperwork. "Where's Riva?"

"She took the kid and left, just like you said. Any idea

where they're going, or am I going to have to track him down again?"

Ian had a pretty good idea of where Riva would take Isaiah. Now all he had to do was follow her and convince her to take her with him. "You won't have to track him down," Ian said.

The sun was setting, sending shades of blush that matched his mother's pink and punch rose bushes streaming across the sky. He turned off the state highway and onto the dirt road leading to Oasis. In addition to setting up his out-of-office response and bringing McCormick, Dorchester, and Sorenson up to speed, he'd downloaded a little research into Riva Henneman to his phone before he left the Block. He used the time at the stoplights to catch up on Riva's new life and learned two things.

First, the county assessor's records indicated she owned just over a hundred acres of rolling farmland with a barn and farmhouse built in the 1920s. Second, unlike Eve or Cady Ward, Riva didn't have much of an online presence. The farm's website focused on the produce and growing methods, the local farm-to-table advocates whose products were used in the restaurant, and the farm's connection with the ESCC. Same went for the social media outlets. They were all under the farm's name, or featured pictures of the kids at work in the greenhouse or kitchen. Not Riva.

Either she was letting her work and the earth speak for itself, or she was hiding.

He parked in front of the house, got out, and looked more carefully around the property. The restaurant was obviously closed, the windows shuttered, the front door locked. No lights in the kitchen area. The house was dimly lit, so he climbed the steps to the front porch running the length of the house and knocked on the door. A magazine sat on the floral cushions on the porch swing.

No answer. Hands on his hips, he turned and looked over the property again.

Riva's voice carried to him on the gentle breeze. Up the hill, he saw her walk out of a small shed, chickens scattering in front of her. Isaiah trailed behind, nodding as she spoke, following her into another small building.

He turned and walked in the direction of the chicken coop. A six-foot-high fence enclosed several sheds that smelled far less of chicken poop than he would have imagined. The hens, he supposed, pecked at the ground, fluffed their wings and feathers, and trotted off in an outraged flurry when he opened the gate.

Isaiah and Riva both turned when he walked into the small building. Riva stepped in front of Isaiah, her arm lifting protectively to clasp his arm and keep him behind her. "What are you doing here?"

Maybe it was the picturesque setting, the spring breeze in the trees, the water babbling in the brook at the base of the valley. Maybe it was Riva, in jeans and a tank top and work boots. Whatever it was, for a split second he thought about the politics of touch, of the dynamics of interpersonal relationships that dictated who could touch whom, when, how. How their previous relationship turned all of that upside down. How Riva wasn't going to willingly let him touch her. How much he really, really wanted to.

"We need to talk," he said.

Chin high, color bright on her cheekbones, she looked

at him. "Go inside," she said to Isaiah without taking her eyes off Ian. "Raid my fridge and see what you can whip up for dinner. I'll be there in a few minutes."

Isaiah scooted past Riva, brushing up against the hens' roosts as he sidled past Ian to the door. The hens clucked and shuffled, creating a rustling sound in the straw.

"Interesting place you have here," he said.

She flushed like he'd insulted her, then lifted her chin. "What do you want?"

"I'm coming with you."

"No. You'll just be a distraction."

"Riva, you don't understand how dangerous this is."

At that she laughed, a sharp, ugly sound that made the chickens squawk. She reached into a roost, shushing a flustered chicken, and pulled out an egg. "Are you for real? Of course I understand how dangerous this is."

"You need protection."

"Again, probably true, but you're not the man to provide it."

"Goddammit, Riva."

"Don't scare my chickens. If you can't keep yourself under control, go wait outside until I'm done."

He took a deep breath. "I'm used to keeping an eye on you."

"Seven years ago you had a right to. Now you don't. How on earth would I explain you to my parents?"

"You're bringing a friend home?"

She laughed again. It wasn't a happy sound. "I'm not a college girl anymore, Lieutenant Hawthorn."

"Okay, I'm your assistant."

The look she gave him was so incredulous he almost laughed. "If I'm going to tell my dad I want into his business because the farm's draining me dry, the last expense I'd carry is an assistant."

"So I'm an apprentice. Doing an unpaid internship."

"You do know how old you are, right?"

"Career change. The farm-to-table movement. Back to the land, and all that," he said, waving his hand.

"For some of us, the farm-to-table movement isn't a *yeah, yeah, whatever* thing," she said, mimicking his dismissive hand movement. "It's a way of life, our calling."

"Of course," he said quickly.

"You must be really desperate if you're willing to show up as my assistant."

He was. Totally desperate to get the bastard who'd corrupted his department and keep her from waltzing off into a dangerous and volatile situation without any backup. "I know how to do searches. Where to look for things."

"My dad's not going to have a composition notebook full of names and dates and connections stashed in a supersecret hiding place under his mattress. He's an early adopter of most electronics. He keeps meticulous records, but they'll be stored on a partitioned hard drive somewhere."

That was exactly the kind of information he needed. A dozen questions rose in his mind, but he set them aside. He needed her to agree; then he'd start asking questions. "Data mining is my specialty. What wouldn't make them suspicious of me?"

"I don't know. I haven't been home much since . . . since then." A foray into one of the nests came up empty. Riva absently stroked the hen's back, then moved on. "Look, you don't know my dad. He'd have to see you as unthreatening."

"Okay."

She tucked her hair behind her ear and looked him up and down, striking sparks along his nerves. He was used to being openly assessed by everyone: his parents, his medical team, fellow cops, criminals, women in bars. Under their gazes he felt like a miracle, an opponent, a potential hookup. When Riva looked at him, he didn't feel like any of those things. He just felt vulnerable. "The philosophy background will help. A desk job would help."

"I have a desk job. I'm a civil servant in project management for the city."

She paused with her hand under a chicken. "Seriously."

"When it comes to boring the life out of someone with metrics and analytics, I'm your man."

He waited. She looked at him, assessing. "Your hair is okay. It's not buzzed like most other cops."

Some guys could pull off the bald, sexy look. Ian couldn't, a lesson he'd learned after losing his hair to radiation and chemo.

"What happens when Dad Googles you?" she asked as she moved down the row.

"I have alternate identities on social media."

She reached under another chicken and came back with two eggs. "Good girl," she cooed at the hen. "I don't want you to come."

The statement came out in a bizarre combination of experiment and defiance; for a moment he saw the girl he'd sent into meets with drug dealers and midlevel suppliers. He didn't respond. The fact that she was thinking about it, arguing with herself as much as with him, worked in his favor. "I know."

She closed the last hutch and folded her arms across her chest. "But you could make me do it. Threaten me like you threatened Isaiah."

He thought of all the avenues, legal, shady, and downright illegal, he could use to make her do it. He could coerce her, threaten her, threaten Isaiah. But he wasn't playing just for the bust. If Riva was going into a dangerous situation, Ian went with her. Period. "There's a proud choice and a safe choice here. Make the safe choice."

"I always felt safe with you," she said.

His heart thudded hard against his breastbone as he remembered the way the air held a charge when she was around, wiring her up for busts, sitting in a warm car together, the radio playing softly, neither of them saying what was on their minds.

All he wanted was to keep her safe. The rest he could work out on the fly. "You are safe with me," he said quietly. "I swear I'll keep you safe."

"Can you cook?"

"I can, but I don't," Ian said. "I can grow stuff, though."

She shooed him forward and closed the door to the chicken coop. "You can?"

"My mother's a master gardener. I'm good with flowers and the basic stuff you'd grow in a vegetable garden."

She looked at him sideways, as if surprised by this. "We've spent hours together, but I don't really know you."

"I'll give you the crash course on the way to Chicago."

She hauled open the screen door and walked into the kitchen, pausing to set the bowl of eggs on the counter, then lean over Isaiah's shoulder. "Chicken with shallots," he said.

"Smells delicious."

"Add more white wine?"

"Up to you. It's your kitchen."

Ian lingered by the door, not sure of his welcome or his place in the room. One hip cocked against the counter, Riva absently stirred a pot of rice with her left hand and pulled her cell phone out of her back pocket with her right. She tapped, scrolled, then lifted the phone to her ear.

"Hi, Mom," she said.

"No, wait," Ian said.

She waved her hand at him to shush him. "How are you feeling? Oh. Well, I'm calling with good news. I'm coming home for the luncheon."

Her voice had the bright note someone used when they were trying to cheer someone up. Even across the kitchen and over the sounds of boiling water and sizzling chicken Ian could tell the conversational rhythms were off, her mother's response lagging, dull.

"We'll talk menu when I'm there, okay? I've got some ideas. Set the table, please. Plates are in the cabinet to your right, silverware in the drawer by the sink."

Focused on Riva's half of the conversation, Ian didn't move. "She's talking to you, five-o," Isaiah said, slinging a glance over his shoulder. "Chop chop."

Ian opened the cabinet and found mismatched china that looked like it had been scrounged from an estate sale, the rims scalloped and decorated with roses, forget-me-nots, apple blossoms. The silverware was the same odd assortment of pieces, some obviously old. The tableware matched the kitchen, with its ancient sink and appliances and cabinets freshly painted in cornflower blue.

"I'll take a look at the recipes. Mom . . . Mom?" She looked at the phone, checking to see if the call had dropped. "Mom, did you take something . . . Never mind. I'm bringing someone with me. A colleague from the farm-to-table movement. He's interested—Yes, he. It's not like that, Mom. He's just a guy I work with. No, he'll get a hotel room."

The voice on the other end of the line had picked up in both tone and speed. "Mom, he doesn't need to stay with us."

"Actually," Ian said, precisely aligning a fork with the rim of the plate. "I do need to stay with you."

At that Isaiah turned around and gave him an incredulous look. The chicken sizzled in the pan. Clearly flustered, Riva patted his hand to redirect his attention back to the pan, and turned the heat down a notch.

"We'll talk about it when we get there," Riva said. "I don't know. Tomorrow? The day after? I've got some things to finish up here."

Ian plucked three napkins from the holder in the center of the table and folded them precisely down the middle to make triangles. "Tomorrow."

The glare she shot him was somewhere between infuriated and murderous. "I've got to go, Mom. I'll let you know. Bye."

She stared at him, color high in her cheeks. Clearly, the logistics of staying in the same house with him hadn't occurred to her. Behind her, Isaiah whistled as he transferred the rice into a bowl, then the chicken onto a pretty platter.

"And that," Ian said, "is why we need to coordinate a plan before we start talking to people."

Isaiah set the serving dishes on the table with a flourish. "Eat now, fight later."

The meal was delicious, as good as anything Ian had enjoyed in the city's best restaurants. The shallots were fresh and sweet, the white wine sauce adding a nice bite. Riva pushed the breadbasket across the table without comment and watched with satisfaction as Ian sopped up the sauce. "I missed lunch," he said.

"No, I'm just that good," Isaiah said. He was still eyeing Ian warily, but something about sitting down together and breaking bread had softened the teen a little. "You're on dish duty."

Ian started stacking plates. "You're going to stay here and look after the farm for Riva?"

"Yeah. I've got this."

Ian wasn't sure if Isaiah was trying to convince himself or Ian, but either way, he was glad. "Good. Pack a bag," he said to Riva.

"Excuse me?"

He turned on the water, plugged the drain, and squirted dish liquid into the rapidly filling water. "You're not staying here tonight."

She glared at him. "What? Afraid I'm going to run?"

"No," Ian said, when he meant *yes*.

"Hypothetically speaking, where am I staying?"

"With me."

"The hell I am."

"For two reasons," he said, over her outraged protest. "First, because yes, I want you where I can see you. Second, we need to get our stories straight before we walk into your parents' house tomorrow."

"We can do that on the drive to Chicago."

He rinsed the plates, well aware of Isaiah watching without commenting. "And we will. We'll go over this again and again, until we're letter perfect."

"No."

She spun and walked away, down a short hall. He slid the dishes into the water and followed her, winding up in the doorway to her bedroom. He looked at her, at the anger and resentment and, yes, lust, too, crackling in her blue eyes, gleaming in her tousled chestnut hair. "Riva."

He stopped. He'd missed so many things, her connection to the bigger drug trade, her family dynamics, and her. Just her. He had to get this right.

"We are about to go after the man you claim is the link between gangs and drugs and police corruption in this city, and one of the biggest suppliers in the region. They will not hesitate to kill us. In a normal situation, we'd spend weeks getting ready. We don't have weeks. We have hours. Pack a bag."

CHAPTER SIX

"If we're worried about our cover story," Riva said, clinging to her patience with her fingernails, "you need to stop talking to me like I'm your snitch. Or your flunky. Or your CI."

She hissed the words at Hawthorn and prayed he'd get the hint and keep his voice down. Isaiah was just down the hall, and right now he didn't know the full story of Riva and Hawthorn.

"You're right," he said unexpectedly. "I'll work on that. Pack a bag, *please*."

He was wearing a look she knew all too well, implacable and all man, prepared to stand there until kingdom-fucking-come. Ian Hawthorn, the control freak. When he looked like that, she stood a snowball's chance in hell of getting him to change his mind. "Fine. Just . . . fine. Wait here."

She pushed past him, ignoring the little shiver that ran up her spine when her shoulder brushed his biceps, and walked back down the hall to where Isaiah stood at the sink. "I'm going with Hawthorn tonight," she said, extemporizing. "We've got some work to do. Don't wait up. We'll probably be late, and I'll just spend the night with a friend in town, then leave tomorrow."

"Okay," he said, absently swiping a slow circle on a dirty plate. He was gazing longingly at the bookshelf overflowing with cookbooks and organic farming magazines.

"Want me to pick out some reading material for you?"

"Yeah. Thanks."

Riva grabbed three titles and wandered in the direction of the sleeping porch, where a single bed doubled as a napping spot or guest room. Hawthorn was watching as she did this. "What? He likes to read cookbooks."

She ducked into her bedroom and threw together a suitcase full of clothes she didn't wear often anymore, skinny dark jeans, ankle boots, fitted sweaters and T-shirts, things she could work in but would also look respectable when she served at the luncheon. Most of her makeup was so old it should be thrown away, but instead she swept it into her makeup bag.

"That's it?" Hawthorn said when she carried the bag through the living room, into the kitchen.

"What were you expecting?"

"More, I guess. My mother travels with enough luggage for the grand tour of the continent."

The first woman to come to mind as a travel companion was his mother? That was interesting. He reached for the suitcase, but she picked it up before he could grasp the handle. "I've got it."

Her heart was thumping wildly in her chest. The reaction was ridiculous, given how much time she'd spent with Hawthorn. Getting in a car, in the dark, to do something dangerous . . . been there, done that, didn't want the T-shirt.

But this was different, for reasons she really didn't want to think about. She hoisted the bag into the back seat, then climbed in the driver's seat.

"I'll follow you," she said. "Where are we going?"

"My place. We might as well be comfortable while we're going over this."

He drove to one of the warehouses renovated into apartments in the SoMa district. The exterior was old brick, the logos for long-gone businesses repainted to add character. He unlocked the door and pushed it open for her. The apartment was new, gleaming granite and brushed steel and track lighting, and preternaturally tidy. Very Hawthorn. Through an open doorway she saw a big bed covered with a dark comforter.

She looked away, cursing the heat blooming on her cheeks. "Where's the spare room?"

"I don't have one. You can take my room."

She was already shaking her head. "I'm not sleeping in your bed."

He tossed his keys onto the counter separating the cooking area from the living room. "I sleep on the couch all the time anyway."

"Afraid I'm going to sneak out in the middle of the night?" she asked, only partly kidding.

"I wouldn't put it past you."

He was dead serious. She leaned back against the breakfast bar and folded her arms across her chest. "We're not doing this if you don't trust me."

"We're doing this whether I trust you or not," he shot back. "Know why? Because you'd walk away and flip me off on your way out the door, but you won't give up Isaiah like that."

"You're right. Because he's a boy learning to be a man, a good man. The kind of man who's a force for positive change in his community."

"I'm doing my job. Which is also a force for positive change in the community."

"The difference," she said precisely, "is that Isaiah won't use people to get what he wants. You will."

"Don't blame me for the choices you made, Riva."

She felt her face go white. This, here, now was where she drew the line. "Have I ever . . . *ever* . . . blamed you, or not taken responsibility for my choices seven years ago." She didn't frame it as a question because she knew the answer. And so did he.

A muscle popped in his jaw before he answered. "No."

"I took full responsibility for what I did. I did everything you asked then, and I'll do everything I can to help you now, because I'm helping Isaiah." She left out the little warning bell going off in the back of her mind about her mother, because while every cell in her body told her something was really wrong at home, she didn't need to tell Ian that.

His jaw was so tight she could use it as a knife. "I know."

"Good. As long as we're establishing boundaries, Lieutenant Hawthorn, I won't sleep in your bed."

He stood in front of her in what she called the classic cop stance, feet spread, legs braced, one hand on his hip where his gun would be. Over his shoulder she could see the SoMa district, lit up and bustling with spring evening traffic. "We need to talk about that."

Talk about his bed? If they talked about it much more,

she was going to grab his hand and lead him there. "Okay, talk."

"Say my name."

What did his name have to do with the sleeping arrangements for the night? "What?"

"Say it. I'm not Hawthorn for this trip. I'm Ian Fallon. If you call me by my real last name after you've introduced me, your dad is going to suspect something. If you call me by my rank, we're in deep trouble." He leaned forward and braced his hands on either side of her waist. "Our lives are at stake. Yes, I want to find out who's supplying drugs to the Strykers, but I also want to keep you—us—both safe. You have to call me Ian. Say my name."

The only sounds in the apartment were the soft hum of the ventilation system and her heart pounding in her ears. Their strange, strained relationship was so intimate in so many ways, but she'd never used his first name. "Ian."

"Again."

Her head snapped up. "Ian."

"Again."

"Ian."

"Good. Now use it conversationally."

"Fuck you, Ian."

He huffed out a laugh. "Polite conversation," he said, and straightened to hold out his hand. "Hi. I'm Ian."

She stared at his outstretched hand. It was just a handshake. Just palm-to-palm contact.

Except it wasn't. It would be the first time she'd willingly touched him. He'd touched her, frisked her, handled her wrists and her arms, guided her places while she was handcuffed, on one heated occasion wired her up for the night. She'd never, ever willingly touched him. Had avoided it all those years ago.

"Do it."

"Stop ordering me around," she snapped.

"Please."

He's just a man. He's just a man in his apartment, holding out his hand. It's like starting over.

Except it wasn't starting over. There was no way for them to begin again, not with their history. All she had to do was pretend he was just a man. Who'd said, in essence, *please touch me.*

Oh, don't go there. Don't go to his voice, rasping and quiet, intimate, one step from a murmur, one step from seduction. She'd had the usual range of lovers, the back-to-the-land movement offering up men who approached sex the same way they approached growing things—with attention to detail and a slow hand. But none of them were Ian. None of them were imprinted on her like he was.

"You get why this is difficult for me," she said.

"Yes. Do it anyway."

Slowly, she reached out and put her hand in his. It was warm, dry, closing slowly and firmly around her palm.

"Our lives may depend on you not flinching every time I come within six inches of you, much less make contact."

"I know. I just . . ."

"I scare you."

"A little."

A shadow crossed his face. "You lose something when you lose control of your body like that."

She inhaled a deep, shaky breath. "Do they teach you that in the academy?"

"Not exactly, but they teach you about power dynamics. I can draw a conclusion. You don't need to afraid of me. This isn't like last time."

"With all due respect, Lieutenant, I'm here in your apartment because you basically coerced me into being here."

"Try that again, and use my name."

"Dammit," she muttered. "With all due respect, Ian, I'm here in your apartment because you basically coerced me into being here." She paused. "Wow. That sounds different when I use your name. Lieutenant Hawthorn has the right to coerce. Ian doesn't."

He frowned, as if the subtle shift hadn't occurred to him before he sent them down this path. "Ian," she said experimentally. "Ian. Ian Fallon. Ian."

She was teasing him now, and she knew it. She was still trapped between his outstretched arms, his face inches from hers, his gaze flickering between her mouth shaping his name and her eyes.

"I'm still Hawthorn," he said.

"Actually, you're not," she said quietly. "That barn door is now open, horse long gone. Ian. Is now a good time to talk about me not sleeping in your bed?"

A muscle jumped in his jaw. "You always did know how to push my buttons."

"Yes, I have to sleep in your bed, or no, I don't . . . *Ian*?"

Something snapped in his eyes, something she'd pushed against and pushed against seven years earlier, something that had been banked back to hot coals but never fully died. He'd been under control before, tightly leashed but vibrating around the edges. A muscle flicked in his jaw as he fought some internal battle. She found herself wondering if this was the time she pushed him too far.

"One of these days you're going to say my name, and you're going to say please, and then you're not going to be able to say anything at all."

Heat spiked through her, searing all the air from her lungs. His voice was low, potent, lacking the ice-cold deadly precision she remembered. It was a lover's voice, an implacable, focused lover's voice, no laughing or teasing or even kindness that she remembered from her previous experiences.

Too far . . . and not quite far enough.

"Is that what you want, Riva?"

She could see in his eyes that he thought he'd won, that by pushing her as far as he had, he'd tipped the balance of power back to his side. She reached deep for the woman she'd become in the last seven years. "You know it is."

He froze.

"It's what you want, too. But we both know it's a really bad idea."

"Not as bad an idea as it was then."

"If that's how you feel, then kiss me."

Fearless, he'd said. Fearless and rash. They were both playing with a fire that could burn them to ash before they even left town. But she wasn't eighteen anymore.

"Just a kiss. That's all. We're both adults now. We can handle a kiss." She tipped her head forward so their faces were mere inches apart, angled just a little to bring their mouths into alignment. "Would it make you feel better if I crossed that line? Give you plausible deniability?"

His breath eddied against her lips. For a dangerous, heady moment she thought he would cross that line and kiss her, a move that would resolve everything and make it so much worse. "No one has to know," she murmured. "I won't tell."

His gaze searched hers. But then the muscles in his arms and shoulders bunched, sending a spike of hot, sweet, adrenaline-fueled desire right to her core, and he pushed himself upright.

Leaving her to seethe in a familiar, seething sexual frustration. "Sleep in your own bed. I'm not sneaking out tonight."

"Again with my name."

She didn't know whether to slap him, kiss him, or scream. The desire to do all three at once while launching herself at him swept through her, momentarily stealing her voice. "Sleep in your own bed, Ian. I'm not sneaking out tonight, Ian."

"Have it your way," he said with a shrug.

Fewer than eight hours into the operation and his self-control was shot.

Ian sat on the edge of his bed and put his head in his hands. On the other side of his bedroom door was his houseguest/prisoner/informant, getting ready for bed. Innocuous sounds like the blinds closing, a suitcase unzipping, feet padding across the floor, water running through the pipes to the half bath off the foyer sent his imagination into overdrive. All he could think about was that at some point in time, she would be out there, taking off her clothes to put on . . . what?

A nightgown? One of those soft oversized T-shirt things that bunched up around a woman's hips while she slept? Pajamas? Maybe she wore actual pajamas, the kind that looked like men's but were fitted to shorter limbs and rounder curves. Soft cotton sleep pants and a faded T-shirt? Fuzzy socks to keep her feet warm?

Maybe she slept in nothing at all.

He clenched his hands in his hair and talked to the floor. Very quietly. "She's not out there naked."

He couldn't be sure of that. This was a new Riva, brashness and boldness dialed up to fifteen on the one-to-ten scale, all woman. It wouldn't shock him at all to walk out tomorrow morning to Riva's bare limbs spilling out from under his extra blanket and sheet, her reddish-brown hair tumbled over her cheek, her nape, the tops of her shoulder blades.

Nightgown. Sleep shirt. Whatever would allow him to tangle his legs with hers and keep her warm while she slept.

Three hours. They'd been in each other's company for less than half a day and the situation was already spiraling out of control. He would have kissed her, was microseconds away from doing it when she'd said *I won't tell*. Those three words brought him up short.

He wanted to tell. He wasn't a man for secrets, for pieces on the side, for crossing lines. If he kissed Riva Henneman, he was going to take that vacation Swarthmore kept nagging him about, take her to bed, and take what he'd wanted for the last seven years. If he did that, he wanted to be able to tell everyone. Not to brag about a conquest—he kept his own counsel when it came to women—but because he wanted her.

But there was no way it could happen. Like Captain Swarthmore had said, the future he wanted depended on being politically savvy.

Face facts. You wanted her the moment you laid eyes on her in Kaffiend. You can't have her. So you just have to get through this.

It was going to be a very long trip to Chicago.

CHAPTER SEVEN

Seven years earlier . . .

A shadow fell over the economics textbook she was pretending to read. Riva looked up to see Officer Hawthorn looming over the table at the back of the pancake house. With one quick glance he took in her face, hair, clothes, the textbook and laptop open on the table beside her.

"You paid up?"

She nodded. Her heart was pounding, her eyes unable to decide where to focus: on his face, or anywhere but his face. How could she have mistaken him for a grad student? The lamp hanging over the booth threw a soft light on his face, but it only brought out the lines around his mouth, the firm set of his lips, the implacable look in his eyes. He wore jeans, the soft caramel leather jacket over a long-sleeved T-shirt and nononsense boots.

Her stomach rolled a slow loop she might be able to chalk up to nerves. There were two problems with that. One, she'd bought drugs from a dealer before without her nerves getting involved. Two, the glimmering sensation coursed through her chest to settle low in her pelvis. Nerves didn't make her body go soft, her lips part.

Desire did.

"Let's go."

She hurriedly closed the laptop and the book, then shoved them both into the messenger bag she carried and followed him through the pancake house. It wasn't busy at this time of night. The perfect out-of-the-way place to meet your cop handler before buying some drugs.

A nondescript car sat around the corner of the building. Hawthorn clicked open the locks.

"Where are we going?" she asked.

"To the meeting point."

He skirted the edge of campus, taking Riva down streets she'd not seen before, using a back route through the science buildings to avoid the worst intersection on campus before turning onto the winding road that led through the park that marked the campus's eastern edge. They pulled into a small parking lot where joggers and runners left their cars before setting out on one of the trails. The lot was empty except for one other car, idling near the dumpster. Hawthorn parked next to it. "Out."

He met her on the passenger side of the car. Riva hugged her arms around her body and shivered in the cold October night while the other driver's door opened and a blond woman got out. "Officer Sorenson, Riva Henneman," Hawthorn said.

"Hi," Sorenson said. "How are you doing?"

"Great," Riva said, mock cheerfully. "Fine. Couldn't be better."

"Glad to hear it." Sorenson opened the back door. "Get in the car."

Riva got in, then slid across the seat to let Sorenson follow her. Once inside, Sorenson opened a nondescript tote. "You're going to do these deals wearing a wire." She pulled out a black square with a cord neatly wrapped around it. "Battery pack. Goes on your waistband. Mic. Clips somewhere under your clothes. The advantage to being a woman is that your bra makes a good attachment point. Men have to have the thing taped to their skin. You would not believe how much they bitch about losing a little chest hair."

"Okay," Riva said.

Sorenson eyed her. "How many layers are you wearing?"

"I get cold easily," Riva said, defensive.

"Lift up your top."

Riva looked around. All she could see of Hawthorn was his back, where he leaned against the side of the car. From the sounds and posture of his body, he was on his cell phone. Awkwardly, she hoisted her shirt above her bra. In less than a minute Sorenson had the battery pack clipped to her jeans and the mic tucked into the spot where her bra cups met. One strip of medical tape snugged the slack cord against Riva's stomach.

"All done," Sorenson said, businesslike. "You can go back to Officer Hawthorn."

She felt like a dog during an obedience trial. Riva yanked her shirt down, got out of the car, trotted over to Hawthorn's vehicle, then opened the passenger door.

Once inside, he looked her over again, gaze lingering on her chest.

"Want me to take my shirt off so you can get a better look?" she snapped.

"I'm checking to make sure the wire's not visible," he replied. "Also, everything you say while we're recording goes into the public record."

Oh, Jesus. *"Are we recording?"*

He reached for the handset. "Are we recording, Jo?"

"Not yet," came the response. "Say when."

Hawthorn looked at her for a moment, then spoke into the handset. "Turn it on when she gets out of the car each time."

"You got it."

"How long until the first meet?"

"Twenty minutes."

He hung up the handset. One elbow on the doorframe, the other on his thigh, he stared straight ahead. Fine. Two could play that game. She opened her messenger bag and pulled out her econ textbook. She couldn't focus on the words. Her head was full of so many details, the way his legs sprawled open, the intriguing, complex meeting point of zipper, belt, and soft cotton shirt tucked into his waistband. The scent of his leather jacket and some sort of cologne, or aftershave, or maybe his shampoo. His skin. She was sure she could smell his skin, faintly musky. He'd done something to make himself sweat during the day, but it wasn't an unpleasant smell. Instead, she found herself wanting to burrow into it, breathe deeply, rub her body against his.

He startled her out of her dreamy train of thought when he reached out and turned the heat down. "You're flushed," he said. "I thought you were too warm."

"No," she said. "I'm . . ."

She was cold and hot, sick with fear and nerves and a growing sense of shame. How could she have been so stupid as to agree to sell drugs for her father? Her psych class had discussed sociopaths; with cold dread she'd recognized all the behavior traits: intelligent, charming, untruthful, egocentric, lacking in remorse. Her whole life he'd played her against her mother, holding out his approval like a toy in front of a toddler, then snatching it away the moment she made a mistake. How was she supposed to know Hawthorn was a cop? Her sheltered upbringing didn't include picking out undercover police officers.

What if this never went away? What if she never learned from her mistakes, never found her own power and courage and confidence?

"You're what?" he said impatiently.

She was terrified, and as turned on as she'd ever been in her life. Her body and brain were in a state of cognitive dissonance she'd never experienced before, animal desire surging hot and fierce through her veins. Her fingers and toes were numb with cold, almost imperceptible shudders running through her shoulders, but her face was indeed flushed and heat pulsed between her thighs.

Awareness flickered to life in his eyes. His gaze skimmed over her again, this time seeing the truth. His hand hovered over the knob, then turned the heat back on.

Present day . . .

Ian was jolted out of a near coma the next morning by his kitchen cabinet doors opening, then slamming closed.

Convinced he should be the only person in his apartment, he lurched out of bed and hauled open the bedroom door. Riva Henneman jumped about three feet in the air and two feet backward, careening crazily off the edge of the sink before fetching up against the counter.

"You scared me half to death!" Her hand was over her heart, her blue eyes wide in a face so pale her freckles stood out.

He blinked, remembered the events of yesterday, and woke the rest of the way up. "Sorry. I was sound asleep."

"Are you still working the night shift these days? It's after eight."

He hadn't fallen asleep until almost four. "Do you need something?"

"Coffee. Desperately. And a shower. Almost as desperately. Um . . . do you mind putting that away?"

For a short, terrifying moment, he thought she was staring at his tented sleep shorts. Then he followed her gaze a few inches right to his hand, loosely clasped around his service weapon. He didn't even remember grabbing it. "Habit," he said shortly.

"You sleep with it?"

"It's close at hand."

"That's not exactly safe gun practice."

"I don't exactly have small kids in the apartment." A thought occurred to him. "Can you handle a firearm?"

"Sure," she said offhandedly. "I'll give you a demonstration if you don't tell me where you keep the coffee."

"In a minute," he said, setting the gun on his dresser for safety. "What kind of firearms?"

She shrugged. "Hunting rifle, shotgun, and handgun."

He might need coffee to deal with this. "You learned to shoot because you live alone in a rural area?"

"No, I learned to shoot because my dad thought guns were cool. Seriously, Hawth—Ian. Can we save the interrogation for after coffee? I have a splitting headache and if I don't get caffeine in me soon I'm going to—"

"Fridge door. Does Isaiah have access to those weapons?"

"Weapon, singular, and of course not." She hauled open the fridge door. Her face lit up when she found the bag of beans in the door. It gave him a moment to look her over. His first instinct had been the right one. She wore a pink T-shirt nightdress that fell to midcalf. It looked soft to the touch and was charmingly wrinkled from the heat of her body. The V-neck showed her clavicle while the soft cotton clung lovingly to her breasts, a thought that threatened to turn his morning erection into an all-day companion.

"I only have a shotgun at the farm." She unrolled the bag and found the scoop inside, then opened the top of the coffee maker and dumped in enough ground coffee to wake the dead. He thought about pointing that out, then thought the better of it. "Normally I keep it under my bed, but when I got home yesterday I unloaded it, locked it up in the gun safe in my closet, and hid the shells in the chicken feed."

"You keep a shotgun under your bed."

"I live alone on a farm at the end of a dirt road. You probably know this, but the sound of a pump action shotgun being racked is the most recognizable sound the world over."

Riva Henneman stood in his kitchen in her nightie, making coffee and talking about guns. Surreptitiously, Ian grabbed the doorframe. Solid under his hand. He wasn't dreaming, but he also wasn't totally awake, so he said the first thing that came into his head. "What do the guys you bring home think about that?"

She ran water into the carafe, then poured it into the reservoir. "Usually they're on the bed, not under it, so it doesn't come up."

She brought them home for sex, not conversation. You only looked under a woman's bed if you were at the joint-cleaning stage, or if you'd landed on the floor during seriously athletic sex. She also must need that coffee. She was answering his questions with a hefty dose of attitude but not outright loathing.

"But I've mostly dated guys in the farm-to-table world, so they know all about shotguns. They'd be surprised if I didn't have a gun in the house."

Maybe he was the only man who found a woman's competence with weapons sexy. Maybe he needed more than four hours of sleep.

The silence stretched between them, gaining an electric crackle as she actually focused on him. No longer distracted by the frantic search for coffee, her gaze sharpened and took him in from head to toe, sliding over his skin like fingertips, starting with his face—eyes, the lines in his cheeks, his mouth—then gaining weight and heaviness, more like it was the palm of her hand that dragged slowly over his chest, down his abdomen to the waistband of the cotton sleep shorts he wore. Her gaze lingered and his cock responded appropriately for what he felt was a really difficult situation: Riva in his kitchen, Riva likely naked under her nightgown, Riva looking at him like a morning quickie would be a great way to kill time while the coffee brewed.

He didn't look away, or shift, or apologize. Instead he

stood under her gaze and felt a rush of pleasure unlike anything he'd known, let desire sweep through his veins and capillaries to pulse at the edges of his skin.

Her gaze swept down his legs to his bare feet, then back to his face. When their eyes met she blushed, hard, like she'd forgotten that at the end of that sexually charged survey of his body she'd have to deal with the man again.

If she asked him now if he wanted that kiss, he'd say yes. One shitty night of sleep and Riva in a nightgown, and his self-control was shot.

Riva ducked her head, letting her hair hide her expression while she pushed the start button on the coffee maker. "I won't be long in the shower. We should get going. It's a solid six-hour drive to Chicago and I want to be there in time for dinner."

When Ian came out of his bedroom, he carried a duffel bag and a backpack. His hair, still wet from his shower, gleamed like the coffee she'd just finished. He wore a pair of flat-front chinos, a thin sweater with the sleeves pushed to his elbows, and brown leather boots. The effect was office drone who rode a motorcycle. A familiar little thrill skittered along her nerves and settled in her chest, making her heart jump.

"Ready?" he asked.

She was sitting on his sofa, trying her best not to fidget herself into a frenzy. Being inside like this made her antsy. She needed fresh air, miles of walking, dirt under her hands, rain on her face. And now she was about to go back to the place that had made her the girl he'd arrested.

"As I'll ever be," she said. He opened the door for her, then followed her down the hallway to the stairs they'd walked up the night before and out to the parking lot. It was a glorious spring day, sunshine pouring down from the skies like light flung at a painter's canvas. She'd spent a fair bit of her time in Hawthorn's car wondering where he lived, how it was decorated, if he had roommates. Never had a sleek condo crossed her mind.

He unzipped the backpack and pulled out his laptop. "You drive the first shift."

She didn't say anything while navigating traffic to the highway. To her surprise, neither did he. She'd half expected him to tell her how to drive, where to go, which route to take. Instead, he fiddled with some electronics she didn't recognize.

"You can ask," he said without looking at her.

"What?"

"You want to know what this is, but you're not asking." His gaze flicked up to hers. "You can ask."

Getting used to a situation where she could treat Ian Hawthorn like an equal was going to require serious adjustment. "I couldn't, before," she said.

"This is a different situation." He plugged a USB cord into the laptop. "We're colleagues, remember? We have to act like colleagues, like you're the boss and I'm the apprentice, or intern, or whatever."

She laughed, merging into traffic on the eastbound interstate. "You are so not an intern."

"Just pretend for a while," he said.

Pretend they didn't have history? Pretend the air wasn't heated and crackling between them? Pretend he'd never cuffed her, never used her as a CI, never changed her life? She blinked. No time like the present. They had six hours to get this straightened out. "Okay. What's all that?"

"Portable secure wifi." The answer came readily to his lips. "I can access national and state databases with secured wifi. Can we share the charger?"

Before, Hawthorn hadn't asked her questions unless it pertained to her readiness to buy yet more drugs from yet another unsuspecting dealer. "Sure. I'm all charged up."

He disconnected her phone, plugged in, and powered up the laptop. She looked at him, seeing him in the sunlight for the first time.

"You keep staring. You can't stare like that. You have to take me for granted."

"I've never seen you in sunlight before," she said.

That got his attention. His gaze snapped to hers; she could see him riffling through his memories of her. "Am I sparkling?"

It took her a second, then she laughed. "No."

"Keep going," he said. "Ask away."

"Pets?" she said, somewhat randomly. It was easy to talk about pets.

"I don't have any now. My schedule's too erratic to be fair to a cat, let alone a dog. We had collies growing up. My mom was around to let them in and out. Dad named them after quarterbacks. Marino, Elway, Montana, Bradshaw. You?"

This was weird. Very weird. "We had a cat."

"What was his name?"

"Mr. Fluffers," she said reluctantly, and watched his mouth slide out of control.

"Mr. Fluffers."

"You got a problem with that?"

"Not at all. A Persian?"

"White. My mom has a Yorkie now."

"A preference for fluffy things she can cuddle?"

"I guess," she said, thinking about her mom's longing to love things. "Why?"

"Because later tonight I'm going to be sitting down to dinner with your parents, under the guise of us being very friendly colleagues. From what you're saying, you don't go home much, let alone bring other people home. I need some of the basics of your story to not fuck this up from the beginning, because fucking it up could put us in a lot of danger."

And there was the Hawthorn she knew, focused on the operation, completely disregarding the personal elements. She hoped the old saying was true, that familiarity bred contempt, but in their case, all it seemed to be breeding was new, complex layers of attraction, desire. On her part, at least.

"My dad may not be the most law-abiding citizen, but he's not going to kill either of us." But even as she said it, she wondered if she knew who her father really was. Seven years was a long time. People changed in that length of time. She had.

"That's not a risk I'm willing to take. You said yourself you haven't been home much in seven years. You may not know what your father's become. Tell me about your parents."

"They're both from Chicago. Mom's from the Gold Coast. Dad grew up in Fuller Park, on the South Side, and got himself a scholarship to Northwestern. He met Mom there."

"What's her family like?"

"Her dad was a banker, on corporate boards, that kind

of thing. He was a perfectionist, which made Mom anxious. My earliest memories are of her always fretting, about meals, about how we looked, the house, traffic, the weather, anything she couldn't control."

He typed something into his laptop. "Maiden name?"

"Montgomery."

"You're an only child?"

"Yes, but not by choice. They tried for years to get pregnant. Mom had so many miscarriages the doctor finally told her to stop trying. I was the miracle baby."

He typed away, scrutinized the data that came back. "If she came from money, why was your father distributing drugs?"

She'd never really thought about it, not until Hawthorn exploded her life. After that, she'd thought about it late at night when she couldn't sleep, trying to make sense of who she was, who she could become, always hoping and dreaming that one day she'd have the relationship she'd always wanted with her mother. "Because he's a sociopath. And because my dad's a sociopath, he took Mom's miscarriages personally. He wanted a boy," she said finally. "Really badly. I used to hear him yelling at her about it, how he worked his ass off to get her what she wanted, and what about what he wanted? Somebody to carry on his work, to follow in his footsteps. It was 'all he asked her to do.' Like the fact that I was a girl was her fault, not his. His moods dominated the whole house. I was little, maybe five or six when I first picked up on this. I felt badly about it, that he was so mad at her, so I tried to make him happy, tried to be the son he wanted. It would work for a while, and then I'd mess up. Miss a couple of shots in basketball, or get elected vice president of the student council, not president.

He'd go back to ignoring me and picking at Mom. Nothing could please him when he was like that. Not her cooking, or the house, or me. By the time I was eighteen, I just wanted him to love us. I was willing to do anything. And, as you know, I did. The end."

"He fixated on a son because . . . ?"

"His ego. Women are weak. We are fatally flawed," she said. She'd heard it a thousand times in a dozen different ways, but it all boiled down to the same thing. Inherent weakness.

"I'm sorry," Ian said.

She focused on the highway zipping away under the wheels of her truck, taking her home. "Between you and a couple of psychology classes, I figured out what was going on. I've tried to set boundaries, take care of myself."

She could feel his gaze against her skin, but he didn't push it. They drove for a couple of hours, Ian typing and clicking, asking questions when data came up. She checked her phone, then flipped up her turn signal to switch lanes in time for the next exit.

"You don't have to drive this cautiously," he said.

"This is how I always drive."

"You always drive the speed limit, indicate turns half a mile ahead, and never text and drive."

"Yes. Because after I met you, I lived in fear of being pulled over. I'd turn and walk away if I saw a cop in SoMa."

"That's not your best move. Make eye contact. We're more interested in the people who won't look us in the eye."

Trust Ian to go straight for the logic and avoid the emotion. She came to a complete stop at the sign at the top of the exit, then consulted her phone and headed south.

"Where are we going?"

"We're getting some lunch."

He looked around the exit. Enormous gas stations sat beside each off ramp, with chain fast food options hovering like fighter planes next to the mother ships. "You're going to eat McDonald's?"

She headed down a county highway, away from the neon and twirling signs. "There's a local place a few miles down the road. I hope you like barbecue."

"Love it," he said. "When my brother was home on leave last year, we tried all of Lancaster's local barbecue joints."

"Fat Shack is the best," she said.

"I prefer Smokehouse, but Jamie would agree with you."

"Home on leave from where?" she asked, interested despite herself.

"The navy."

Something niggled at the back of her mind, a memory she couldn't make gel into a thought. "I could see you in the military," she said. "Why didn't you join?"

"I thought about it," he said. His jaw was tense, his voice emotionless again. She didn't ask. She wanted the right to question him, and for him to see she also exercised another option: the right to keep silent and allow someone some privacy.

"You can ask, if you want."

"You obviously don't want to talk about it. Sometimes even people who know each other well respect boundaries. I'm making a point," she said.

"I can see that," he said mildly. "Here's your point.

Things are different now. You can ask questions, refuse to answer them, decide where we eat, which, for the record, I would have let you do seven years ago, except all you said when I asked was *I don't care*. That's your point. Let me know when you've got it."

She pulled into the dusty gravel parking lot next to a low-slung white building with picnic tables dotting the grass and a big smoker behind the kitchen, cut the engine, and turned to look at him. "What happens if I admit I get it?" she asked.

He didn't pretend to not understand her question. Instead he turned the full force of those hazel eyes on her. It was like turning a gas burner from off to high, heat radiating instantly. "We figure that out together."

A minivan pulled into the lot next to them, startling Riva. The side door opened and a pack of kids poured out, the older ones helping the younger ones out of car seats and down the step to the gravel. "Let's eat."

They ordered at the window, through which they could see the kitchen in full swing. Riva studied the operation, then made a conscious decision to shut off her work brain and ordered ribs, fries, and an iced tea.

"Make that two," Hawthorn said. "Inside or out?"

Inside was dominated by two large televisions turned to competing news stations. She peered out the back window and found picnic tables covered with cheery red-checked vinyl tablecloths held down by large squeeze bottles full of the house varieties of barbecue sauce. Inside meant they wouldn't have to talk. Outside would soothe her soul.

"Out," she said, then added, "If that's okay with you."

"I prefer it," he said.

By unspoken agreement they ended up at a table shaded by a big oak with freshly minted leaves tossing in the breeze. Riva tucked her hair behind her ear and dug in her purse for her sunglasses. "It's pretty," she commented.

"How did you find this place?"

"I keep a list of recommendations I get from a bunch of different places. Customers, distributors, other growers, the internet. Last night I picked out a couple on this route."

"How did you get into the farm-to-table movement? Before you bite my head off, a colleague would know that."

She used the waitress arriving with their food to consider how to answer this question without giving too much away. "When I dropped out of college, I went to work at the natural foods market, mostly because after I had spent a lot of time thinking about a prison cell, I wanted to work outside."

He picked up a knife and fork to cut the meat from his ribs, but then set the knife down when the slightest pressure sent the flesh sliding right off the bone. "I didn't know you dropped out."

"I did," she said matter-of-factly. "I had to learn what I wanted, who I was, because all I knew was how to be what Dad wanted. I liked being outside, and felt stifled in classrooms, so I dropped out. That was the first step."

"Now you have Oasis and the farm. That's a lot of progress in seven years."

"I started doing what I wanted to do, shaping my own future," she said. "A future that includes kids like Isaiah. It's one I can give my whole heart to."

"Sounds like a pretty good life to me," he said quietly.

The rest of the drive was uneventful, but not as awkward as Riva expected. Lunch taught her that their shared history made things like sitting in a car together and having a meal together less stressful than it would have been with a near stranger. She knew Hawthorn, how he moved, how he looked when he was angry, or focused, or even amused. For better or worse, they had history.

The afternoon sunlight was fading when she merged into the traffic heading into Chicago. She pulled up alongside an old house in the historic neighborhood of Logan Square, and shifted into park.

"Why not the driveway?"

"The truck's leaking oil." She clambered out and shut her door, rounding the hood to stand by Ian. "Dad won't like a big stain on the driveway."

"Anything else I should know before we go in?"

Before she could answer, the front door opened and a yipping ball of hair topped with a bouncing pink bow barreled down the sidewalk toward them. "Oh, Sugar! Come here! Riva! Riva, honey, grab her!"

Riva sat down on her heels and opened her arms, collecting a squirming ball of teacup Yorkie to her chest. "Hello, furball." The tiny dog writhed and wagged and licked her face, giving Riva ample time to note how white her muzzle was, the cloudy spot on one eye. "Yes, I'm happy to see you, too."

Her mother minced down the sidewalk toward her, dressed in princess-pink ballet flats, ankle-length pants, and a cashmere sweater with frills at the hem, neckline, and button placket. Her hair was carefully done, her makeup impeccable. "Oh, dear," she fretted from halfway through the flowerbeds lining the path. "I should get her leash."

Sugar, more interested in the newcomer than Riva, strained out of Riva's arms. "She's fine, Mom. A little help here?"

Hawthorn reached out and caught the dog before Riva dropped it, cradling it in his left arm. The tiny thing braced its front paws on his chest and strained up to sniff at his jaw.

"She likes you," her mother said to Hawthorn. "She's normally very reserved. I'm Stephanie."

"Nice to meet you," Hawthorn said, shaking her hand like he wasn't holding a tiny, ridiculous dog. "I'm Ian."

"Welcome, Ian," she said, tearing up a little. "Any friend of Riva's is so very welcome here. Oh, darling, it's so good to see you!" She hugged Riva, squeezing her shoulders tightly. "How was the drive?"

"Fine. Traffic was light." Riva was surprised to hear her voice was level. She leaned back and studied her mother's face, trying not to look like she was checking the state of her pupils. They were contracted, but the sun was in her eyes.

"Oh, look at me, leaving you two out here on the walk! How stupid of me. Come in, come in."

"I'll get the bags," Hawthorn said.

"I'll get mine," Riva replied. Which was how they ended up following her mother up the sidewalk, each of them carrying a suitcase and Ian with a Yorkie.

Inside the house's two-story entry, her mother was fluttering around Ian, not quite finishing sentences about the house or offering him something to drink while Ian looked around without seeming to do so. Riva knew only because she'd seen him do it dozens of times. For the first time, the plan became real.

"Mom, we should get these suitcases out of the foyer before Dad gets home. Where do you have us?"

"Oh, you're right. Your father doesn't like a mess. Come upstairs," her mother said.

"You can put Sugar down," Riva said to Hawthorn.

"She's fine where she is," Hawthorn replied.

As she followed him up the stairs, his shirt shifted a little, exposing a leather tab clipped to his waistband. Riva saw the dull gleam of steel. With her free hand Riva reached up and tugged swiftly on his sweater, hiding what she now knew was a concealed weapon.

Her mother opened a door. "We renovated three bedrooms into a two-bedroom suite with a shared bathroom. For when the grandchildren come to visit. Riva, you're in here."

Riva followed her mother into a lovely guest room with a big four-poster bed and dresser on the far wall and a little sitting area clustered around the fireplace. The uppermost branches of the redbud tree were visible through the windows at the back of the room. "The nights are still cool enough for a fire." Her mother opened the door next to the fireplace. "Bathroom's through here, and Ian, you're in the adjoining room. I'll leave you two to get unpacked. Come on, baby," she cooed, kissing Sugar's head. "Come with mama."

Hawthorn handed over Sugar. Riva looked at him.

Despite her best efforts, she was alone in a bedroom with Hawthorn.

CHAPTER EIGHT

The door closed behind Riva's mother, leaving Ian and Riva in the bedroom together. Riva's color was high, her eyes not quite meeting his, looking around the room at the ruffled curtains, the carpets on the dark hardwood floors, the chairs with throw pillows grouped around a rug in front of the wood-burning fireplace. The windows were old, tall and narrow, letting in lots of light weirdly refracted by the wavy glass.

She was, he realized, looking anywhere but at him. Or at the bed. For a long, searing moment he let himself imagine Riva in that bed, her hair a tumbled red-brown tangle around her face as she slept, her lips soft, her face relaxed, not tense and angry and distrustful. Then, because he was an idiot and a masochist and into wanting things he could never have, he added a fading flush to her cheeks, reddened skin on her chin and neck from the scruff around his mouth, from his kisses as he made love to her while the fire crackled.

He'd give anything to see her like that.

Anything? Including his career?

He cleared his throat. "That went well."

"I'll ask her to move you." Riva stared at him.

He resisted the urge to shove his hands in his pockets. "It's better if you don't."

"You do understand that she's given us adjoining rooms because she's so desperate for grandchildren that she'd encourage a colleague to knock me up."

He thought he knew the depth and breadth of his desire for Riva, the way it tasted, smelled, felt as it pooled in his body, overtook his brain. He clearly suffered from a failure of imagination, because not once had he imagined her pregnant or holding a child. His child. The child they made together. He didn't let himself think of that kind of future, because his body was a ticking time bomb already.

But now it was there, Riva's slender body ripening with a baby.

And suddenly something that had been abstract and off-limits before—a wife, children, a future—swam into sharp HD detail. He'd been young when he got cancer, so getting married and having kids was never at the front of his mind. As he grew older and watched his friends pair off, get married, start families, he'd been content with what he had: a future with the LPD and politics. But at the words "knock me up," a howling regret surged inside him. Because he could imagine Riva married, pregnant, teaching her kids to gather eggs, feed the sheep, weed the garden.

She was staring at him. In their new and improved relationship, that counted as a quip, and quips deserved fast, snappy responses. "I do know," he said. "But that's why it's beneficial. If we need to talk after lights out, I don't have to creep down the hall to your room and raise suspicions."

And he could keep an eye on her, for two reasons. The cop in him wouldn't put it past Riva to sneak out. The man in him balked at the thought of leaving her unprotected.

"We're going to share a bathroom."

"I promise to put the seat down."

She shot him a glare. "That's not the problem."

"So what is the problem?"

More glaring.

"I'm not dense, Riva. We're going to be sharing a bathroom, which means getting naked to do things like shower. Our bedrooms are separated by only a couple of doors. There's a fireplace in yours. Very romantic. That's the problem."

She deflated a little. "I just didn't think we'd be this close."

"It's not as close as the front seat of my car."

"True."

The tension crackling in the air between them ebbed, leaving Ian in the near-constant state of arousal Riva inspired in him. But obviously she needed some space. "I'm going to go for a run," he said abruptly.

"I don't run," Riva said, warning clear in her voice.

"You don't have to come with me," he said. "Thanks for your help on the stairs."

"No problem," she said. "I'm going downstairs to try to salvage dinner."

"What?" he said, caught off guard.

"Dad's criticized Mom's cooking for so long she's basically terrified of her kitchen. They order out a lot.

But she'll feel like she needs to cook because that's what Dad thinks a family should do. I need to intervene before she gets started."

He schlepped his suitcase and laptop bag into his bedroom, which was smaller but contained a similar volume of chintz and ruffles, and changed into shorts and a T-shirt. His suitcase had a small, secured compartment for his Sig P938. Ian locked it away. The laptop he left closed on the small desk by the windows. It was password protected, with an encrypted drive. When opened, the screen showed only the operating system's logo; nothing connected it to the city of Lancaster, much less to the police department.

When he trotted down the stairs to the entryway, he could hear Riva in the kitchen. He followed the sound of her voice and found her and her mother sharing a glass of wine. Riva stood behind the kitchen island, which looked like an operating table in a Swedish-designed spaceship, surrounded by gleaming white cabinets that could contain dishes or a pantry or the fridge or a body. She had managed to maneuver her mother to the opposite side of the island, commandeering the cooking space. Onions sizzled on the stove.

"I'm going for a run. Need to work out the travel kinks," he said. "When should I be back?"

"We'll eat around seven," Riva said.

"Great."

"—seems like a nice man" was the last thing he heard before he jogged down the front steps and onto the sidewalk.

I am a nice man. I'm a very nice man. Just not to your

daughter. With your daughter I was a cop first, an ass-hole second, and a man third.

"Things are different," he said as he picked up his pace. Now she'd slept in his apartment. Now he'd seen her morning look, soft and sleepy and dangerously de-caffeinated. Now she'd seen him rock hard and ready for her.

The "short version" of her life sent a little stinger of regret for the way he'd treated her through his chest. Being a miracle was a double-edged sword. His family was so grateful he had survived the cancer they still lit candles and wrote notes to the doctors who treated him. Riva was a miracle, too, but all it got her was manipulation and guilt. His respect for her was growing by leaps and bounds.

The Hennemans lived in the Logan Square neighborhood, in a house remodeled to within an inch of its life, and remodeled well. He'd done some research on the real estate situation, and found that Rory Henneman had gotten in early and cheap in what was now a very desirable neighborhood. He made a mental note to ask about that at dinner.

The second interesting thing about the house was that the property was in Stephanie Henneman's name only. Not Rory's. He wondered if Riva's mother even knew about that. If she'd come from money, she should have some in her own name, but all of Henneman's accounts were in his name only.

He sprinted the last quarter mile back to the Hennemans' home, slowing when he reached their block to catch his breath. He let himself in through the back gate to familiarize himself with the yard. The house was an interesting mix of Victorian—porch that curved around the front and side, detached garage, peaks and dormers on the uppermost level—and modern finishes and styling inside, all white trim and dark hardwood floors and gray tones in paint and carpets. The yard was no different, with the big trees common to an older neighborhood towering over a Japanese garden, teak benches and burbling fountains, a rock garden, and a big expanse of grass. Probably for the grandchildren.

He heard a male voice and paused outside the door. The tone was low, even pleasant, but the words caught his attention. ". . . what's your excuse today, Stephanie?"

"Dad, I—"

"Shut up, Riva. I asked your mother a question. I want an answer."

Ian couldn't hear the response, but Rory must have gotten one because he said, "Another headache? Is this a menopause symptom? That's the third one this week!"

"Dad, really, I wanted to cook for you and Mom. Show you what I've learned."

Ian's stomach turned over. Gone was the confident, assertive tone he'd heard in the kitchen at Oasis, or the in-your-face attitude she'd used during the heated negotiations about where she would sleep. Riva's voice was colorless, small, almost pleading.

"What you've learned is what any home ec major from the nineteen fifties learned in high school," Rory said, razor sharp, dismissive, and mocking.

He hadn't met Rory Henneman face-to-face, already had good reason to think he was scum, but in that moment, Ian hated him. He stopped himself just short of using his cop's knock on the door, noiselessly making his way back down the path, then whistling as he approached the door. His tactic worked; Sugar greeted him with a flurry of barking and scrabbling claws. "The damn dog's good for something" came through the door.

"Hey, Riva," he said through the screen door. "Can I come in?"

"Let the man in," Rory said over a ringing cell phone. He sounded magnanimous, the lord welcoming the visitor to his castle. If Ian hadn't heard the previous conversation, he would have thought Rory was the nicest guy on the block.

As she fumbled with the door latch, Stephanie's pupils were black holes in her eyes. In the dim kitchen light, the effect was eerie enough to make the hair stand up on Ian's arms. "Hey, girl," he said, and bent down to scratch Sugar's little head.

Riva raised her brows. *Did you hear that?* He gave her a slight nod.

"Dad's home," she said in a normal tone. She glanced significantly at a closed white six-panel door and mouthed, *He's in there, with his laptop.* "He had to take a call. Ten minutes until dinner."

"Great. I'll take a quick shower."

He divested himself of Sugar and took the stairs two at a time. Nine minutes later he walked back down the stairs in chinos, another of his nondescript thin sweaters over a T-shirt, his boots, and his Sig. He followed the sound of voices to the dining room, white paneling with plum paint above and white crown molding, where Stephanie was fussing over china and linens while Riva set platters of food on various trivets.

He forgot about that when he got a good look at Riva, hair clinging to her temples, face flushed, and forehead pinched with worry as she set a pot roast on the last trivet. "Here we go. I hope it's good. Dad, this is my colleague, Ian. Ian, my father, Rory Henneman."

"Nice to meet you," Rory said, giving Ian's hand a firm shake.

Riva's father wasn't what he expected. A couple of inches shorter than Ian, he wore nice jeans and a button-down with the logo for Henneman Vending embroidered on the pocket. He had Riva's chestnut hair and blue eyes. All it took was the handshake, that brief, two-, maybe three-second moment when their hands clasped, and Ian felt a vibration at the base of his skull, like someone had slid an ice pick in between the bones. It didn't happen often—a couple of times when he'd walked into a domestic murder scene when the killer was still there, another couple of times when he was working on the street. He'd been expecting a run-of-the-mill guy looking to get rich. Instead his early warning system blared *dangerdangerdanger* until his nape all but vibrated with it.

Then Rory dropped his hand and the moment broke. "Thanks for opening your home to me," Ian said.

"Any friend of Riva's is welcome here. This smells delicious." Rory glanced at his wife, then at his daughter. "What is it?"

"It's pot roast," Stephanie said brightly.

"I can see that," Rory said, but Ian saw Stephanie flinch ever so slightly. Rory's gaze was watchful, like a big cat hunkered low in the grass, picking out the slowest in a herd of gazelles. "What's it seasoned with?"

Stephanie froze for just a moment, eyes wide, unblinking. Ian doubted she even knew she'd done it; the movement had the sharpness of a spinal reflex. "Um, garlic, and rosemary, and . . ." She looked at Riva.

"Go ahead, Mom," Riva said.

Stephanie laughed, then reached down and rubbed Sugar's little head. "You tell him, dear. I can't remember."

"It's a paleron, not a rump roast, rubbed with salt and pepper, then seared, then roasted with the celery, rutabaga, carrots, and mushrooms in a really good cabernet Ian picked out on the way up here."

Rory smiled. "At least someone knows what we're eating," he said to Ian.

"Please, go ahead," Stephanie said belatedly, gesturing to the steaming platters.

Ian's mouth filled with saliva as he transferred a succulent piece of beef to his plate, then passed the platter to Stephanie. The smells were incredible, hints of spices rising from the crust on the meat, the vegetables retaining some of their crispness yet yielding easily to his fork.

Rory slowly chewed a bite of beef. "So this is what you've been doing in Lancaster?"

"This is it," Riva said lightly.

"Is this what you're cooking for your mother's . . . luncheon?" There was no way to tell if he approved or not.

"We're still talking about menus, but Mom, I'd prefer to go shopping the morning of the luncheon and make something from whatever's fresh at the stands."

"Don't you need to send out menus with the invitations?" Rory again, undermining in the most solicitous tone possible.

"So we'll send out menus that say 'The meal will be cooked with ingredients harvested only hours before. Bring your appetites and sense of adventure!' "

"Maybe you should stick with the caterer," Rory said.

Ian slid a glance at Stephanie, mechanically slicing

away at the beef with an equally mechanical smile on her face. So far none of her food had made it to her mouth.

"Up to you, Mom," Riva said. Her tone was bright, but forced. Ian bent his head over his food, using his peripheral vision and hearing to take in data.

"I'm sure you'll be fine," Rory said. "Maybe your mother will learn something from you." The stinger froze Stephanie's hands for just a second. "This isn't bad. Where did you learn to cook like this?"

"The people I met through the co-op," Riva said, her color high, her voice forced into an eagerness that made Ian seethe for her. "Most of them loved to cook and cared passionately where the ingredients came from. We used to joke we spent a quarter of our paychecks on rent and the rest on food."

"How's the restaurant doing?"

"Oh, you know . . ." Riva said, pushing her roast around on her plate, a false cheery optimism in her voice.

Ian shot her a look over the asparagus. Back at the Block, when she'd said she would ingratiate herself with her father to get the information he needed, he'd blithely agreed. But after a mere fifteen minutes in Rory's company, he knew there was no way he'd let Riva put herself at risk like that. The man was manipulative, egocentric, and cruel, which made him dangerous to Riva in more ways than one.

"We've added one or two spring preview nights a week, until the harvest really gets steady and productive. Then in the summer we'll be open Thursday through Saturday nights, with special events on Sundays and Wednesdays. I've got some kids from a community center working for us."

"We?" Rory asked with a glance at Ian.

Riva blushed and tucked her hair behind her ear. "It's really a community effort. That's part of the reason why I'm back. Chicago has a strong urban farming initiative."

"Ah," Rory said sagely, as if this made more sense than coming back to help Stephanie with the luncheon. "Now I get it."

Time for Ian to jump in. "I'm mostly observing at this point," Ian added. "Riva tells me you have your own business. Candy and vending, right? That's cool. How long have you had it?"

"Since before I had Riva. I'm my own boss, and I'm competitive. I like to kill what I eat, not punch a clock and take a paycheck."

Ian quickly discarded the idea of giving Rory his cover story and instead stroked Rory's ego. "When Riva told me about your business, I checked on what the city does for vending. We use the same company that staffs the cafeteria."

"That's pretty common. The big guys come in and get the vending as part of the food service contract. We just have to scrap a little harder for market share. I've bought out a couple of guys who couldn't make it work."

Ian filed that away. Buying out legit businesses meant getting cash somewhere. Loans from banks, or an infusion of cash from another, less legal source?

"How many guys do you have working for you?" He added another smile to tone down the way his voice drifted toward an interrogation.

Rory spent the next twenty minutes explaining his business in detail. The number of drivers he had and the number of routes they ran. What made stops profitable. This fit Ian's plan perfectly. He wanted attention directed away from Riva, to himself. The safest thing was for him to gain Rory's trust and get access to his office for a thorough search. The door was closed, but the second he got a chance, he'd take a look, see what kind of security the laptop had and whether he was using a server.

"It depends on what's in the machines," Rory was saying. "That's our second-biggest problem after the Aramarks and Marriotts. People want healthy food now. The business used to be candy and soda, maybe muffins that would last for a week in a machine. Now people want fresh. I'm replacing candy machines with ones that dispense fruit and vegetables, those microwavable oatmeals, organic snack bars, that kind of thing."

"Sounds more labor intensive," Ian said. "Fruit has a shorter shelf life than Twinkies."

"It is," Rory agreed. "You better believe it is."

"I've got some ideas for healthy snacks with a decent shelf life," Riva interjected.

Ian shot her another covert look, but Rory ignored her. "What do you do now, Ian?"

"Right now I work for the city," he said. Rule number one of undercover work was to avoid volunteering more information than had been asked for, and keep the story simple.

"No wonder you're looking to make a change," Rory said. "Bureaucracy kills me. Once you go into business for yourself, you'll never go back. Doing what, exactly?"

"Analytics, mostly. Data analysis, monitor metrics, search for ways to improve services while keeping costs down."

"Sounds exciting." Just a hint of regret that Ian didn't get to work at a real job.

"Yeah." He kept his tone moderate, but added a little

ruefulness to it. He was starting to get a handle on what made Rory tick. "I have a degree in philosophy—"

Rory laughed. "Much of a job market for that?"

"Not really, so the minor in statistics came in handy. Mostly my job's about looking at the big picture, then breaking down the variables to improve efficiency."

"Government is a good place to start for efficiency improvements."

"I know, right? But you'd be amazed at how inefficient most business processes are. The little details in terms of service delivery or waste really add up."

He cut a piece of celery, added a bit of meat to his fork, and chewed the mouthful while watching Rory. Ian the skinny analytical office drone now had all of Rory's attention.

Perfect.

"So you're interested in farming?"

He leaned forward and injected a frustrated note into his voice. "I have to try something. A couple of friends of mine recommended Riva's restaurant. I went, and was really blown away by how good food could taste when it was a couple of hours out of the ground. It got me out of the statistics and back into philosophy. What's the purpose of being alive? It can't be all spreadsheets and meetings."

"Damn straight it can't be." Rory topped off Ian's wine but didn't offer it to Riva or Stephanie. The women at the other end of the table had ceased to exist.

"Riva's brought me along on a few of her day trips to farmers' markets, CSAs, supplying restaurants. I want to get a feel for the business side of things because that's where I can really help. How does it all work? How do you handle fluctuations in supply and demand?"

"You don't," Riva interjected.

He looked at her.

"You don't manage for them. You flow with them. If late frost get the peas and kale harvest, I adapt what I serve." She flashed him a little warning smile.

"What about the restaurants you supply?"

"They adapt, too. Obviously they want some information. What are we planting? Some ingredients are the same, spinach and Swiss chard, carrots and peas and broccoli, but I sit down with the chefs I supply and talk about what their creative vision is for each season. Together we'll come up with seasonal menus around what we plant, and we keep them up to date on how the growing season is going, what pests we're seeing, how we're handling them. I always throw in a few things I think will do well, just in case. We can use a low tunnel to warm the soil and protect against frost, but nature happens. Insect invasions happen. Part of the farm-to-table ethos is a willingness to enjoy what you're served rather than dictating the experience. If you want consistency, there's always the McDonalds drive-thru."

"It's that flexible?" Ian asked, astonished.

She shrugged. "Some of the best dishes I've served have come from an afternoon browsing at the farmers' market."

Rory sat back and swirled his wine in his glass. "Do you play any sports?"

Bad Ian for taking his attention off Rory. It was time for another fast decision. "Basketball in high school," Ian said. "Around the time I lost interest in my job, I took up boxing."

Bingo. Rory's eyes lit up. He said, "I sponsor a couple of local boxers."

Ian knew that. A deep search had turned up Rory's name associated with a local boxing organization. The name disappeared pretty quickly, but he'd taken a chance. "Did you see the Spence-Algieri fight?"

"Yeah. From the first row."

"You went to New York for that fight?"

"I did. Spence put on a clinic. I was close enough to get hit by flying sweat. You should come by the gym. Watch my boy train. He's getting ready for a fight next month."

There it was, the crack he needed, his way in. There was no doubt that Rory, with his total lack of emotion and an eye to the long game, was behind the corruption in the LPD and the new pipeline of drugs Kenny and his guys ensured flowed unimpeded into Lancaster. He looked at Riva. "What do we have planned?"

She wasn't doing anything as obvious as glaring at him, but he'd spent enough time with Riva in a pissed-off state to know when she was seething and holding it back. "We need to work on the menu for the luncheon. Prep will take all day the day before. Day of is booked, of course. And I've got meetings set up with half a dozen local operations. There's probably time for some visits to the gym," she conceded.

"Any dessert with this?" Rory asked.

"Just ice cream. Actually, can I take a raincheck, Dad? Remember Kelly, my friend from high school? We made plans for me to come over and meet Wyatt."

Me? Not we? Who the hell is Kelly? Or Wyatt?

Rory waved his hand like he was dismissing an underling.

No way was Ian letting Riva head out into the Chicago night without him. "Let me grab my wallet and phone."

Riva reached for his plate and silverware. "You really don't want to do that. It's going to be all nursing and the consistency of poop and sleep schedules."

Alarms went off in his head. Maybe this was just Riva trying to get some time by herself, or maybe something more complicated was going on. Either way, she wasn't going out at night without him. "I'd like to see more of Chicago."

"You're sure?" Riva said, warning in her voice. "Last time I talked to her it was forty-five minutes of mastitis details."

He'd been around pregnant cops and new mothers, and cops had no filter when it came to body fluids. But one of the admittedly few perks of going through chemotherapy and radiation was the total inability to be grossed out by basic bodily functions. Add a few weeks on patrol and he'd developed a cast-iron stomach. "I'm sure."

"Fine," Riva said. "I'll load the dishwasher and we'll go."

"Your mother can load the dishwasher," Rory said as he pushed his chair back. Ian glanced at Stephanie. Her eyelids drooped at half mast, and all she'd done was rearrange her food on her plate. "I'll help her. Then she's going to bed like a good girl."

CHAPTER NINE

Riva stood beside her truck, dinner congealing in her stomach. Her father's vicious stunt with her mother left Riva torn between staying to protect her mom and leaving before she started screaming at her dad. Conflicted, she lashed out at the only person available to her. "What were you doing in there?" she hissed. "That's not what we agreed to!"

Ian reached for the door handle. "Locks? The situation has changed."

She pushed a button on her clicker. "How?"

"I met your father, that's how." He hoisted himself into the passenger seat.

"Stay out of this, Ian. I can get what we need faster and with less suspicion. Just be yourself. It's hard enough having you around, but when you stop acting like a cop, it throws me off," she said as she backed out of the driveway. "You were talking. Smiling! You smiled almost all the way through dinner!"

"I smile," he said. "Smiling at people is an easy way to lower their defenses and appear nonthreatening."

And there was the emotionless strongman she knew so well. "I know that," she said. "Women do it all the time. But I've never seen you smile like that."

"Like what?"

Easy, warm, friendly. Like he wasn't carrying the weight of the world on his shoulders, like he wasn't cold and hard, a robot. "Like a human being, I guess."

He turned his head and looked at her, his eyes unreadable behind his mirrored shades. The deep lines bracketing his mouth had disappeared with each smile at her father. She'd never thought they were laugh lines. They looked like the kind of mark left by prolonged exposure to pain. "I'm human."

"And you like boxing?"

"Not only do I like boxing, I actually box."

"Of course you do. " She clenched her fingers around the steering wheel. "Oh. That's what you're doing. You're setting yourself up as someone he can impress."

"He likes an audience."

"Yes, he does," she said.

"What did your mom take while I was gone?"

Riva blew out her breath. "I don't know," she said, trying to keep her voice from shaking. The situation was worse than she'd thought, her mother thin to the point of brittleness, unable to remember a short list of ingredients. "She's been taking medication for headaches. I need to check what's in her medicine cabinet. Do pain pills make you nauseated?"

"Even high doses of ibuprofen can. They're hard on your stomach. But we've got a pretty serious prescription painkiller addiction problem in Lancaster right now.

Your mom looked like she'd taken something stronger than Valium."

"She gets nervous. Would a doctor prescribe prescription painkillers for nerves?"

"A good one wouldn't," Ian said.

"There's so much you can do for pain, and headaches, and nerves, through diet. But that would make her stronger, more independent. He wouldn't want that," she said to herself. Her father wouldn't want her mother well enough to think about choosing a different life, maybe with Riva.

They drove in silence for a minute, then Ian said, "You're white-knuckling that steering wheel at twenty-five miles an hour. What's wrong?"

She almost laughed. He'd known her in the time she thought of as After. The moment Ian Hawthorn took out his handcuffs and arrested her started After. After Hawthorn she developed her own sense of self. After Hawthorn she set boundaries. After she saw the consequences not only of her actions but also of her attitude. Her hero worship.

Now Ian was seeing who she was Before Hawthorn. When she was weak. Malleable. Easy to manipulate and convince. Before she gave up everything about herself in an effort to win what her father withheld: love, affection, attention, approval. She didn't like having anyone, much less Ian, know exactly how stupid she'd been, how little sense of self she'd started with.

"I can't believe I didn't see him for what he was," she said finally.

"Don't beat yourself up over it. You were a kid. Impressionable. He used you."

"I'm not beating myself up over it," she said. "And don't think I haven't noticed that you didn't agree to back off."

"I thought you were going with the business-in-trouble approach."

"I am. The first step is to look like I'm supersuccessful. Then I'll go to him and tell him I was just trying to protect Mom from the truth because she can't handle it, but really, I'm a failure and I want to make more money by going into business with him instead. Initially we'll work with some of the vending ideas. That's going to play to his ego, if we can package Rolling Hill Farm products and sell them in his vending machines. But I'll also suggest I can help him move drugs, too."

"Why start that way?"

"Because he likes to help you when you've fallen. And he likes it when we both agree that Mom is weak and helpless."

"Good plan. Great initiative. You're not doing any of it."

She narrowed her gaze. "Excuse me?"

"He thinks I'm a desk jockey looking for excitement. He's already got inroads in the police department. Getting an in at city hall would be his next step. All you need to do is to hang low and be my cover. I'll get what I need and it's safer for you."

"You think he's going to trust you, just like that."

"You said your dad is the kind of man who wanted a son and didn't have one. I think he likes being the top dog, but he's getting up there in years. I think he's looking for someone to raise up, pass the business on to. I can be that person."

They were waiting at a stoplight. Riva leaned forward and rested her forehead on the steering wheel. "I tried," she said to the dashboard. "I tried to be what he wanted. You, of all people, know exactly how hard I tried."

To her utter shock, Ian's hand patted her hair where it spilled over her shoulder. "You were never going to be what he wanted," he said. "Because it wasn't about you. It was about him."

"Classic narcissist," she said, but her brain was otherwise occupied because he was now stroking her hair, softly, slowly, gently. The motion was both soothing and exploratory, like he'd been curious about the texture under his fingers.

"Exactly." His voice was just as distracted. "I thought it would be warmer."

"What would be?"

"Your hair. What color is this? It's not red, and it's not brown."

"Chestnut. It's chestnut brown."

"It looks like a deer's pelt. Reds and browns and some gold."

She didn't want to get out of the car. She didn't want to do anything that would shatter this unexpected and unexpectedly sweet moment between them. Ian was touching her, his voice low and curious and absorbed, and she thought she might fly to pieces right here in her car. It wasn't possessive, or dictatorial, or demanding. She could almost feel his fingers trembling through the fine strands of her hair.

"I used to think about your hair," he said. "You wore it straight. I wondered if it was naturally wavy."

The image of Ian thinking about her hair swept through her. She closed her eyes. "I straightened it back then. Now I'm outside too much to make the effort worthwhile. Humidity. Wind. You're familiar with the humid subcontinental climate, right?"

"I like it this way." Still soft. Still low. Now intimate. "Unruly. It suits you."

She turned her head and looked at him, her hair sliding down her back, leaving his hand on her shoulder. Ian's gaze lingered on hers, an odd note in his expression. Was that possessiveness?

She was ninety percent sure the friction in his apartment had been for show. Now she wanted to know. "Have you ever wondered what it could be like?"

"I've spent the last seven years wondering." His voice was low, fervent, unwilling.

The truck interior was so quiet she could hear her shallow inhales and the sounds of a spring night, crickets, kids playing. His fingers drifted along her collarbone, sending sparks skittering along her nerves. She was surprised her skin didn't light up, especially when he lifted his hand to brush his thumb across her lips, then her cheekbone. But while she wasn't the frightened virgin he'd arrested, Ian still made her pulse leap, her senses go on high alert.

He noticed. Of course he noticed. "You okay?" he asked.

"Yes. Just . . ."

Her phone dinged with an incoming text. *Grant home early = unusual = family night. Raincheck?*

She sighed. The last thing she wanted to do was go home again, but maybe it was for the best. She could go upstairs and sit with her mom, ask questions, figure out what was going on.

Ian put his hand back on his thigh. "What's up?"

"Kelly wants to postpone. Her husband works all the

time, but he's home early tonight, and they want to spend time together as a family."

No problem! she texted back, using exaggerated punctuation to hide her disappointment. "It's not surprising. I basically dropped all my high school friends when I quit college. We reconnected on social media a few months ago—"

Three dots appeared almost immediately. *Let's go out. Not lunch. Lunch is boring. Drinks and dancing sound good?*

That sounded fantastic to her. "How do you feel about nightclubs?" she asked with a smile.

"Fine," Ian said. No hesitation.

"Seriously?"

"Very seriously."

"You dance. You don't just hold up a wall and watch."

"I dance."

Sounds great. Let me know what night works! I'm bringing a friend.

"Where are you going?" Ian asked when she started the truck.

"Home," she replied.

Ian looked around. "Does your father work from home or does he have an office?"

"He's got an office at the warehouse, but he's usually in a truck, visiting current customers or trying to drum up new ones. That's why his laptop is always with him."

"A personal vehicle? Or a business one?"

"Depends. Probably his truck, unless he's running a route. He's the vacation coverage for his guys. It keeps his hand in the business. I think he works from home, too."

"Let's cruise by the warehouse, get the lay of the land. What about this club he was talking about?"

"The boxing club? It's not far from the warehouse, actually, in the West Loop area. Dad bought space there maybe twenty years ago. It's an easy commute and close to the interstate, which makes it easy to get to different stops."

She merged into traffic. Ian watched out the windows, holding on to the handle above the door. She had no trouble imagining him in the same pose in a patrol car.

"What are you doing?"

"Memorizing the intersections." He looked at her. "Habit. You always know where you are in case you have to call for backup. You'd be amazed how many calls we get where people can't give us an address, much less cross streets. Does Kelly know?"

"No," she said, surprised. "You said I couldn't tell anyone."

"While you were a CI up to the trial. After that, you could tell anyone you wanted."

"Would you want to tell anyone?" She tried to soften the edge to her words, but failed. "Would you want anyone to know that kind of thing about you? That's part of the reason I left my old friends behind. I was different, and I couldn't tell them why."

A shadow crossed his face, like he knew all about keeping things close to his chest. "Does anyone know?"

"You. Me. Sorenson. Whoever else in the LPD. The ADA. That's it."

"No one at the ESCC knows."

"No one," she said quietly.

"How did you explain dropping out of college?"

She shrugged. "It wasn't for me. Rolling Hill Farm and Oasis fit me much better. Ultimately I want a national reputation as a leader in the farm-to-table movement. We're here."

CHAPTER TEN

"Pull over there," Ian said. He pointed at an empty space at the curb, opposite a brick building with three loading doors facing the side street. Black lettering identified Henneman Candy and Vending. He looked around, taking in the street, the buildings, the sound of laughter and music coming from the main street. The neighborhood reminded him of SoMa, shops and dining and clubs only a couple of blocks away from light industrial zoning. He had to be on his guard, because no good would come of thinking he knew this situation, this town.

This woman. He'd wanted her badly enough before, but now . . . now she was even more dangerous. Grown up. Working in a career he admired. Sexy as all hell, especially the way she drove, parallel parking the truck like a boss.

She shifted into park and looked at him. "Why aren't we going in?"

"Wait a minute."

He needed a moment to process this, because there was so much more to this situation than he'd suspected. Riva had never told anyone. No one knew what she'd done wrong, and what she'd done right.

He could relate. He didn't tell people about the cancer, either. For a long moment he considered telling her, but then, across the street, a set of headlights flashed on and stayed on.

All his senses went on high alert. Riva followed his gaze. "Who's that?"

"Stay in the car," Ian said.

He got out and walked down the center of the street, making it easy for the car's occupant to get a good look at him. After a moment the lights went off and the driver's door opened. Ian felt his muscles come to attention, but then his eyes adjusted to the dark again and he recognized the man now standing in the shadows beside the car.

"Hey, Micah." He held out his hand.

"Ian. Good to see you again."

Following Captain Swarthmore's advice, Ian had reached out to the Chicago PD via a contact he'd made at a conference the year before. Shorter and lighter than Ian, Micah kept his dark hair swept back from his face and had a quick intelligence under a cop's habitually guarded expression. "Who's that with you?"

Ian looked over his shoulder and beckoned Riva out of the truck. The door slammed, then he heard her booted feet on the gritty pavement. "Riva Henneman, this is Micah Sewell. He's with the Chicago police."

"Hi," Riva said warily.

"This is a courtesy call, to let them know we're on their territory."

"Okay," Riva said. "Do you usually do these calls late at night in the West Loop?"

Micah smiled and looked around. "This is what the outside world looks like? Fascinating. I don't get out much. I'm in cybercrime."

"Micah and I met at a conference about technology and law enforcement."

"You guys go to conferences?"

He had to laugh at Riva's flabbergasted tone. "We go to conferences for the same reason anyone else does. To exchange ideas, experiences, and talk about best practices."

"I do love me a good best-practice conversation," Micah said. His demeanor was casual but his face was as watchful and wary as Ian's. "Bring in ISO 9000 and I'm in heaven. What are you doing on my turf?"

"We believe an individual with a known connection to this warehouse is supplying the biggest gang in Lancaster with heroin and cocaine."

"And you haven't contacted my captain to set up a joint operation because . . . ?"

"Because cops are involved."

"Yours or mine?"

"Mine. As far as we know."

Micah blew out his breath. "Shit. Which means we're probably involved, too."

"That's why we're meeting here, not in a conference room at your headquarters."

"Why call me?"

"Because I trust you," Ian said simply.

"You have proof of any of this?"

"Of the corruption, yes. Of the supplier's involvement, no. That's why we're here."

Micah looked at Riva. "We. A quick check of the records pertaining to this address lists the owner, one Rory Henneman, who has a wife, Stephanie, and one daughter, Riva. You're giving up your father?"

"Yes." Riva's voice was steady.

Wisely, Micah didn't ask any more questions. Plausible deniability mattered in situations like this.

Ian looked at Riva. "Do you have keys to the warehouse?"

She nodded. "I'll have to disable the security system, though, or Dad will get a notification on his phone."

"Call him and tell him I wanted to see it."

Riva stepped off to the side and initiated the call. Ian kept one ear tuned to her tone of voice and as much of the conversation as he could catch.

Micah sighed. "Jesus, this is a bad idea. What are you thinking, running an off-the-books operation with a civilian who's got a personal connection to the suspect?"

"She's totally trustworthy," Ian said.

"She better be. You're trusting her with your life, and probably the lives of other cops."

Ian gave him his *no shit, Sherlock* look.

"What do you need from me?"

"Information."

"Get some to give some."

Ian handed Micah a USB drive that contained what he'd learned so far about Rory. "You'll keep this between us?"

"For now," Micah said. "I'll look into things on our side. Quietly. Before you ask, we don't have surveillance cameras on this particular street."

"Which makes it perfect for someone coming and going with drugs or cash."

Riva tucked her phone in her back pocket. "Dad said that's fine. He seemed pleased by your interest."

Micah lifted an eyebrow at Ian. "I'm thinking about getting out of my desk job with the city and starting my own business," Ian said.

Micah's laughter boomed down the street, rolling off the brick buildings. "Desk job," he snorted.

"Any suspicions?" Ian asked Riva.

"No. I think I called in the middle of a Cubs game. He wasn't too chatty."

"Have fun, kids. I'll be in touch. You know how to get ahold of me if shit starts to go south." Micah got back in his car.

Ian followed Riva around the corner to the eight-foot-high chain link fence topped with razor wire surrounding the parking lot. "Your dad means business."

"It's a building full of candy and soda. We used to have a couple of break-ins a month before Dad added the razor wire and upgraded security." She entered a code into the keypad built into the fencing. A click, and the latch gave.

"What happens if someone destroys the keypad?"

"It locks, rather than unlocks, an alarm goes off at the security company, and Dad gets a call."

He followed her across the parking lot. A row of white box trucks was parked noses out on one side of the building. On the opposite side was a door marked OFFICE. Riva headed straight for it. Another keypad, and then a key to unlock the door.

She flicked on the lights. There was a desk, a couple of filing cabinets, the usual office supplies, a calendar on the wall, but the room had an air of disuse to it. "Does your dad do much work here?"

"I think he rotates through the routes so he can stay in touch with customers, but otherwise, no. When things started getting tough in the vending business he started working from his car. He was always drumming up new business, tweaking contracts with clients. Or so we thought."

"When did you figure it out?"

"I was sixteen, maybe. I overheard a few things, put some pieces together." She unlocked yet another door and reached in front of Ian to flick on a series of overhead florescent lights. Eight-foot-high shelves ran on three sides of the space. Stacked on the shelves were boxes and boxes of candy and soda. In the middle were neatly parked white cube trucks, all with black Henneman Candy and Vending lettering on them. The space was immaculate. Not a single candy wrapper or box on the floor.

"You were literally a kid in a candy shop," Ian quipped.

She didn't smile. "You'd think, right? But Dad rarely brought anything home. We girls had to keep an eye on our weight."

"No offense, but your dad's some kind of asshole."

"I know that now."

"Any other entrances besides the office and the bays? A back door?"

"Through there," she said, pointing to a gap between shelving units.

Ian opened the door and peered down an alley. "We're parked that way?"

Riva ducked under his arm for a look. "Yes."

He was filling in a map of the West Loop in his head, places of interest. "Good. Okay, that's all I needed."

"You're not going to search his filing cabinets or his desk?"

"They're locked."

Riva dangled her keychain in front of his face.

"He really trusts you."

"No," Riva said matter-of-factly as she switched off the bank of lights and relocked the door. "He can't imagine that I'd betray him. There's a difference."

She unlocked the filing cabinets and her father's desk. Ian pulled on a pair of gloves and rifled through the drawers. Nothing jumped out at him except a nine mm handgun in the bottom desk drawer.

"I'm pretty sure that's registered," Riva said.

"Any others?"

"Maybe. He used to stash a shotgun behind the seat when he ran the routes. He probably still does."

"Great," Ian muttered.

"He got held up. Twice. Then he bought the shotgun."

"I still can't figure out how he got connected to the Sinaloa cartel," Ian mused. "Maybe one of their affiliates demanded protection money?"

"I don't know. I do know Mom went into hysterics both times he was held up. I was eleven."

Ian filed that information away. "Lock up again," he said. "Let's go."

Traffic was light this time of night, a few cars meandering along, souped-up cars drag racing off the stoplights, music thumping from the open windows.

"Thanks for not calling me an informant."

"You're not an informant this time," he said.

As he watched her drive, all the tension seeped from his muscles, leaving him, if not relaxed, then in a strange place of ease and calm. He'd felt this before, during the cancer treatment. It was as if his brain had two speeds; it was either white-knuckled to keep total control of everything, or suddenly just gave up, threw up its hands and let go. Riva was a good driver, cautious and methodical. He wasn't responsible for Chicago, even the south side of Chicago. Right now he was safe, Riva was safe, they had a plan, and her hair glowed like a banked fire in the streetlights.

He was so tired of fighting this. So tired. He'd been sitting in cars with Riva Henneman for what felt like years, fighting an attraction that never went away. He was twenty-five again, angry and aching and as turned on as he'd ever been in his young life, wanting her. Loathing himself for wanting her, because as fucked up as he'd been, that was one line he wouldn't cross.

It hadn't stopped. The edge was just as sharp, the ache as permanent as his fear. He'd begun to wonder if pulling out the knife between his ribs would heal him or leave him to bleed out on the floor.

You could find out.

The voice of rationalization was familiar. It was the one that said getting blackout drunk didn't matter, having sex with random women, driving like a demon on speed, lashing out at his parents, his brother, none of it mattered, because he had been sick. He rationalized a lot in those years.

She parked in front of the house, turned off the engine, and looked at him. "You've been awfully quiet."

"You still jump a little when I touch you," he said. "If that happens in front of your father, he's going to get suspicious and we'll both be in danger." What he meant was, *I want to kiss you, strip you, find out what this thing is between us I can't explain or hide anymore.*

"I know." She drew in a deep breath. "I thought it was fine after the drive. I thought it was better."

Brow furrowed, she got out of the car and headed up the walk. Ian followed her, watching her hair swing with the sway of her hips. The house was quiet when Riva unlocked the back door and shut off the alarm system. The light over the stove bleached the kitchen's Scandinavian surfaces to moonlight, but left the rest of the house shrouded in darkness.

"We have to deal with this," he said finally.

She turned to look at him, and in that single glance he could see all her defenses were down. They were speaking in hushed tones, standing close enough to hear the other without waking her parents, faces as close as lovers'. The hair on his arms quivered at her nearness, the electric connection sending a shock straight to his heart.

"It goes back a long way," she said.

"I remember," he said.

Seven years earlier . . .

Riva opened the car door and slid into the front seat, unable to stop the soft moan she made when the heated air made contact with chilled skin.

"What the hell are you wearing?"

She looked down at herself. Despite the dip in temperatures from cool to cold, she wore only boots, jeans, and a fitted cardigan over a tank top. "Clothes?"

"You should be wearing a winter coat."

She looked him over, eyes skimming the leather jacket, his sprawled thighs in the jeans that were thankfully more form fitting than the baggy sweats and tracksuit pants favored by most of her male classmates. "Hmmm," she said mock playfully. "You're most definitely not my dad."

He looked at her. The dome light faded off, leaving only the dashboard lights and the soft radio program in the background. "Watch your mouth."

His voice was low, even, and as chilly as the wind outside. It was a dangerous game she played. "You want me to look like I've just run down from my dorm room to make the buy, right? That means no coat."

But it could mean more than a thin gray sweater over a tank top and a pair of jeans.

"You're too casual about this. Get your head in the game."

She got right in his face. "You think my head's not in the game? Your game is the only place my head is right now. Your game dominates my every waking moment and most of my nightmares. I'm playing your game like my life depends on it, because it does. The only thing worse than death is spending forty years in prison."

"Stop acting your age. Nothing is worse than dying."

"Like you'd know," she scoffed. "Like you've ever faced that choice."

He stared straight ahead. "Every day of my life."

"Because you're a cop. You chose to be a cop! No one sat you down and said be a cop or go to jail!*"*

At that he swiveled and leaned over the center console. "You chose to sell drugs to college students."

"I know I did!" She was so close their noses were almost touching. All it would take to send them both up in flames was a quick tilt of her head, a slight tip of her weight forward to bring their mouths together. His thin,

mobile mouth against hers. But she couldn't bring herself to do it. That would cross a line, send this deeper when all she wanted was to be rid of him.

Except all she wanted, equally as badly, was to be with him. A hotel, his place, the back seat of his car. Her body pulsed with desire, lighting up her nipples, her skin aching for his hands, her sex slick and swollen for his cock, her hands trembling, her emotions in knots. She hated him. Hated herself for making such a stupid decision, and hated him for catching her at it and for offering her a way out. Once he was done with her, she had plans. She'd be the straightest arrow ever shot from a bow, but she wasn't about to tell him that. He was both her downfall and her salvation. She could forgive him for being one, but not both.

"I know I'm here because of my own stupidity. But nothing in our agreement gives you permission to act like my goddamn father, telling me to wear a coat and be home by ten."

He hadn't moved. His face was taut with tight control, a potent combination in a man. "Take your shirt off."

"Excuse me?" she said, incredulous.

Utter astonishment furrowed his eyebrows, then he blinked. He closed his eyes and exhaled long and slow through his nose. When he opened his eyes again, all the fury and desire were gone, replaced with a calm, dark emptiness that broke her heart. "That came out wrong. I'm going to wire you up. That's all. Sorenson usually does it, but we're shorthanded tonight. She's across the park, ready to make the arrests. I'll call her over."

"No," she said. "It's fine. It's almost time for him to call. Go ahead. It's fine."

"How about you just lift your sweater . . . that's far enough."

She'd exposed maybe two inches of her belly, just barely enough for him to clip the battery pack to her waistband. He straightened the wire, then gave it to her. "Run it up under your top."

She managed to work the wire under the hems of her tank top and sweater, then reach down between her breasts and grab the clip. But the tiny mic kept slipping from her sweaty fingers as she tried to fasten it to her bra. "I can't . . ."

His gaze caught hers, hazel, molten, aware of the shattering desire between them, acting on none of it. "I'm going to touch you, okay? Just for a moment."

His hands lay on his thighs. He waited until she nodded her consent, then raised them. They were warm on her bare skin, raising goose bumps as he used medical tape to affix the wire to her abdomen. She lost all ability to reply when he slid the tips of his fingers under the lacy cup of her bra to pull the fabric forward and clip the mic to it. Her nipples peaked. She felt it. He saw it. A muscle jumped in his jaw.

She'd known this before she'd dressed for another fun evening with Officer Hawthorn. She was taunting him the only way she could: with her body. She wanted to make him lose his composure, see the dark red stain on his cheeks, his jaw tighten, his cock strain against his fly. The chemistry in the car was palpable, hot and seething and electric enough to make the hair on her arms stand up, never mind her nipples, or the sweet throbs of heat between her legs, all she could think about when she lay in her dorm bed at night . . .

Present day ...

That's how crazy she'd made him, driving him to the point of thoughtlessly barking out a command without any regard for how it would sound to her. But rather than cowering, she'd called him on it. The confidence was there, just buried deep.

She rubbed her forehead with the palm of her hand. "Trust me, I remember. I just don't know how to get past something like that."

All she had to do was trust her body, not her brain. Which sounded simple enough. Ian knew it wasn't.

"Let's try this," he said, and kissed her. All it took was ducking his head a little, angling his mouth just enough to brush his lips across hers. It was chaste, brief and warm and dry, and yet somehow also just like getting a gun pointed at him. His heart rate went fast and irregular, and adrenaline washed into his system like a flash flood. Her mouth, her wide, mobile, indescribably lush mouth was under his lips.

And then it wasn't. She'd pulled back a little, as had he. Her gaze locked on his. His brain just stopped and stared, hyperalert, like a deer surprised at a watering hole. This was one way, one very primal, all-or-nothing way to get Riva over her fears, her visceral reaction to his touch. But she had to want him.

Her eyelids fluttered open. She licked her lower lip like she was chasing the taste of him. "I've waited seven years for you to do that." Another unconscious glide of her tongue, the pink matching the heat rising to the surface of her skin, but her gaze was cloudy, troubled. "Do it again."

He wanted to kiss her, touch her, get so deep inside her that he drove those clouds away, but first, he wanted some privacy.

"Upstairs."

She nodded, led the way. In her bedroom the windows were open, the night breeze lifting the gauzy curtains. A fire had been laid in the fireplace, but wasn't lit. The mound of pillows and thick duvet seemed daunting, like finding the mattress would require excavation equipment and hard hats.

He closed the door behind them. She stood in the no-man's-land between the door, the bed, and the fireplace, head high, gaze fixed on him, body tense and poised for movement. "What else have you been waiting for?" he asked, deliberately keeping his voice calm, gentle. Locking down the desire running wild inside him.

Her fingers flexed and her hand lifted, then relaxed at her side again. Holding back. "Everything," she said.

He didn't respond. The air held that charged-up vibration between fight and surrender, like the outcome wasn't a given at all. He crossed the floor to stand about a foot in front of her, on the very edge of her personal space, then lifted his fingertips to her cheek. The skin was so soft he almost didn't register it under his touch. He brushed his thumb once over the corner of her mouth and watched her lips soften. He let gravity slowly drag his hand down over her jaw to her throat, then over her collarbone to the deep V of her henley, where he paused. She was trembling.

"Riva. Are you with me?"

CHAPTER ELEVEN

"Yes. It's just . . ." She heaved in a deep breath. His hand rose and fell with the movement. Her heart was pounding so hard he could see her breast quivering with each rapid beat.

All the muscles in his body were tensed to take a step back, end this, when she spoke. "It's all messed up in my head," she said. "Can I . . . ?"

"Whatever you need." The screaming voices in his head could just sit down and take a number. He'd been waiting for this for years. Another few minutes wouldn't matter.

She reached out and put her hand on his hip, right below his waistband. He could barely feel her touch through his jeans, and maybe imagined her thumb rubbing over his hipbone. He ran his fingertips up her breastbone, then back down to hook in the V-neck and the front of her bra. Exerting the smallest pressure imaginable, he coaxed her a couple of inches closer, bent his head, and kissed her again. He kept his mouth soft, enticing rather than demanding, and was rewarded with her lips parting under his.

The tentative touch of her tongue triggered something in him, too. Time kept slipping like a stripped gear. Riva as a teenager. Riva as a grown woman. Himself as an angry, hot-tempered young cop, trying manhood on for size in a way he'd never expected, even resented. He'd been out of alignment since the diagnosis.

Then Riva closed the distance between their bodies, and everything *snick*ed into place, key in lock, bolt shot home, brain shut down. She was going for this, all in. No regrets. No hesitations.

He wrapped his arm around her waist and spun them around, backing her into the door. "Shh, shh," she whispered as the wood thudded against the frame. "Ow. Hard. Door is hard."

He winced and pulled her a little closer. "Right. Sorry. I got a little carried away there."

"There's a nice, soft bed right over there," she said.

He caught the edge of the duvet and gave it a big flip. Throw pillows scattered to the wind. Riva toed out of her boots, then knee-walked to the center of the bed, then turned and reached for him. He hastily got rid of his own footwear, then knelt on the bed in front of her.

It seemed as natural as breathing to weave their fingers together, palms cupped up. He bent to her, capturing her mouth with warm, tempting kisses, waiting, waiting, until his hand lifted involuntarily and slid into her hair, capturing the strands against her jaw. The other hand, still joined with hers, slid around her waist to pull her closer. He kept on kissing her until her fingers tightened in his and her free hand started to roam, trembling and hesitant at first, then gaining confidence to tug his shirt free from his jeans and flatten against his side.

Her touch was searing. Electric. It wasn't always easy to be naked in front of a woman; between the appendectomy scar and the port scar, this moment usually brought things to a screaming halt for a moment. Still, it had to be easier for him than it was for Riva. He broke contact and reached behind his head to yank the shirt off. Her eyes widened, her gaze skimming over his chest, but she didn't ask, just swept her own shirt over her head, leaving her hair in tousled disarray.

He used chest and hands and hips to urge her down onto the mattress. Stretching out full-length against her was like taking serious voltage. He'd never been more aware of body contact. He pressed his erection into her hip, tucked his knee between hers, and went back to kissing her.

By the time he'd finished, her mouth was hot and soft and open, smearing messily against his as her body lifted infinitesimally into his. Determined to discover what she liked, he trailed his lips along her jaw to her ear. What would make her purr, gasp, arch into him? He wanted to know, had to know.

She went still when he brushed his lips over her ear, tipped her head to the side when he closed his teeth on her earlobe, but the press of his tongue to the soft skin just below her ear made her shudder, then sigh. She was ticklish; a light touch on her ribs made her squirm, but when he firmed up, it was like her entire body went molten. Her thighs had parted a little more, giving him room to roll more closely into her body. Instead, he kissed his way down her torso, his mouth hot and open and wet around the edges of her bra, then her navel, pausing at her belt.

He looked up the soft curves of her body and found her staring down at him. "Turn over," he murmured, working consciously to make it a suggestion, not a command, or an order.

She looked surprised, a little hesitant, but did. Maybe putting her body in his hands had become automatic, but he didn't take it for granted. Instead he shifted up her body, keeping his thigh between hers and draped himself over her back. He swept her hair away from her nape and pressed a kiss into the vulnerable skin.

Beneath him, her body went still, something he noticed when the soft give and take they'd developed halted. Suddenly, he was breathing into tense muscle and locked joints.

Interesting. Fear or desire? He did it again, this time lingering so his breath washed over sensitive nerves, adding a tiny edge of his teeth. A full-body shudder, then a low moan and she went soft under him. While he watched, a shiver raced over her shoulders and lifted the tiny, delicate hairs on her nape.

A feral surge of desire swept through him, canting his hips until he was grinding against the round curve of her ass. To regain his control, and torture them both, he repeated the kiss on every bump in her spine from her nape to the top of her tailbone. When he reached her bra strap he unfastened it, nudged it aside, and went back to dropping kiss after kiss down her back until he'd reached her jeans.

"Turn back over," he said.

She did, her hair spreading over her face until she pawed it back, then pulled off her bra. He didn't want to stare, but found he couldn't help himself. Her skin was so pale, the tips of her breasts a dark rose and peaked. She shifted, spreading her legs, making room for him to settle between them. Involuntarily he pushed against her, the movement tidal, deep. He took his weight on one arm and teased the skin above her waistband with his other hand, keeping his kiss as light as his touch. He traced her hipbone, her ribs, then swept up to cup her breast.

She wrapped both arms around his neck and arched into the touch. Again, his control nearly failed him when she wrapped her leg around his hip and pulled him closer, the quick rise and fall of her abdomen brushing against his, heightening the sense of constriction in his jeans.

Then her hands were between them, working away at her button and zipper. He sat back, helped her get her jeans off and discard them on the floor by her bra, leaving her bare from head to toe. Cold air swept over them as he lost the plot for a second, again caught up in the simple beauty of her body.

"You too. Please."

The words were almost inaudible, but she was with him. He unbuckled his belt, unzipped, got through the awkward moment of getting jeans and boxers off over his erection. Naked in front of her, the moonlight picking out the stark red scar from his port, the thinner, older scar from his appendectomy. But she wasn't looking at those. Instead her gaze skimmed like warm silk over his shoulders, his arms, his abdomen.

She was looking at him.

"Come here," she said.

He settled against her, letting the feel of her bare skin

against his wash over him and be distinct data points. Her bare thighs against his. His cock, trapped between her soft stomach and his. Her nipples, tight little points against his chest. Her hands, one at his nape, the other at the small of his back. Her pulse was pounding in her breast again. He kissed her, ignoring the need throbbing in his cock, soaking in the texture and taste of her mouth, the sensation of having Riva under him.

Don't get too carried away, said voice of reason in his brain. *Right now you can pretend this doesn't mean anything. Hell, you've been pretending that for years. But you go any further, and you're in uncharted territory.*

Tearing himself away from temptation, he shifted to one side and skimmed his hand down her torso, following the curves he'd seen only in his fever dreams. His mouth hot and open over her, he stroked the trimmed curls covering her mound, then dipped his fingers into her folds.

The first touch made her shudder, lift, spread, opening her so his fingers delved into slick, swollen folds. He groaned, rested his head on her forehead, and closed his eyes as he dipped into slick heat, circled her opening, then trailed up in search of—

There. She arched. Her fingernails, short as they were, bit into his shoulders. He circled the tight bud, ruthlessly focusing on her response to hold back his own primitive instincts, but nearly lost it when she started to gasp. He covered her mouth with his own and kept a steady pace, watching her muscles tighten, her body quiver, and the pretty pink orgasmic flush bloom on her face and throat. She was tender and strong and earthy, fully present in her body. Her fingers tightened on his shoulder and biceps, her hips lifted into each stroke, and he was lost. Her release looked less like letting go and more like annihilation.

The orgasmic tension in her muscles slowly slackened. Her hands released their grip on his shoulders. She stared up at him, eyes wide, defenseless.

So that's how it felt to cross the line and jeopardize his career. He'd just have to pretend a little harder, when he got home.

But right now he wasn't home, and he'd do it again in a heartbeat, because for the first time since Riva had reached for his hand to write her phone number on it, she was soft and relaxed against him. No tensed muscles ready to fly, no conflict in her eyes. Heart pounding, body aching, he bent his head and rested his forehead against hers.

It felt so goddamn right.

"Ian," she whispered. Her hand drifted down to his hip. "What about you?"

It might literally kill him, but he shifted to the side. "There's no rush," he said, though it cost him. He was as aroused as he'd ever been. "We don't ever have to do that, if you don't want to. I'm going back to my room to make some notes," he continued over her soft protest. "You should get some sleep. Tomorrow's going to be a long day."

He got out of the bed and snagged his clothes from the floor. When he left her she was sitting upright, the sheet and duvet clutched to her chest, hair tousled, glaring at him.

CHAPTER TWELVE

Riva surfaced from a deep sleep to the muffled sound of her alarm going off under her pillow. She silenced it, then stared at the screen. Four forty-five in the morning. Head raised, she listened for any sign of alert life in the suite's other bedroom. All she heard was muffled sounds from the floor below her, the clink of a coffee mug against the countertop, then water running.

She shoved her hair out of her face as she swung her legs over the side of the bed, then paused again. Still no noise from Ian's room. His light had been on when she'd finished showering and gone to bed. She was running on about five hours of sleep. Ian was running on less. Maybe that would keep him out of her hair for the next fifteen minutes.

He'd been in her hair last night. A sense memory triggered a hot little thrill, of Ian's hand gathering her hair before his lips brushed her nape. She associated his hands with power and control, so the firm touch—

No. Stop there. Not now. Stay focused.

Tiptoeing across the plush area rug, she turned the knob and opened the door slowly. No light from Ian's room, no rustle of bedclothes, although she suspected him of Spidey senses and the ability to Apparate from one spot to another. She stepped into the hall, looked and listened. No Ian, no voices downstairs.

Just her father.

Ian wasn't going to like this, not one bit, but what mattered in the long run was making sure she had enough evidence to get Isaiah free from the LPD's clutches and back in a kitchen, where he belonged. She padded down the stairs and turned the corner to the kitchen. Her dad was standing by a steaming French press, focused on his phone. For a moment Riva looked at him in the dim light over the stove. He wore khakis and a Henneman Candy and Vending button-down, and his belt matched his work boots. His hair, the same shade of chestnut as her own, was liberally streaked with silver. His knuckles were thickened from a lifetime of working with his hands, loading and driving a truck, schlepping boxes of candy from the truck to the vending machines.

He looked so ordinary, so human. He was anything but.

She cleared her throat and rubbed her eyes as if wiping away sleep. "Morning, Dad."

He spared her a single glance. "You're up early."

The important thing was to sound like the girl she used to be, desperate for his attention and approval, uncertain and afraid. Going for deferential, she took a hesitant step into the room. Getting him to talk to her would work much faster than Ian's plan, and besides, she should have done this seven years earlier. This was her responsibility, not Ian's. "We didn't get much time to talk last night. I thought maybe I'd run a route with you today."

She used to do that all the time during school breaks, go out with him on a route. She was so proud to go. Each year she waited anxiously for the moment he got her a shirt just like his but in her size, with her name and the logo on it. The receptionists would fuss over her, and her dad would stand by, proud as any father could be, while she restocked machines, collected the coin bins, or ran back to the truck for an unexpectedly low item.

She'd loved him so much. Pleasing him, earning his approval, was the only thing that had mattered to her.

"Not today," he said, dismissing her. "You should spend your time getting a handle on your mother's little lunch deal."

She could make a lunch for eight worthy of a magazine spread in a couple of hours. "I've got a pretty good idea of what I'm going to do, and I'd rather—"

"Hey, do you think your friend upstairs would want to come work out at the gym tomorrow?" He depressed the plunger on the French press and opened the cabinet for a travel mug. "I've got a fighter who could use a different opponent."

Think fast. He doesn't respect people who plead. "I'm sure he'd love that," Riva said. That would be a good way to get Ian out of the way while she searched for her father's laptop. "He was pretty impressed with you. I'll text you and let you know."

Her father flicked a glance at her as he poured coffee. "I really need to go."

She waited a second, her toes curling away from the

tiled floor, and played her next card. "Business isn't as good as I said it was," she said finally.

His eyes sharpened. "That so."

"Yeah. I didn't want to worry Mom."

"Do you need money?"

"No. No loans. You built Henneman Candy and Vending without help, and I will, too. I need . . . to expand my business."

"Into vending?" He snapped the lid onto the travel mug. "The bulk of my business is still the stuff that's bad for you."

"Not that business, Dad."

He went still, and for a moment Riva thought she'd pushed him too far. The darkness in his eyes had a knife edge and the power to slice her to ribbons. "I'm not sure what you mean."

"Dad," she said quietly. "I know I screwed up in college. But I'm stronger now. I could be useful."

He hadn't moved. "What would your boyfriend think of that?"

Riva smiled. "He's not my boyfriend. I get a call a week, more in the summer when the weather's nice, from people like that, who never risk everything to make something of themselves. He's just a desk jockey thinking the grass is greener on the other side of the cube wall."

"Your mother hopes he's your boyfriend. I caught her looking at wedding venues."

"Tell her to stop. We're not dating, much less getting married," she said, ignoring the little twist in her heart.

Her father snapped the lid on the travel mug and gave her another one of those long, unreadable looks. Like he was gauging whether or not to trust her. "Maybe you both could be useful."

She frowned, hoping she looked like a better actor than she felt. "How's that?"

"Lancaster has potential. We've been trying to lock down that market for a while. We've made some friends doing it. Enemies, too. A friend with the city wouldn't hurt."

Nothing specific. Nothing incriminating. "Got it," Riva said, even though she had nothing.

"He works in IT? They can't pay him much."

"No idea," she said. "If he quits, he's giving up a pension and government benefits, so backfilling with cash wouldn't hurt."

"You probably didn't plan it, but your job's a good one. It's a legit cover for money coming in, and you move around every day, like I do."

"That's what I thought," Riva said, trying to infuse excitement and pleasure into her voice. Her dad would like the ego strokes.

"Our last try at laundering the money fell through. Management problems. Nightclubs are risky." He shook his head. "You're a known quantity. Let me talk to some people."

"Great," Riva said. "I'll be around for a few more days. I could stay longer, but Ian has to get back."

His name came out without hesitation. She still wasn't thinking about last night, but she did notice that. Saying his name no longer tripped her up.

"I'll call you later."

"Love you, Dad."

He let himself out the back door. Riva stood in the

kitchen, listening to all the familiar sounds of her childhood—his boots on steps, the garage door opening, his car engine turning over, tires on the cement, then the Doppler sound of the engine fading like her last hopes.

He hadn't denied it. At some level she'd thought he'd either deny his involvement, or say he'd gotten out of that gig when the business got back on its feet. But he hadn't. He was either so confident in his ability to remain hidden in plain sight, or so delusional that he didn't even deny it. She rubbed her forehead and then she did the only thing she could do in this moment. She went back to bed.

Several hours later, she awoke to bright sunshine, birds trilling obnoxiously in the oak tree by her window, and the scent of Ian Hawthorn's sweat and skin drifting from her pillow to her nose. Earlier she'd been still shrouded in shadows and too focused on her father to think about the night before. But daylight brought with it a new awareness, of the relaxed muscles in her shoulders and back, and the little flashbacks to Ian's mouth on hers, his hands on her skin, whispered words in her ear.

Water ran in the pipes leading to their shared bathroom. He was awake and in the shower, a thought that conjured images of water flowing over Ian's lean, hard muscled body. Now she knew exactly how he looked, the way the planes of muscle shifted under his skin, the coiled strength hidden by bland, unremarkable office-drone clothes. There wasn't an ounce of fat on him. The way his muscles flexed and bunched reminded her not of a World Wrestling Entertainment steroid junkie but of a stealthy predator, dangerous, silent, disarmingly supple but fast and with razor-sharp teeth and claws. A jaguar, she decided. A lynx. Fierce. Feral. Deadly.

Stop slotting Ian Hawthorn into the wild kingdom.

The itch she'd been unable to scratch for years should have been satisfied, but felt incomplete. She'd thought it would be wild, passionate, hastily banging into doorframes and tripping over their clothes in a frenzy to get skin to skin and down to business. She'd thought it would be almost separate, each striving to come, an explosion of long-delayed tension and desire.

Instead, he'd turned all his relentless, focused attention to her pleasure and taken nothing for himself. She found she wasn't surprised, would have been more shocked, in fact, if he'd been selfish in bed.

There's no rush, he'd said. They didn't have to ever have sex. Did he really mean that?

The little voice in her head wanted to know if it had worked, wanted to see him, see how she felt near him, if her body would give in to the little opportunities to brush against him.

Out of habit she reached for her phone, where she found texts from Isaiah and Kelly. Isaiah had sent her a conscientiously detailed update on the farm, including the temperature, humidity, barometric pressure, state of mind of the chickens, egg count, and a rundown on every plant in the greenhouse and fields. The last messages were pictures of what he'd cooked for dinner.

I'll finish the chores early today. Want anything else done while I'm here?

She had a laundry list of projects to do around the farm, but none of them appropriate for an eighteen-year-old to tackle on his own.

Three new recipes, she sent back. *Work with what will be ready to harvest in a couple of weeks. And turn the dinner pics into a collage and post them on the Oasis site. Build that buzz.*

Kelly's text had come at five forty-two in the morning. *Want to go out tonight?*

You were up early. ☺ Let me check with Mom, but probably. Dinner?

Three bubbles appeared immediately.

Wyatt's up with the sun these days. Let's hit Lit tonight! I haven't been out clubbing since before I got pregnant.

Lit was their old hangout, a leftover from high school when they'd trowel on the makeup, dress up, and put their fake IDs to good use. She texted back *Sounds great!*, then looked up from her phone when the water in the bathroom shut off with a *thunk*. Was it her imagination, or could she hear the towel rubbing against his skin as he dried off? The fan was running, so probably it was just her overheated imagination triggered by the faint scent of his sweat in her sheets.

She needed to make puff pastry dough, so she was going to have to leave the bedroom. Soon. The question was, beat him downstairs or let him go down and get some coffee? She knew very little about how Ian handled mornings. Ian between six p.m. and two a.m. was a familiar, open book, but mornings, that time of day when people's temperaments varied most, when they were grumpy or rumpled or disgustingly cheerful, she had experienced exactly one time with Ian.

That one had involved boxer briefs and a gun.

She needed coffee, so she got up, splashed water on her face, and brushed her teeth, then dressed for the day in jeans, a tank top, and a sweater for the chilly morning. Her skin was clear, slightly pink, her eyes wide, her gaze soft. She pulled her hair back in a ponytail. "Woman up. He's arrested you. Fooling around doesn't even compare. You got through that, and you'll get through this."

She couldn't remember what she'd thrown into her suitcase the night Ian had come for her, so she rummaged through her clothes, searching for something slinky and suitable for a night of drinking and dancing, and found a sky-blue camisole, a black skirt she used to waitress in, and her peep-toe nude heels that went with everything. Problem solved. Ian's bedroom door opened, then closed, and his footsteps faded down the stairs. She left the clothes on the bed, shoved her phone in her back pocket, and darted after him.

In the kitchen Ian was perched on a bar stool with Sugar on his lap while her mother fretted in the fridge. His jeans were worn white in all the interesting places and another soft, light sweater. He met her gaze without giving anything away. "Morning," he said quietly.

Her heart was pounding. Terrible news from the kitchen. Fooling around with him only left her wanting more.

"Good morning," she said, because not responding would be awkward. "Let me, Mom."

Her mother lifted her head from peering into a crisper and stared at Riva. Today her pupils were normal, responding to the changing light, her gaze alert but full of pain. Riva knew that look, bewildered, confused, hurt by her father's abrupt withdrawal last night at the dinner table. The pattern played out over and over again, the attention like a searchlight, intense and powerful and addictive, focused on everything that mattered to you, then the abrupt drop when nothing you do or say or think can be right, much less get his attention back. It had taken her years to see the pattern, then believe it was true, then learn how to fight it. "I can make you two breakfast," she said, and the tentative note in her voice cracked Riva's heart.

She kissed her mom on the cheek and gave her a quick hug. "Looks like a good night of sleep was all you needed. Let me make breakfast while you tell me your vision for the luncheon. It'll be faster if you talk and I cook."

She took her mother's place in front of the fridge, took stock of the ingredients, then looked over her shoulder at Ian. "How do you like your eggs?"

He looked up from tightening the tiny pink bow in Sugar's hair. "How are you making them?"

She hated that he'd started the day pandering to her. Everyone had an opinion about eggs. She'd spent hours arguing with friends over the merits of poached versus soft boiled and which bread to use to sop up a warm, runny yolk, and knew people who flatly refused to eat eggs at all unless they were fried into Frisbees. "I was planning on soft boiled over a potato hash, but I can adjust depending on how you like them."

"Sounds great."

Her mother reappeared from the office with a big binder and a tablet. Perching on a stool at the end of the breakfast bar, she opened the binder and ran Riva through a dizzying array of images, recipes, and themes she'd collected from the internet and various luxury-goods magazines. Ian set Sugar on the floor and ignored her raised paws, demanding that she be picked up again.

"I'll cook," he said. "Talk me through it."

"That's really not necessary, Ian," her mother fretted.

"It's no problem," he replied. "I've made hash and eggs before."

He actually was competent in the kitchen. Riva directed him to pans and knives and cutting boards, watched him dice potatoes and onions and clean up as he cooked. It was a nice counterpoint to the frenzy her mother was spinning herself into as she talked about china, linens, flowers, and themes.

"What about that one, Mom? Add the greens and give them a quick stir to soften them with the potatoes' heat. You have similar dishes."

Her mother considered the image, of blue Italian china with contrasting patterned napkins. "One egg or two?" Ian asked.

"Two. It smells really good. More coffee?"

"Coffee for everyone, I think. Cream's in the fridge." Ian poured coffee and put the cream and sugar on the table while Riva served up the hash, added an egg to two of the plates and two eggs to the third. "Breakfast is ready, Mom."

They seated themselves in the breakfast nook, her mother sliding her binder next to her plate like Riva used to do with a book when she was a girl. "I like it, but I'm afraid it's too busy."

Riva was cheered by her engagement and enthusiasm, like her mother was a completely different person this morning, alert, attentive, maybe even able to make a decision. "Okay, so we do the blue dishes with white linens and flowers. Or that one." She pointed at an image of a single tulip bound to snow white napkins with a matching ribbon. Place cards sat above the napkin, and flowers spilled exuberantly from small white pitchers stacked on cake platters. "You have that gorgeous white Asprey service. It fits well with a simple, elegant spring theme. I'll work with what I find at the co-ops and farm stands right now, and you can mention the urban gardening movement."

"I don't know, dear. I just can't seem to make a decision. But these women have worked very hard to bring the dinner dance together, and I want to thank them."

Ian was quietly eating his hash, but Riva could feel his attention on her. "It doesn't seem silly at all. Thanking people who work really hard to raise money for underrepresented populations is very important. I know you want to do your best."

Her mother was eating with more appetite than she had at dinner the night before. "This is delicious, dear. I had all this in the fridge?"

"It's two kinds of potato, olive oil, some salad greens, a bit of feta cheese, fresh pepper, and soft-boiled eggs. Easy peasy," she said lightly.

"Thank you," her mother said to Ian. "Rory says I'm such an airhead."

"You have a good eye for centerpieces," he replied. At her mother's raised eyebrows, he added, "My mother likes to host her garden club friends. She'd like those."

Her mother perked up. "Where are you planning to serve?" Riva said.

"In the backyard," her mother said, her voice growing in confidence. "I thought several tables under the oak trees."

"Perfect!" Riva exclaimed. "The lawn looks fantastic and the trees are in full leaf so it won't be too sunny.

I'll source the flowers and the ingredients while I'm out the next few days."

"We really should talk about the menu," her mother said.

"Mom. I made this" —Riva gestured to their empty plates—"with what you had in your fridge. Once I get into an urban garden's co-op, the sky's the limit. Trust me."

The sunshine settled like a soft blanket over the breakfast nook while her mother wavered. "All right," she said finally. "The Asprey and tulips. You two go on. I'll handle the dishes."

Riva had managed to avoid looking right at Ian through the meal. This might not have been her best choice, as she'd collected instead a collage of odd images. His forearms, exposed by his sleeves, pushed to his elbows. The way his sweater sat at his hip, caught by the pocket seams of his jeans, and the slight bulge of his fly. The fabric, stretched taut over his shoulders when he chopped onions and sprinkled feta over the eggs.

She forced herself to look at him, to meet his gaze like he was a colleague. "Ready?"

He held her gaze effortlessly. "I need an hour or so. I've got a couple of things to check in on at work. Are you ready?"

She'd completely forgotten about the puff pastry. "That's fine. I'll whip up quick puff pastry."

They stood up at the same time and inevitably crashed into each other. She let out a bright, tinkling laugh totally unlike her; he gripped her upper arms to keep her steady. Involuntarily she startled, staring up at him, wide-eyed.

He let her go, but totally in character. "Oops," he said, relaxing his hands as he stepped to the side before leaving the room.

"No worries!" Riva said, still bright, still artificial. Her heart was racing, and a light sweat broke out between her breasts, prickling at her nape. She stacked the plates and tried not to flinch at the clatter the silverware made. Speaking of nerves. . . . "Mom, are you still taking the Valium?"

"Sometimes, honey. You know how anxious I am, and I've started getting headaches, too."

"Are you taking anything else? Anything stronger?"

"No. Although sometimes the pills do affect me in funny ways. I feel worse when I take them, not better."

She made a mental note to get upstairs and go through her mother's medicine chest at the earliest opportunity. "I'm worried about you. You seem fine now, but last night—"

"Last night I just needed to go to bed, like your father said."

"Do you know if anyone has any food allergies I should be aware of?"

Her mother closed her notebook. "He's very nice. He's obviously attracted to you."

Riva stifled a hysterical giggle as she set the plates to one side, then gathered flour, salt, ice water, butter, and her mother's food processor. "Gluten-free? Raw? Vegan?"

"Riva. Your father says infertility runs in families. I hate to think I . . . if you even think you want children—"

Her husband was getting deeper and deeper into drug trafficking, the man staying in her guest suite was investigating the crime, and her mom was worried about whether Riva could have children. "Mom, I'm really not thinking about that right now."

The sharp tone in her voice silenced her mother. But she sat at the breakfast bar, watching as Riva pulsed together the flour and butter, added the water to the flour and pulsed again, then rolled it out.

"You make it look so easy," her mother said.

"I could teach you," Riva said casually as she folded the dough into thirds. "You could come visit me, and we could cook together."

"Your father says I'm hopeless in the kitchen."

Stupid and *hopeless* were at the top of the list of words her father used to belittle her mother. "Dad says that, but it's not true." She wrapped the roll of dough in plastic, then looked into her mother's eyes. "Come back with me, Mom. Please."

Her mother laughed uneasily. "What would your father say?"

"We don't have to tell him."

A bright, wild hope flared in her mother's eyes. For a moment Riva thought she was going to say yes, but then Ian's boots clattered down the stairs. "I'll be in the truck," he called. When Riva looked back at her mom, the hope had died.

"Ian's a nice man," her mother said, changing the subject. "You haven't dated anyone, not even casually, since before you dropped out of Lancaster College."

Riva put the wrapped dough in the fridge to chill, then washed her hands. "Ian and I might be attracted to each other, but you can't act on every attraction. Sometimes things just aren't meant to be."

Sorrow darkened her mother's eyes. "I'll clean up. Go visit your gardens."

Halfway between the kitchen and the foyer Riva stopped, reaching blindly for one of the pristine white spindles as she took a deep breath. There was no going back now.

She hauled open the front door, fending off Sugar's break for freedom with her foot as she stepped onto the porch. Ian was waiting by the truck, arms folded across his chest, legs crossed at the ankle, gaze directed at his boots. He looked up as she walked down the path.

She hoisted her bag higher on her shoulder and fished in it for her keys. "If I give you addresses can you plug them into your phone and navigate?"

"Sure," he said.

"We're headed for Seventy-Sixth and Racine. Urban Canopy," she said, then steered down the street.

CHAPTER THIRTEEN

Ian focused on the blue dot in his maps app. At least his phone knew where he was. After last night with Riva, he wasn't sure he knew which way was up. Doing the right thing had only left him with an aching groin and a new endless loop of Riva playing in his head. "Head to the interstate. Why are we going here?"

"They're one of the best urban farm and community agriculture organizations in the region. Totally focused on economic and social sustainability, plus they have a cool CSA that includes produce from locations farther away. And they've got a compost component. Basically, they're about ten steps ahead of Lancaster, which means I can learn from them."

The department's outreach efforts gave him a superficial familiarity with Lancaster's urban farming movement, but he asked about the specifics, letting some silence linger between her answers and his next question to give the tension somewhere to dissipate. Getting her talking about her chosen career path eased the tension in the car to the point where she was breathing again.

She pulled into the parking lot and headed for the door embedded in a gigantic mural of mushrooms painted on the red barn, where Andy, the site manager, met them. Ian followed a few steps behind, giving her the space she obviously wanted and needed this morning. She introduced herself, then Ian, then focused on Andy with a single-minded intensity on the thorough tour of the facility that included discussions about the indoor farm, lighting, technology, yields, natural fertilizers, volunteer schedules, delivery arrangements, and the ever-present need for more funding.

He watched her without bothering to hide his interest. She lit up like this, smelling growing plants, examining lights, listening to their guide's knowledgeable, enthusiastic patter. This was where she was home. In places like this she didn't have to hide. Here, all anyone cared about was nurturing plants, people, the earth.

She took a deep breath. "Do you smell that?" she asked.

Ian inhaled. Dirt, damp, a rich humus smell of vegetation decomposing into life. "Yeah."

She shot him a smile, bright and clean, like she'd forgotten who she was, who he was, what they were doing. Observing from a distant corner of his mind, he smiled back, like he'd forgotten all these things too.

Then her gaze went hot and fierce. Like she'd remembered not that he'd arrested her but other, more pleasant memories, ones she wanted to recreate and expand.

She absently brushed the dirt from her palms. "I'm sourcing produce for a charity luncheon in a couple of days. Would you have anything to spare that would feed ten? The attendees are the subcommittee chairwomen for Memorial Hospital's annual dinner dance fundraiser. I'd like to showcase the city's urban garden movement."

Andy's face had started to close off when he heard the short timeline, but he perked right up again at the word "showcase." "Most of our weekly harvest is allotted to the CSA deliveries and the farmers' markets. But that's a pretty small order, so we can probably help you out. Let me introduce you to Debbie. She runs that side of the operation."

Debbie was indeed delighted to hold back the ingredients for a salad, and put Riva in touch with a farm near the Wisconsin border that could supply the pork for the tart and a variety of cheeses. "Are you visiting any other urban gardens?"

"I was thinking Growing Home?"

"Excellent choice. They've got an amazing program and partner with a legal aid group to help get records expunged or sealed."

"That's one of the reasons I wanted to stop by. One of my partner organizations is interested in adding that particular service. A conviction makes it so hard to get a job."

"I'll call Lamar and let him know you're coming. Good luck. Call me if you have questions or want to talk something through."

She waved cheerfully as they headed back to the truck. Once inside, Ian pulled out his phone. "Address?"

She gave him the address, and he directed her out of the parking lot. "Are you bored?" she asked.

He settled back in his seat and thought about this for a second. "No," he said.

"You sound surprised."

"Maybe a little. Shutting off my work brain isn't easy, but you've managed to do it."

"You're welcome."

Midday traffic was light as they drove to Growing Home. Lamar, the site manager, was expecting them. He'd been primed with the request for ingredients. "Any chance to expand our brand awareness and open new doors for fundraising," he said with a self-deprecating smile. "Grants are getting harder and harder to come by these days."

"It's a tough climate," Riva agreed. She held out her hand to include Ian. "My colleague, Ian."

Lamar's gaze swept over Ian. Ian knew he'd been made as a cop. "Where y'all from?"

"Lancaster. About six hours from Chicago." Not his jurisdiction, in other words.

Lamar pursed his lips and nodded slowly.

"We're just here for a tour," Ian said. "No surprises."

"And the ingredients," Riva said. "Definitely those."

They got a tour, Ian making sure to stay in Lamar's line of sight and take absolutely no interest in anyone or anything not related to dirt, plants, and the process of turning seeds into food then getting them to kitchens and restaurants around the city. The people working at the site eyed him with the wariness common to people who grew up with cops in their faces but without the sharper edge that indicated fear or guilt. Toward the end of the tour, Riva sat down with their chef and talked ingredients and recipes with an absorption that fascinated Ian.

"You remind me of a kid focused on a video game," he said as they were leaving. Lamar was going to deliver the ingredients the morning of the luncheon, and Riva had that distracted expression that meant she was processing the conversation with the chef.

"If I add pears to the green salad . . ."

"That place had an interesting vibe," Ian mused as he fastened his seat belt. "Can you find your way home or do you need directions?"

She surfaced long enough to look around. "I can find my way home."

"This kind of business would make a great cover for moving drugs," he mused.

Her head whipped around so fast he thought he heard something crack. "It was just an observation," he said.

"Good," she said, her color high. "Because that wasn't why we were there."

Riva, however, set off his radar. "Something you want to tell me? About Isaiah, maybe? Or the ESCC?"

"No!"

"Pull over. Right now."

She swerved into a gas station parking lot. "What?"

"What, what? You tell me what. Now, Riva."

"I hate it when you use my name like that," she muttered. "Fine. I got up early and talked to my dad before he left for work this morning."

"And?"

"I told him the farm wasn't doing well and I wanted to get in on his business. His real business. Not the vending-machine cover business."

Ian glared at her. "I know that was the original plan, but plans change."

She shook her head. "I can do this faster than you can. He already trusts me, and he'd believe I couldn't make it on my own—"

He cut her off. "That was before I met your dad. If there's a safer way to do this, then we'll do it. Aligning me as a connection inside City Hall is safer."

"For me. Not for you. If they find out about me, Dad has some leverage. If they find out about you, you're dead."

"I'm trained and paid to take that risk. You're not."

"With me, there's less of a risk in the first place."

A man walking by with a gigantic soda and a bag of chips stared at them. "Lower your voice," Ian said.

"I can't go back now," Riva said. "I'm less of a risk to him than you are."

"But I'm a bigger prize, and we both know how your dad feels about winning."

Her shoulders slumped ever so slightly. "Yeah. You're probably right. But that's not going to stop me. The point is to do this as quickly as possible. I'm really worried about my mother. This app says there's a Vietnamese food truck that gets great reviews a few blocks from here. You up for pho?"

They needed to talk about her mother, but for the moment he nodded, keeping quiet until they'd ordered from the food truck and found an empty table in the small park near the food truck. The paper bag contained chopsticks and a spoon useless for gathering up the noodles. Ian fumbled with the chopsticks until he'd gotten the hang of lifting a dripping portion of noodles and beef to his mouth. "Tell me more about your mother. She doesn't show up on anything but social media and charity profiles."

"She's been a homemaker since before I was born. Her dad didn't raise her to have a career, and my dad didn't want her to have one."

"Does she know about your dad's side business?"

"No."

He gave her a look. Denial was fine when nothing was on the line, but right now, they needed to be realistic. "You sure about that?"

Another mutinous glare. "What are you saying?"

"I'm saying that she shows all the signs of someone who's dealing with serious cognitive dissonance." He slurped up the noodles, then wiped his chin. "She wouldn't be the first wife to turn to painkillers, or to polish her husband's tarnished reputation with good works like raising money for a drug treatment wing at a hospital."

"She doesn't know!" She set down her chopsticks and folded her hands, sugar sweet except for the fury turning her lips white around the edges. "Someday someone's going to get into all your personal business and drag it out into the sunlight and point out the flaws and mistakes."

"You can do it, any time you want."

She stared at him.

"All you have to do is tell Captain Swarthmore about last night. I probably won't lose my job, but I'd lose any shot at promotion. For kicks, the media would be all over my life and everyone in it."

She looked away, then fiddled with her paper cup of iced tea. "I wouldn't do that."

"You could."

"I wouldn't." Her color was high. "Last night was between you and me. No one else needs to know about it."

He chose his words carefully. "You still looked a little startled this morning."

She poked moodily at her chicken, then plucked a

mushroom from the broth and ate it. "It's different when you touch me now. I want to know . . . what it could be like if you really let go."

"I did let go."

"Not really." She flicked him a glance, like she was worried about his ego. "It was good. I'm not criticizing. It was fine."

"Every man dreams of hearing that," he said, squinting into the sunlight. " 'Fine' means you added a few things to the grocery list and made a mental note to get your tires rotated."

"Hardly," she retorted. "Stop trying to distract me."

Of course she wanted all of him. Riva wouldn't accept anything less. "I understand."

She spoke haltingly. "You were careful. With me. I appreciate that. I'm not complaining. I just . . . you're always holding back with me. Do you think I can't handle you?"

He was having trouble breathing. So many questions, none of them ones he should ask. His heart was going to come right out of his chest. "Maybe you're not the only one remembering the way we used to be."

She flashed him a look, blue eyes, tousled chestnut hair, trying to find her way through this. "This is where you tell me that you fantasized about tutoring an inexperienced girl in the ways of lovemaking."

"I didn't." He took a deep breath, forced himself not to check out the skyline she found so entrancing, looked her right in the eyes. "I fantasized about this."

Her brow furrowed as she pointed at the remains of their lunch. "What? This?"

"About meeting you again. When you were older. About you liking me, instead of looking at me like I was your worst nightmare. About somehow finding a way to ask you out. I didn't fantasize about having sex with a girl who was completely under my control. It was wrong on so many levels that I knew I wouldn't be able to live with myself if I let my mind go there. You were eighteen, but I was older and a cop, and it was my responsibility to keep things in line. We could have so easily crossed that line, Riva."

"You fantasized about this." She looked at the table, strewn with the remains of their takeout lunch. "About, like, a lunch date?"

"Any kind of date. The biggest moment was you not turning white and bolting when you saw me again. After that, I was all smooth lines and cool banter. Getting a yes was easy."

She was staring at him, really looking at him. "Not sex."

"No."

"Wow. Now I feel like a total creeper."

It was his turn to half laugh. "I was aware of the attraction between us."

"Do you always talk like you're writing a report?"

He locked his gaze with hers. "You turned me right the fuck on. I've never been so attracted to a woman. It started the moment we made eye contact at Kaffiend. Intense, devastating, all consuming. I thought I'd never get out from under it. Is that better?"

Her breathing was rapid, shallow. "How did you not think about it?"

"I just didn't."

"That's some amazing mind control."

"I've always been focused."

Her eyes narrowed. "And there you go again, back

behind the walls." He expected an explosion, but she just stared at the sky, lost in thought. "I guess your fantasy met reality that night at Oasis."

That actually made him laugh. "Yeah."

"Kitchen fires and getting thrown out of a restaurant are a great way to reconnect. Unless, in your mind, you were saving me from something."

He would have given up his entire salary not to react to that comment, but the gods weren't smiling on him. He flushed, beet red by the stinging heat in his cheeks and ears.

Her laughter was half crowing, half sheer delight, loud enough to turn heads at tables around them. "Okay, now you have to tell me. Car accident? Burning building? Stalker? All of the above?"

"Sometimes we just met at a bar."

She laughed harder. Getting defensive wasn't helping him here, so he finished his noodles and waited for her to settle down. When she did, she flicked him a glance. "I want my startle reflex gone."

"It takes time," he said quietly. Riva needed to learn to turn into his touch, to seek it, to arch and purr under it.

"How do you know that?"

"There's a reason why we put recruits through a training academy." He was sidestepping the answer. He'd learned that long before he joined the LPD. Staring at an IV line into his port, knowing it dripped poison into his veins in order to kill the cells gone rogue in his body, was the biggest mind fuck he'd ever come to terms with.

Wrapping his brain around the complex, fragile relationship he was forming with Riva would be the second biggest.

"Any ideas?" Her tone was light, like they weren't talking about how to come to terms with a power imbalance, like they weren't talking about how to have sex without her getting shocked out of the moment every thirty seconds.

Possibilities ran through his mind. He could get a hotel room, plan a nice dinner beforehand. He'd start with her hands, gentle touches, nonthreatening, undemanding. Sharing a shower wasn't a bad idea, either, something physical but not sexual. He could focus on this, double down, spend hours seducing her until all she thought when his skin touched hers was *yes, there, more*.

But then he remembered why they'd met again, their purpose in coming to Chicago. They didn't have time to take a weekend off and hole up at an expensive hotel. "Nothing that doesn't totally ignore why we're together again, and here."

She sighed. "Our timing is crap."

"But this time—"

He stopped. This time wasn't all that much different from last time, and they both knew it. It wasn't timing. It was them.

"Yeah, there's no way to finish that sentence," she said. Moving briskly, she collected their paper bowls and took them over to the trash can beside the food truck. "I'm still a CI you arrested, and you're still moving up in the police department. Ready to go?"

"You're going out with Kelly tonight, right? Drinking and dancing."

"We're going to Lit." She gave him a defensive look. "It was Kelly's idea, but I'm totally up for blowing off some steam. You can stay home, if you don't want to come."

Memories returned in flashes, some HD sharp, others fuzzy edged and slurred voices. The wall of noise made by hundreds of people packing into a tiny space and the music thumping over, around, through them. A chemical mixture of smells, perfume, cologne, hair gel, hair spray, detergents, sweat. Alcohol searing into his gut, then through his bloodstream to the very edges of his skin until the boundaries between him and the rest of the world blurred into a smear. A haze of desperation, provocation, and artificial shrillness rising like the tide until everything went black.

It never stayed black.

He realized he was staring blankly at the gas station sign, and Riva was staring intently at him. He cleared his throat. "Does it fit with your usual routine when you come home?"

She looked away. "This is the first time I've been home since . . . since then. Kelly was my best friend in high school and we've stayed in touch on social media. She was a bit of a wild child. Mom didn't like the idea of me sneaking into clubs, so meeting up with her is a plus with Dad. He'll see it as me siding with him over her. Kelly doesn't get out very much now that she has Wyatt. I want her to relax and have a good time."

"You haven't been home in seven years."

"No."

She hadn't bothered to tell him that. He felt a muscle in his jaw pop when he gritted his teeth. "You didn't think showing up out of the blue would look suspicious to your dad?"

"No one can predict what will look suspicious to him. Unpredictability is a big part of how he keeps us off balance. Plus, if I come home for Mom but then start doing business with him, he'll feel like he's controlling me again. I told you I'd thought about this."

"He's not going to be happy if you start asking questions about your mother."

"I'll deal with that when it happens." She still wouldn't meet his eyes, but tension radiated from the set of her jaw. "I have to do something. I've left her here, with him, for too long."

Ian rolled his shoulders to knock the tension from them. Riva's mother's plight hadn't been a part of his calculations on how this would go down, but helping her mother obviously mattered to Riva as much as protecting Isaiah. "Fine. We're going out. *We*," he stressed. "This isn't negotiable," he added when she opened her mouth again.

"Fine."

In between nailing down the order for her mother's lunch, Riva had picked up ingredients for dinner. He watched her drive back to the house, biting her lip as she navigated through traffic.

"What's on your mind?"

"Dinner."

"What are you going to make?"

"I'm going to give the menu a trial run," she said. "That will reassure Mom, and let me fine-tune before the big day."

He thought of the bags of fruits, vegetables, and herbs sitting on the truck's back seat, all needing to be washed, scraped or scrubbed, then chopped. "I'll help," he offered.

She blinked at him. The seat belt bisected her torso, creating a sweet little bulge on either side. It was kind of endearing. "Thanks."

"You're welcome."

They carried the bags into the house, Riva calling, "I'm home," as the screen door closed behind them. No mini mop greeted them.

"Maybe she's taking her for a walk?"

"Unpack everything," she said. "I'll be down in a second."

Riva's feet hurried up the stairs, growing fainter as she made the turn for the third floor. Her voice was too muffled for Ian to hear the tone of the conversation, much less the words, so he hastily emptied the carrier bags and folded them.

Riva's steps paused on the second floor; when she reappeared in the kitchen she was barefoot.

"Mom says she's got a migraine," she explained, her forehead wrinkled with concern.

"Are the headaches new?"

"Yes. She was anxious, not headache prone."

"If she's taking something stronger, it could be withdrawal symptoms," Ian said. "She'll be down for dinner." He kept his voice down. "Anyone else in the house?"

"No. We'll see Dad pull into the driveway from here."

"I want to search his office."

"He'll have the laptop with him."

"Probably, but I'm doing it anyway. Whistle or something if anyone comes to the door."

She looked like she was about to protest, but instead closed her mouth. Ian pulled on a pair of gloves to do a quick search of Rory's home office. As he opened drawers and searched behind knickknacks and books on the shelves, pictures on the walls, he heard Riva running water in the kitchen, drawers opening and closing, the *whump* of a gas stove lighting.

Nothing. Nothing obvious in the warehouse, and nothing here. He needed to get a look at the upstairs suite, but that wasn't happening today, with Stephanie and the dog asleep up there. Sugar would start yelping if he even set foot on the stairs.

"You sure you're up for being my sous chef?"

"That's the person who does the prep for the chef, right?"

"You know the difference between chopped, diced, and minced?"

"Uh," he said. "They're not all the same?"

She sighed. "Lucky for you I like teaching. Put on an apron."

CHAPTER FOURTEEN

Cooking dinner with Ian Hawthorn. Never in all of Riva's fantasies about Ian had cooking a meal with Officer Hawthorn come up. Maybe she needed to expand her horizons.

Working with sharp knives meant keeping her mind on her work, and in this kitchen, it was a pleasure. Whoever designed the kitchen remodel had had a chef in mind. The cooktop was built into a workspace across from the fridge, with the ovens built into the wall adjoining. "Let's start with the tarts. Wash and slice the new potatoes and shred the Emmentaler."

She handed him a knife and turned back to the puff pastry dough, letting her mind wander as she assembled the tarts. Like any other experience with Ian, this one was causing some serious cognitive dissonance, not least because she'd never expected to bring a man home.

Forget the fact that the man you've brought home isn't actually a boyfriend, much less a serious one. Ignore that. Instead, think about how normal this is. You're worrying about your mother's Valium-induced stupor, your father's ability to find any weakness or flaw and exploit it for his own amusement. You're worrying about having sex without your parents hearing.

"How's this?"

Think about Ian, calmly slicing potatoes while NPR plays in the background. Think about how normal that could be.

She came back to herself with a start. Ian stood at her shoulder, the first stalk of celery nicely minced. His hazel eyes were calm, like he was relaxed, enjoying himself, just hanging out with a friend who might become something more than a friend. She was having a hard time reconciling curt, resolute Officer Hawthorn from her past with Ian, who seemed to have an incredibly thick skin and a limitless supply of patience.

So forget Officer Hawthorn. Let Ian be Ian. Just for now.

"Good," she said. She took the knife from his unresisting fingers, chopped the dill and mint just a little more, then held it out to him. "That's better."

He tipped his head down, in that one movement making her extremely aware of their height difference, and murmured, "It is."

"What?"

His fingers brushed her palm as he claimed the knife. "You didn't flinch."

He didn't push. Smart man, because the whole scene was doing the work for him. The spring afternoon pushed into evening, the golden light gilding the gray-painted chairs and table, the granite counters, Ian's hair as he worked. Cooking smells had long anchored her memories, and this was no exception. The dance they did in the kitchen, his skin against hers as he passed her a bowl of chopped strawberries, her hand on his back as she passed behind him, moving from fridge to sink. The muscles were firm, lean. The look on his face as he stirred, concentrating, but without the intense focus he'd worn in the car years ago. Then he'd looked hard, combative, unyielding. Now his defenses were down. All he was thinking about was the process of preparing food.

She wanted more of everything, the scents of the food, the warm spring air, Ian working quietly by her side. So she opened all the windows and let the twilight sounds stream in, adding a layer of lilac to the atmosphere.

Her mother came downstairs as she pulled the three sample tarts from the oven; her father pulled into the driveway not long after.

"Should I set the dining room table?"

"Let's eat in here." She opened the cabinet holding her mother's everyday dishes and grabbed dinner plates, bread plates, salad plates. "Here. Silverware's in that drawer, and place mats are in the sideboard."

Dinner was awkward. Her father took one look at her mother's glassy eyes and swaying stance and said, "Looks like another early bedtime for someone." It was the tone a parent would use with a cranky toddler.

Her mother's eyes widened slowly. "But I'm not tired," she protested faintly. "I had a headache, so I took some medicine. I want to stay up with Riva—"

"You are tired. It was a big day for you." He tossed keys, wallet, cell phone carelessly on the counter. "You chose the china, right? That's a big day for some people."

Her mother blinked slowly, then looked at Riva. "We

did," Riva said brightly. "The Asprey, remember? It's your favorite."

"The Asprey. Yes. I'm really not tired, Rory. I want to stay up and spend time with Riva."

"Maybe tomorrow night. Tonight you'd best eat, then get upstairs."

"No," she said. "I'm fine."

Rory pursed his lips, then studied her over the rim of his whiskey glass. "How does Sugar look to you, Riva?"

Oh, no. "I noticed the white in her muzzle," Riva said, "but she still seems pretty chipper to me."

"If you were around more, you'd see the difference. She's started having accidents."

"One or two," her mother protested. "Only because she got locked in the closet in the basement. I couldn't find her for the longest time."

"She was only in there ten minutes," her father snapped. "She's old."

Riva's heart wrenched to think of that poor little dog, locked in the dark, and her mother frantically searching for her. She had no doubt who'd shut Sugar in the closet.

"I think it was longer," her mother replied, but her gaze had taken on a worried, unfocused look. "I'm sure it was."

"It wasn't. When they start to have accidents, it's time to put them down."

"Rory, please, it was just a couple of accidents. I've been taking her out more often."

"What if she's in pain?"

Her mother's eyes teared up. "Don't say that. Don't say she's in pain."

"She might be, and couldn't tell you."

"Dad, I'm sure she's not in pain," Riva said.

"Remember when she was limping a month or so ago? Like she'd hurt her hip trying to get into your lap?"

Her mother's face went white. Riva had no doubt in her mind that Sugar's injury wasn't accidental.

"She's not a young dog anymore. You should think about putting her out of her misery."

For a long moment no one spoke. Then her mother said, "I am rather tired. I'll go to bed now."

She reached down and picked up Sugar, then turned and shuffled along the hallway, one trembling hand trailing along the wall for balance. Silence reigned in the kitchen when they heard the click of a latch upstairs.

Other men got angry over normal things. The wrong kind of whiskey in the drinks cabinet, or running out of expensive cigars. An ink stain on the caramel leather seats in the car. She'd once watched a man climb out of his Hummer and go off on his pregnant girlfriend because she'd hung a waffle-weave shirt on a hanger which left a dorky lump in the fabric on his bulked-up shoulders. But not her father. He dug into the things she or her mother loved, like china or food, feigned an interest until they thought he shared their joy, then twisted it and used it until what they'd once loved was ruined. After this, her mother would never enjoy her pretty china sets again.

"China. We've got five different china services. None of them change the way the food tastes," he said to Ian.

Riva's heart was pounding its way out of her throat. She risked a glance at Ian. His face was as blank as a wall, a look she knew very well signaled barely contained fury.

"You didn't have to do that, Dad," Riva said. It was

risky, contradicting her father when he was in a mood like this one. "Sugar seems fine to me. Mom could have made it through dinner. It might have done her good to eat something with people, have a conversation."

He wheeled on her, face dark with rage. "How would you know?"

She felt Ian stiffen and shift his weight in her direction. "I'm just saying, maybe a change in diet or some alternative treatments for her headaches, acupuncture, that sort of—"

"Who's going to take her to the appointments? Not me. I've got a business to run. Not you. You haven't graced us with your presence in seven years. A good daughter would be here to help her, take her shopping, get her out to a museum or something. You say you want to help me run my business? That's how you help. I don't have time to babysit someone who should be able to take care of herself. And don't get me started on that stupid little dog shitting in my house."

Any more of this and Ian was going to step in. "You're right," she said quickly. "I haven't been around much. I'll just take her a plate and come right back down."

"The hell you will."

Ian flicked her a glance. *Don't. Not yet.* Burning with rage and humiliation, Riva sat back down and tried to figure out how to salvage this. "Remember what I said this morning? Maybe I need to get more involved at home too."

"You bet your ass you do, girlie." He held her gaze. "What kind of china do you have?" he asked.

He wasn't ready to let it go. Dangerous. Very dangerous. Lie? Tell the truth and play it up? Down? "I bought a box of odds and ends at an auction when the farmer between my farm and the highway sold his place."

"It doesn't match."

"No. Most of the serving pieces came from department store brands in the 1950s, back when department stores used to make their own."

Her father turned to Ian. "How does the food taste on those plates? Is it any worse because it's served on junk-sale dishes?"

"I've only had one meal at Riva's farm, and someone else cooked it," Ian said. "One of her working students. What was it, Riva?"

"Chicken with shallots" Riva said. She could have kissed him for turning the conversation to her farm. "The working student program really took off this spring. Kids from food deserts come out to the farm and work through the entire growing cycle, from preparing the soil for planting, to harvest, then to prepping the food for the table."

The moment vibrated like dropped pan. *Come on, Dad. Turn on a dime. Be an unpredictable bastard.* Then her father said, "What's a food desert?"

"Inner-city neighborhoods, mostly. Places where grocery stores have given up because the profit margins aren't high enough, so most of the food is either prepackaged or from fast food restaurants. These kids are unfamiliar with fruits beyond apples or bananas and have almost no knowledge of most vegetables, much less how to grow or prepare them."

Her father was losing interest, but at least his rage had subsided.

"How big is the urban-garden movement?" Ian asked

casually, giving her something to talk about but matching Rory's demeanor.

"It's really growing," she said. "Just about every major city has a few gardens with outreach programs to restaurants. Chicago's one of the biggest. It's still kind of under the radar, because it's not directly connected to job training or GEDs or after school programs, but Growing Home in particular has made that kind of outreach a big part of their efforts. Lots of inner-city kids get involved."

Take the bait, Dad. Take the bait.

"Sounds like there are some interesting growth options in the model," her father said.

"Absolutely," Riva said, nodding like a bobblehead doll. "Consumers want organic and fresh food, grown by people they know, and the work itself can be really transformative. It's a win-win."

"Let's talk about that later."

"Sure," Riva said. Her heart was aflutter, and her smile far too wide for the circumstances. Her heart, she found, was racing well into the red zone.

They sat down and Riva served the food. "What am I eating?" her father said.

"A rough draft of the menu for the lunch," Riva said. "We visited a couple of the bigger co-ops today, Growing Home and Urban Canopy. I'm going to develop the menu from what's available right now. What do you think?"

"It's good," her father said grudgingly. "What's in the salad?"

"Potatoes, romaine hearts, cucumbers, radishes. The dressing is made with white wine vinegar and Greek yogurt."

"You helped make this? Was that a big day for you?"

Ian shrugged. "It was fine," he said. Nothing in his tone hinted at his total absorption with chopping the strawberries, or crimping the pastry, or the way his hand lingered over hers as they passed bowls back and forth. "Interesting. I guess."

"You kids have plans for tonight?"

"Kelly wants to go out." The salad was dry on Riva's tongue, not even the sweet pear juice breaking through to ease the bitterness. She set her knife and fork on her plate. "Having me in town is a good excuse for a girls' night."

"Are you going on this *girls' night*?" her father asked Ian.

He laughed, just a hint of self-consciousness in the chuckle. "Tell me you have a better offer."

"Not tonight, but tomorrow night come on down to the gym. My guys will be doing their workouts then."

"Sounds great," Ian said.

Riva looked at her watch. "We should start getting ready."

Ian reached across the table and lifted her plate. "I'll clean up. I only need a few minutes."

BH, or Before Hawthorn she'd spent hours thinking about her appearance. Her hair, thick and wavy without intervention, had been the bane of her existence, requiring regular straightening and curling up again when the humidity went over forty percent. She'd dressed to show off her assets, a flat stomach, slim hips, and accentuated what she didn't have with a pushup bra and a low-cut top. She'd been pretty, if the definition meant "looked like everyone else out there."

Then she started working at the co-op, then as a

working student on farms around Lancaster, and her fashion attention shifted to Carhartts and muck boots, which long underwear insulated the best, and what brand of gloves provided both mobility and warmth. And she'd started eating, first other people's good cooking, then her own. The flat belly was gone. So were the slim hips. She carried a little extra flesh around her hips, which pooched into a muffin top when she wore her matchstick jeans. She hadn't exactly let herself go. She'd just started thinking about other things besides her appearance.

"At least you've got boobs now." She yanked the sky-blue camisole over her head, shimmied into the black skirt, and crammed her feet into the nude heels, then took a couple of minutes to remember how to walk in them.

Ian's footsteps rang lightly on the stairs, then the door to his room closed. She hurried into the bathroom, then knocked on the door, shrugging into a cropped, fitted jean jacket as she did. "I'm almost ready," she said, low voiced.

"Give me a second," he replied.

Riva pulled out her makeup bag. She'd spent too much time outside without sunscreen today, so her nose and cheeks were a little pink. Eyeliner, dark shadow, mascara. Glossy lipstick. There was no time to straighten her hair, so she went the opposite direction and spent thirty seconds spraying, scrunching, and tousling.

The door opened midspritz. Ian waved his hand in front of his face. "That stuff stinks."

Riva turned and stared. He'd added a skin-tight gray T-shirt to the jeans and a wide brown leather belt. The brown leather jacket from her dreams dangled from one finger. The T-shirt lay lovingly against his ribs and abdomen. A memory spiked through Riva, halting her breath.

"Be careful," he said.

One leg out the door in the cold, steady November wind, she paused and looked at him. "What?"

"Be careful. This guy's higher up the totem pole. If they make you, they won't hesitate to kill you. Stay in my sight at all times. Whatever you do, don't get in his car."

"I know. If I get in his car and you guys have to come get me, I blow the operation. I'm not going to do that. Believe me, I want out of this as badly as you do."

"No. If you get in his car, we might not get to you in time, and he might kill you. Do. Not. Get. In. His. Car. I don't care how cold you are. Fucking walk away before you get in his car. Do you understand?"

The coat. This was all about the coat, the one she wasn't wearing because she'd wanted to provoke him. He was worried about her being warm enough. She stared at him. He'd never said anything like this before. "I understand. Besides, the only car I'm getting in and out of these days is yours."

He let her go. "Hold on, dammit."

When she looked back he was shrugging out of his coat, banging his elbow against the Chevy's steering wheel as he did. He held it out to her. "The only other jacket I have in this car has LPD on the back. You can't wear that."

The gesture sent a shiver of delight through her. "Does this mean we're going steady?"

She'd meant to tease him, to lighten the mood a little, but instead his face closed off. "I'm protecting my asset," he said in a voice as biting as the wind outside the car. "You're no good to me if you freeze to death."

"Hello?"

Riva slammed back into the present. Ian was looking at her, one eyebrow raised, as if he'd said something and she'd missed it because she was lost in the memory of the smell of that coat, leather and Ian's skin and a faint scent of something that could be cologne.

"Okay. Fine. Good," she said nonsensically.

"Did you hit your head or something?"

"I remember that jacket," she said. "From before."

He paused in the act of shrugging into the jacket. "Yeah. I've had it for a long time."

"The nights were cold, so you made me wear it. It smelled like you. Remember?"

The leather settled around his shoulders. "I remember," he said quietly. "You'd give it back and it would smell like your perfume."

"You said—"

"I know what I said," he growled. "Let's go."

Her father stood in the kitchen, a glass of whiskey in one hand, his gaze glued to his phone.

In that moment Riva wanted desperately to defy her father, stay home, and protect her mother. She'd bake fresh cookies and get a pint of really good ice cream, and go upstairs to watch the home makeover shows her mother loved. Only after her father had abandoned her to Ian's not-so-tender mercies did she realize what she'd lost by choosing her father over her mother, how screwed up it was that she'd even thought she had to make that choice.

But if she stayed home, she'd lose all the progress she made ingratiating herself back into her father's confidence. If she stayed home, she lost the chance to get her mother free forever.

Right now she had to think about the case. Letting her father win this tiny battle was the sacrifice to make to ensure he wouldn't freeze her out. Give a little to get a lot.

"Don't stay out too late," her father cautioned. "We'll run a route tomorrow, show you how a real business runs."

For a split second, Riva couldn't figure out what he was talking about. She knew how the business ran. She'd done the books, run routes, placed orders, managed the warehouse. But her father wasn't looking at her. He was looking at Ian.

"Sounds great," Ian said. He sounded excited, even a little eager.

Back down the flagstone walk to her truck, parked at the curb. Riva hitched her skirt up to the tops of her thighs and clambered into the driver's seat. Her hands were shaking as she jammed the key into the ignition.

"Has he always been like that?"

She turned the key with more force than necessary. "Like what?" she bluffed.

Silence. She finally turned and looked at him. "Yes. I didn't really understand until . . . until I left for college. I'm not just doing this for Isaiah. He's all but destroyed her. I want him to go away for a very long time."

"That's why you keep setting yourself up as his partner in Lancaster."

She had to be very, very careful here. "Seven years

ago I was too weak to get myself out," she said as she pulled out onto the street and headed for Kelly's place. "If he hadn't refused to help me when you arrested me, God only knows what I'd be doing right now. I'm stronger now. I just hope I'm strong enough to get her free, too."

"You were stronger than you think you were," he said. "I put you through hell, and you never hesitated."

"What choice did I have?"

He didn't answer that. He'd made sure she had no choice at all.

"I can't take credit for what I did when my back was to the wall, because I put my back at that wall. I couldn't help her before. I can now. I know it's not part of the plan, but I'm not leaving without her."

"Hey," he said, reaching out to tuck her hair back from her face. "Plans change. You worry about your mom. I'll worry about your dad. Okay?"

Not trusting herself to speak, she nodded. He didn't say anything else on the way to Kelly's. The front door opened before Riva had shifted into park. Kelly paused in the doorway to kiss Grant and Wyatt good-bye. Grant waved at Kelly, waving Wyatt's fat little fist for him as Kelly walked backward to the truck. Riva flung open the truck's door and trotted up the sidewalk to hug Kelly, hard. "It's so good to see you!"

"I know, it's been forever!" she said breathlessly. "Was I even pregnant the last time you saw me?"

"I don't think so," Riva said, laughing. "You look amazing!"

"You do, too. All that sunshine and work outdoors really agrees with you. You're, like, healthy looking. Come say hi to Grant and meet Wyatt!"

Riva's heart was pounding as she followed Kelly up the walk, but Grant didn't seem to see anything odd in her sudden reappearance. Wyatt was fussy, reaching for his mother, whimpering when she kissed his cheek but Grant successfully distracted him with a stuffed rabbit. As the front door closed she felt a swift pang of longing. Maybe someday she'd meet someone who wouldn't care about her family, her past.

Ian had watched the reunion from the truck's cab, and was waiting patiently for them. Kelly climbed into the back seat and looked expectantly at Riva.

"Kelly, Ian. Ian, Kelly."

"Hi," Kelly said, then gave a breathless little squeal and reached between the seats to squeeze Riva's shoulder. "I'm so excited! I haven't seen you in, like, years. Remember buying those fake IDs from that kid in chemistry class? What was his name? He was supersmart and superstoned for most of school."

"Noah." Her ears were burning. Nothing like sitting next to the straight-laced cop who had arrested you for selling drugs while your best friend talked about all kinds of illegal activities. "His name was Noah and can we talk about something else?"

"Oh, come on," Kelly said. "That was, like, eight years ago. Ian doesn't care, do you?"

"Nope," Ian said cheerfully.

"Noah had some kind of laminating machine, or something, and could mock up an ID, no problem. He used to do out-of-state IDs because the bouncers never knew what was an authentic Maine license, or Utah. He was pretty good at it. I wonder what he's doing now? He's one of, like, six people in our class who isn't on Facebook, including you."

"I do social media for the farm and the restaurant," Riva protested.

"But how do we keep up on *you*? What *you're* doing?"

"The farm's social media," Riva said. "That's what I'm doing."

"Ian's on social media," Kelly said, scrolling down on her phone. "Fallon, right? In Lancaster. I sent you a friend request."

"Got it," Ian said, thumbing through his own phone. "And now we're friends."

Kelly kept up a running series of questions about the farm and Ian's pictures until they pulled into Lit's parking lot. After Kelly slid out of the truck, Riva leaned over. "You have social media set up?"

"Of course. It's the first thing anyone checks these days. Most people accept friend requests from anyone. We've found outstanding warrants when they post pictures of themselves out in public, and used pictures of stolen property as evidence."

It was a little early, so the line to get in wasn't long. The bouncer gave their IDs a cursory glance. "How depressing. We must actually look our age," Kelly said. She headed straight for the bar.

"Hold on a second," Ian said. "Who's driving?"

"Not me," Kelly said. She leaned over the gleaming metal bar and signaled for the bartender. "An apple martini, please. Riva?"

"I'm driving," Riva said. "It's my truck."

"I'll drive," Ian said. "You two should have fun tonight."

She narrowed her eyes at him.

"Keys." It wasn't a request. It was a command, part cop, part protective man.

"You're wonderful," Kelly gushed, casting Riva an unsubtle look. "That's really great of you. What are you drinking?"

"A mojito," Riva said, giving in to the inevitable and handing Ian her key chain. No way was Ian Hawthorn getting drunk under these circumstances. "But I've got to be able to work tomorrow, so I'm not getting trashed."

"Just loose." Kelly handed over a credit card to start a tab. Ian ordered a beer.

They checked out the scene while they finished the cocktails. "Wow. Was it always this rundown?"

Riva smiled. The place really hadn't changed, the dance floor a little more scuffed, the finish on the bar a little more worn. It had the look of a place that went big with a particular age group and had never found a way to change with the times. "Remember how cool we thought we were?"

"We're still cool," Kelly said loyally. "Let's dance!"

Riva looked at Ian, but he seemed to be quite content to nurse a beer and stake out a table between the bar and the dance floor. She let Kelly tow her to the dance floor. Once out there, she lost herself in the music. She'd always loved dancing, and for a while, thanks to the alcohol and the rhythm, her brain pushed aside the nagging reminder of Ian's presence.

Until her gaze caught his across the room.

The look he flicked her, green-brown, molten, promising a level of heat and risk and desire she'd never felt, halted her breath midexhale. Images swept through her mind, the metal door hard against her shoulder blades, his hands snagging in her tangled hair, his cock grinding into her abdomen. His mouth would be hot, his skin would taste of salt and soap.

She left Kelly dancing with a younger guy, obviously alone, and obviously not interested in anything more than a partner who knew how to move, and pushed her way through the crowd to his table. "Hi."

"Hi."

"Ask me to dance with you."

He looked at her. Based on the residual foam in his glass, he was still nursing the same beer while she was two mojitos and an hour of dancing into the night, an assessment he made with one single flick of his gaze. "I don't think that's a good idea."

"Think of it as part of your cover." She let her gaze travel the length of his body, from hazel eyes to the deep creases along his mouth, across his muscled chest to his buckle to his boots, then back up. He shook his head.

"You know what I've figured out? You're afraid. All the time. You use your rules and your goals and your attitude to hold it back. The question is, why?"

Wow, the mojitos were doing a fair bit of talking for her right now. When he said nothing, she turned to go back to the dance floor. He reached for her wrist and brought her up short. "I'm afraid for you. Two dinners with your dad and I know we've got good reason to be on high alert right now."

She laughed. "That's just life with my dad. Come on. Are you afraid for me, or of me? You don't have any reason to be afraid of me. Unless . . ."

Unless she could hurt him somehow. Unless he felt more for her than he'd ever let on. Unless this wasn't just physical chemistry between them. "Unless . . ." she said again, this time in a stronger voice.

He stepped into her personal space, using his body

to guide her back toward the dance floor. "Dance with me, Riva."

His body and the pounding rhythm derailed her train of thought. "Sounds like an order. Ask me."

He laughed, half turned away, and ran both his hands through his hair. She felt an unaccountable urge to smooth down the tousled strands but held back. Ian needed to stop locking away his emotions.

He also needed to ask. For himself, for her, for the fragile, reckless thing shimmering between them. There were a dozen ways she could have made this take a different path, things she should have said at certain moments, or not said, touches she should have resisted, doors she should have left closed, much less not walked through. This was one of them.

"Ask me," she whispered.

He stepped into her personal space until her cells were vibrating in his direction, magnetized and drifting, all but closing the gap between them. Then he did this thing she felt before she saw, using his shoulders and his hips to get closer without confining her, much less touching her. He bent his head, and all she could think was how badly she wanted him to close that distance, how she wasn't flinching.

"Riva, would you dance with me?"

His breath eddied against her cheek as he spoke, and oh, oh, oh, this was new, different, dangerous, because that single step into vulnerability turned the tables on her. She blinked, drew in a shuddering breath, because this . . . this was intimacy. Pulsating lights, throbbing music, a crush of people could have made it sterile, disconnected. Instead, she felt lit up, like his heartbeat was making her rib cage jump and thud, not the bass.

"There. Was that so hard?"

"I'm afraid of myself. I'm really afraid of you."

It was an admission of vulnerability she hadn't expected. Fear of failure, fear of letting the department down, fear of getting played again were all logical fears, common fears. But afraid of himself? Or her?

Now wasn't the time to talk, not with the music dialed up to jet engine levels. Now was the time to move. On tiptoe, she said, "Then we both need this," then grabbed his hand and led him to the dance floor.

There was always that transition moment, dancing with someone new, that moment where you figured out where to put hands, how close was close enough to dance but not so close you set off proximity alarms. All she could think about was the slight pressure of his fingers around hers, not a cop's dispassionate touch and definitely not making her flinch.

When they'd established some space for themselves on the crowded floor, he started moving to the beat, finding a rhythm with his hips with an ease that all but made her jaw drop open. The song had a faster beat, a souped-up synth pop song extended for a club mix, the kind of thing it was easy to sway and shuffle to, maybe lift your arms for a little extra something.

Ian was doing all of those things, but with a total lack of self-consciousness. His eyes were closed, a little half smile on his face, like he'd rediscovered something he used to love.

Then they opened again, found her standing stock-still in shock. He slid his hand to the small of her back and bent his head to her ear. "Come on, Riva. Dance with me."

Danger! Danger! Danger! her brain flared, not like

a car alarm but like lights and sirens. Uneven terrain, edge of a cliff, rogue wave, metal glinting in the hand of a stranger in a dark alley, this moment could make or unmake you. But it wasn't the risk of his hand on her body. This was deeper, different. This was never going away, and suddenly she didn't know if she could handle what she'd asked for.

Without waiting for her response, Ian slid his arm around her waist, dropped low to align their hips, and transformed the thumping bass into a sexy bump and grind that was pure rhythmic invitation.

This was Ian as she'd never seen him, connected to his body in a way that felt real and honest and true. The boy had *moves* based on total comfort in his body, not looking cool or impressing girls but rather on feeling everything the music pushed at them in waves. A not-quite-subtle twist of his hips unlocked hers, as if her body was connected to his, easy and loose and uninhibited. Freefall. His arm dropped away, replaced by glancing, seductive bumps, hips and thighs and shoulders, bare hands brushing bare arms. They'd left their jackets in the truck. Sensations heightened. His jeans against her bare legs. His arms, rough with hair, against hers. All five fingers flattened against the small of her back for a second, two, three, while he slid his thigh between her legs and shimmied. She lifted her arms, closed her eyes, and swiveled in a circle in front of him, tossing her head so her hair whipped across her cheeks and mouth.

Electric heat shot through her, followed by syrupy desire searing over newly sensitized nerves. From there it was nothing to wrap her arm around his neck and cling. One hand rested on her hip, fingers trembling, the touch light, at the edge of his control, but when she pressed her open mouth to his pulse, he pulled her close enough that they were simulating sex on the dance floor. She turned feral, grabbing his shoulder, his hip, grinding against him.

She'd fooled herself into thinking she knew him, understood him. But the reality was Ian was hotter, wilder, more intense, more sexual than she'd ever imagined. This was the man underneath the cop's rigid, controlled exterior?

She pushed away, gaining precious inches of distance. He surfaced from the spell they'd cast, gaze heavy lidded and possessive. For tonight, she was the girl she'd never been, out with a friend, attracted to a hot guy, not a care in the world.

"Come home with me," she said. "Ian. Come home with me."

"I thought you'd never ask," he said.

CHAPTER FIFTEEN

The practicalities of taking Ian home meant she had to find Kelly first. She tracked down her friend leaving the women's restroom, scrolling through texts from Grant. "Wyatt's having a hard time going to bed without me," she said, her brow furrowed with concern. "Do you mind if we bail early?"

"Not at all," Riva said, relieved.

They found Ian leaning against the wall by the door, arms folded across his chest, one booted foot braced against the wall. Women leaving tended to look him up and down, seeing the tight T-shirt, sweet leather jacket, and an undeniable presence and confidence. He ignored the looks, the whispers, scanning the crowd until his gaze locked on Riva.

A hot thrill shot over her nerves, then pooled low in her belly. The truth was, getting comfortable with Ian's touch didn't ease the ache deep inside her. It only strengthened it, gave it the weight and heft of steam rising from a boiling pot.

Ian escorted them through the parking lot, one hand hovering at the small of Riva's back. She climbed into the passenger seat, Kelly in the back. Ian started the truck, adjusted the seat and mirrors, then paused. "Wallet and phone check, ladies."

Kelly held up her wristlet and cell. Riva pulled her phone from her front pocket. "My purse is in the console."

Satisfied, Ian pulled out into traffic. Riva kept the conversation going with Kelly by asking a few questions about Wyatt's latest developmental milestones. When they arrived at Kelly's house, Ian started to open the door. "Stay put," she said. "I've got this."

She guided Kelly up the sidewalk and knocked on the front door. Grant opened it, a burp cloth over his shoulder, Wyatt sleepy and adorable in pj's, sucking his thumb, red eyes and head on Grant's shoulder. "He wouldn't go to sleep without you," Grant said, swaying side to side. "We've been walking the floor."

"Oh, sweetheart," Kelly said, whether to her husband or her son, Riva couldn't tell. She held out her arms, careless of Wyatt's runny nose and tear-stained cheeks rubbing against her silk top. Riva felt a little heartsick, watching the family reunion.

"I'll call you later," Riva said.

"Bye, hon," Kelly replied.

One down, one to go. Riva trotted back to the truck and got in. Ian backed out of the driveway and turned for home. He already knew the route.

"Where *do* the good boys go to hide away?" she asked, the lyrics running through her brain.

Ian huffed, a smile curving his lips. "No idea."

"Why are you so careful about drinking?" Riva asked idly. "Because you were worried about me? You could have had a few. I was okay to drive by the time we left."

He turned and looked out the front window. "It was no big deal. I never have more than two."

"That's arbitrary. Why not?"

"I used to get so drunk, I'd black out."

She turned to stare at him. Ian, blackout drunk? She couldn't imagine it. "You did?" she said cautiously. "Like, in college?"

"Around that time, yeah."

That was before she'd met him. "Any particular reason, or just because that's what all the cool kids did? I can't imagine you doing what the cool kids did."

Silence. All the heat and passion they'd found at the club was cooling rapidly in the spring night.

"Oh, so you can know all my secrets but I can't know yours? That's why I do things like talk to my dad without telling you," she snapped. "And yes, I know exactly how immature that sounds. But we're in this together, and you don't even trust me."

He turned down her street, driving slowly through the pools of light and dark, light and dark as they approached the house. "I trust you. I can count on one hand the number of people I trust." He held up his right hand, thumb out. "My dad. My mom. My brother. Sorenson." He stared at his curled pinky. "You."

One of those things was not like the others. "Come on," she scoffed as he parked in front of her parents' house and killed the engine. "You work with cops. How can you get more safe than a bunch of armed men and women trained as first responders?"

He slung around in the seat to look at her. "I trust

Dorchester and McCormick, a few other guys in the department. But not like I trust my family, or you."

But not enough to tell her everything. "Ian. That's crazy." She opened the door and slid out of the truck, intent on getting inside, getting some water into her system. The world tilted a little, but whether from the mojitos, the dancing, the spring night air, so sweet and cool and seductive, she couldn't tell.

Ian came around the hood of the truck and stepped in front of her. "I know it's crazy. I keep trying to make it not be true. But even when you were my CI, I trusted you."

She made a sound that was part snort, part laugh, part desperate huff. "I can't think why."

"Because you were a good person who'd done a bad thing, not a bad person. That's why."

"You must know lots of good people, Ian," she said. "That's not a good reason to have trusted me."

"I can't explain it," he said slowly. "I just did."

He looked down at her, his own face hidden by the trick of the lighting; they were between two lamps, and the porch light was behind him. But she got the sense in the way he held his shoulders, in the flex of his pectorals, in the soft curl of his fingers as they rose to her face, that he didn't need a reason. Not now, with chemistry swirling between them, a single touch away from catching fire.

His hand hovered for just a second along her jaw, then settled so gently it took a moment for her nerves to register the contact, even in their hyperaware state. Then his thumb brushed over her mouth, pressing gently at her tensed lips, retreating to stroke again, press-stroke-press-stroke until her mouth softened with a quiver.

"Better," he said.

Then he stepped forward, bent his head, and kissed her. Both his forearms rested against the truck's frame on either side of her head. Except for the contact between their lips, he wasn't touching her anywhere, but she was effectively caged by his arms, his jacket, the awareness of his torso and hips and thighs as mental presence.

"What . . ." she murmured, not even sure what she was asking, only that feeling his lips move against hers was making her hot.

"Nothing. Stop thinking. Just feel."

This time his lips urged hers to part. He drank her shuddering little sigh, gave her the tip of his tongue in response. It took her a few moments to realize the kiss had no purpose other than pleasure. It wasn't a prelude to sex. He wasn't shutting her up. He wasn't even gentling her to his touch. He was just kissing her because he wanted to kiss her, because they'd been dancing, because the spring night was intoxicating, because they could. His mouth was firm, warm, seductive, blowing on the banked coals of desire until she was clutching at his waist, tugging his shirt free of his jeans to run her palm up his lean, muscled torso.

"Let's go inside," she whispered when he broke away to drop a line of kisses along her jaw.

She half expected him to say no, but he didn't, just took her keys and unlocked the front door. In the part of her brain still capable of thought she noticed that the only thing swirling in the air was a desire so pure and potent it drowned out everything else. He seemed desperate to kiss her, touch her, cupping her jaw with his hands, dropping kiss after kiss after kiss on her lips as they twisted and turned as they moved through the entry and up the stairs. He kept them moving while she kept them from banging into surfaces, first one hand, then the other braced against the doorframe, the wall, the banister.

It was a fast, fierce battle to get naked, Ian stripping off her top and bra to smooth his hands over her waist and up to her breasts, his mouth claiming hers again and again before he fisted his hand in her hair and pulled her head back to trail hot, wet kisses down her throat. His mouth on her nipples sent a slow, heated throb through her sex and had her scrambling to take off his shirt and unhook his belt buckle.

This was supposed to be about burning off tension. Instead, it threatened to burn them both to the ground.

His cock sprang free when she pushed his jeans to his knees, which buckled when she gripped it. "Give me . . . Jesus, Riva, hold on a second!" The words were almost a plea, one she ignored in favor of stroking his length while he kicked out of boots, jeans, socks, and underwear. With one arm he hoisted her right off her feet and carried her to the bed, dumping her there unceremoniously to shove her skirt to her hips and tug down her panties. He dropped to his knees and set his mouth to her sex, his sure, slow tongue sending heat spiraling through her before the memory of the last time, when she'd been left satisfied and unsatisfied, flashed into her brain. Her knees drew up, toes curling as she reached down and gripped his wrist.

"No. Stop. Inside me," she demanded. "I want to come with you inside me."

The look in his eyes told her she'd blown all the logical circuits in his brain and left him with nothing but primitive responses. He crawled on top of her, using his hips and thighs to spread her wide, notching his elbows above her shoulders to hold her in place and his cock against her sex, kissing her while he rocked back and forth. The hard, hot length against her clit tormented her until Riva was lifting her hips, winding tight around him. The kind of accident she was too old to have happen was getting closer and closer, the kind of accident where he slid into her welcoming body.

She tore her mouth free from his. "Wait," she gasped. "We need to have a conversation."

"Now you want to talk?" he said, his shoulders and chest sheened with sweat.

"I'm on the pill. I had my annual exam last month. I'm clean." His gaze burned into her soul. "Are you?"

Ian stared down at her. "I'm due for some bloodwork, but haven't had it done recently," he said. "I'm always safe, but I won't take that risk."

"Okay," she said. "Condoms?"

He sat up, allowing a rush of cooler spring air into the duvet cocoon they'd made. In the moonlight she saw the sex flush high on his cheekbones and spreading down his throat. His cock was dark red, erect. In between those two flags was his scarred chest. "Don't go anywhere."

"Not going anywhere," she said.

He strode through their shared bathroom and into his room, where she heard rummaging sounds. In a few moments he returned, pulling back the covers to kneel between her thighs.

"Took me a second to find them." He tore one package free from the strip and tossed the rest on the nightstand.

Riva glanced at the condoms fetched up against a

stack of coffee table books meant for decoration. "Optimistic."

"Contingency plan," he countered, and rolled the condom down his shaft, then braced himself on his hands by her shoulders and kissed her.

He gripped his shaft and aligned their bodies. Despite her leg hooked around his hip and her unintentional whimpers, he restrained himself to short, purposeful thrusts that breached her defenses an inch at a time, holding back the power of his hips. Only when he was buried inside her did he stop.

She was trembling. Sweat bloomed on her temples, between her breasts, and her hair stuck to her heated cheeks.

He lowered himself to his elbows. "Okay?" he whispered.

"Um . . . maybe."

He chuckled, pulled out, and slid in again. "Now?"

"Again."

He obliged. She opened her eyes. "Can we be done being careful?"

There was nothing like it, the sensation of thick cock stretching her as he set a rhythm. At first she could look into his eyes, but after a few strokes her gaze slid between focused and unfocused until the sensations won and her eyes slid shut.

She quickly lost herself in the powerful build, the peak growing closer and closer as he drove into her. He shut his eyes, slowing his rhythm.

Her fingers dug into his biceps and lower back. "God, Ian, stop holding back!"

"Want this to last," he murmured into her ear.

"I want to come," she said. "I want to come with you inside me. Ian, please. Please."

"Fuck." He bent his head and surrendered. His next thrust held enough power to make her throw her head back and cry out, so he did it again, and she was lost. Her fingers tightened on his shoulder and biceps, her hips lifted into each stroke, and then she was lost in a release that felt like annihilation.

Sunlight pierced Ian's eyelids, setting off a dull throb of a headache before he'd even opened his eyes. He patted blindly for the pillow next to him, bringing it up to cover his face as he tried to figure out how he felt about putting his body, his emotions before his career.

All he'd meant to do was show her that he trusted her, that she meant more to him than what a big arrest could bring his career.

He hadn't meant to go quite so far, reveal quite so much.

He let his memories of last night bloom in high def behind his eyelids. Riva, in a cobbled-together outfit, her hair witchy and tousled, signaling trouble. Nursing a beer while he watched Riva dance, alone and unafraid. Then Riva got in his face, and he got in hers, and then they were dancing.

Dancing. More like foreplay on the dance floor. He'd thought it would be a good way to get her over the fear of him touching her, because good dancing was all about glancing little bumps and sidesteps, grinds that melted into shimmies and shivers. It seemed so simple. Dance with her, so she'd get used to his hands on her body. Dance with her, because he could.

Dance with her, because he wanted her body against his more than he wanted to breathe. Whether she noticed or not, he'd kept eyes on Riva the whole night. Eve Webber had been kidnapped out from under Dorchester's nose. Ian wasn't letting the same thing happen to Riva. But last night was a big warning sign, because the more time he spent with Riva, doing normal things like a road trip, cooking, dancing, the more he thought about the future. After the diagnosis, he'd stopped thinking about the future, or one that he wanted, anyway. Anything analytical, like plotting his promotional path, was fair game.

But his heart? Wanting something for his heart and soul? No more.

It was a blunt-object strategy. When he'd thought about what he'd lost—his commission in the navy and a shot at a SEAL team—he got blindingly furious, then got blindingly drunk. Substituting anything else for that future just reminded him of what he'd lost, with the same result, regaining consciousness with hours gone.

Problem defined. Solution?

Stop wanting. Stop desiring. Stop longing, yearning, hoping, dreaming. Just stop.

The police department was a home he could return to, a place he could do some good, with people who understood but wouldn't cut him any slack. His strategy had worked until the night seven years ago when Riva Henneman had looked up from her laptop, then looked him up and down.

He'd seen an easy arrest, an inexperienced girl in over her head he could turn to his advantage. He'd gotten a dangerous quicksand of forbidden desire, one that should have gone away when she dropped off his radar.

That was the problem with dangerous things. They

never really went away. They went dormant, but inevitably the clock started ticking again, counting down to the inevitable. Like Riva.

Where was she? He swung his legs over the edge of the bed and sat up and headed for the bathroom, where he saw a damp shower and towel and caught a whiff of her soap and a fainter scent of her skin. She was up and gone. He showered quickly, then dressed in jeans, T-shirt, and a thin fleece. The smell of bacon frying drifted up the stairs and along the hallway.

Someone was making breakfast. A good breakfast.

He trotted down the stairs in his stocking feet, following the call of bacon and Rory's voice.

Riva and her dad both looked up when he walked through the door. "Morning," he said.

Riva stood at the stove, bacon and hash browns frying in the same grease. Potato peels lay piled in the sink; she'd scraped and shredded the potatoes by hand. She wore a light brown cotton dress gathered at the sleeve and neckline with elastic and at her waist by a belt. Embroidered flowers tendriled along the neckline and down to the skirt. "Good morning," she said, the line of her mouth tense.

"Morning," Rory said, smiling wide. "Have fun last night?"

"Yeah," Ian said. "You know what it's like when office drones let loose. Sorry to hold everyone up."

"I'm happy to wait for this kind of breakfast," Rory said.

"Where's your mom?" Ian asked.

"Still in bed. She's not feeling well."

That explained the tension in Riva's shoulders. She dropped two slices of bread into the toaster. "Fried eggs okay?"

"My favorite," her father said.

Riva smiled and handed him a piece of bacon. She handed out plates as the toast popped up, serving herself last. "You're taking Ian out on a route today?"

"If he still wants to go," Rory said, making short work of the delicious meal.

"Absolutely," Ian said, following Rory's lead and eating far too quickly for his taste. The eggs were perfect, sprinkled with avocado, tomatoes, and feta cheese. "If you don't need me today."

"I'm going to tinker with the recipes a little, keep an eye on Mom, maybe take her to lunch," Riva said. "Go ahead. I know you're interested in this."

It was a huge act of trust on Riva's part. He nodded. "Thanks."

"Not worried about losing him to his own business?"

"The goal is to lose him to his own business," Riva said with a smile. "We need more small farmers, but if he decides to do something else, that's his choice."

"Ready when you are," Rory said.

Rory apparently thought nothing of leaving Riva with a messy kitchen and a mound of dishes, so Ian shot her an apologetic look and followed Rory out the back door. He pulled his phone from his back pocket and texted Riva.

Tell me if you go out.

Three dots appeared immediately. *Will do.*

"So," Ian said easily as he climbed into Rory's Mercedes. One quick glance told him the laptop was on the back seat. "Tell me all about Rory Henneman. Did you always want to own your own business?"

Rory slung his arm over the back of Ian's seat and swiveled around to reverse down the driveway. "Not much to tell. I've lived in Chicago all my life. My mom raised me in Fuller Park. She worked two jobs, sometimes three, to feed me and my brothers and sister. I saw pretty early that the best opportunities were for people who took risks, not working for someone else."

"Did you go to college?"

"Yup. Started my first business while I was in school."

"What was that?"

"Selling textbooks. This was back in the day when kids used textbooks, not e-books. I'd buy them for more than the school paid and sell them at the beginning of the next term for less. The next I branched out into setting up swaps, again, pre-Craigslist. I found storage space for people who didn't want to haul their stuff home every year. I ran a taxi service, and sold candy out of my bag. That and the truck became the foundation of Henneman Candy and Vending."

He drove easily, Ian noticed, one hand on the wheel, the other on his thigh, confident of his knowledge of the streets, the neighborhood, his place in it.

"How did you meet Stephanie?"

"One fall break I drove her to the airport to catch a flight to see her boyfriend out east. That was on a Wednesday. I knew the minute I met her I was going to marry her. I picked her up on Sunday and took her to dinner. Monday she called the boyfriend and broke it off. We've been together ever since." He gave Ian an easy, charming smile. "I know what I want and I go after it."

"Pretty romantic," Ian said.

"Her parents hated the idea. She's from an old family in Chicago, lived in Gold Coast, private schools and all that. They threatened to cut her off. She didn't tell me that until after the wedding. That's how infatuated she was, determined to stand up to her family."

If Rory had planned on an influx of old money to fund his dreams, only to find that his heiress came penniless, that might explain the tension between him and Stephanie. Then again, guys like Rory didn't need an excuse to torment someone. "Did they?" Ian asked.

"Yeah, but they came around when Riva was born. We were okay. Lean years make for good memories when you finally make your name."

"Riva's your only?"

"Eleven miscarriages before the doctors told us to stop trying. She couldn't carry a baby to term."

"Riva's pretty amazing," Ian said. "What she's doing, the kind of life she lives, it's hard work. But she never complains."

"I'd hoped she'd do what I did."

"Open her own business? She did that."

"Marry up. The kind of man who could support her. Not one of those trust fund kids who've never worked a day in his life, but an entrepreneur. The kind of guy who makes stuff, creates jobs."

"Maybe she will," Ian said. Lancaster wasn't a big city like Chicago, but it had an old money crowd. One introduction at a fundraiser for the ESCC or Oasis, one guy smitten with Riva's work ethic and determination, and she could find herself married to more money than Rory could imagine. In fact, he couldn't believe it hadn't happened already.

Why wasn't Riva dating anyone? Aside from that offhand joke about guys not seeing the shotgun because they were in the bed, not under it, she'd never mentioned a boyfriend. Because he hadn't asked? Or because there was no one to mention?

He made a mental note to ask the next time they were alone.

"I asked around about you," Rory said.

Ian laughed. "Asked who?"

"I know some guys in Lancaster. I looked into business opportunities when Riva went to school there. Made some contacts."

Ian's heart hurled itself slow and hard against his rib cage. *THUD. THUD. THUD.* Would he know if Rory had taken his picture? Ian had never seen him aim a cell phone at him, but that didn't mean anything these days. All it would take to blow this sky high was Rory taking his picture and sending it to Kenny.

What if Rory had separated him from Riva in order to kidnap her? "So you've discovered my secret."

Rory didn't blink. "Maybe. What's your secret?"

"I don't work for the city. Lancaster outsources their IT work. I work for one of the subcontractors on the accounting side."

"That would explain why none of my contacts had ever heard of Ian Fallon."

"It's just easier to say I work for the city," Ian said. He pulled out his phone and sent Jo a text. *Hey, how's your mom doing?* It was a lame code, dating back to their high school days, before either of them got cool enough to invent something sophisticated. They'd started it when they were hiding late nights out from their attentive, hard-to-fool parents, and never got out of the habit.

Rory gave him an assessing glance. Ian tried his best

to look malleable, easy to persuade, and a little desperate. This was the tricky part. Guys like Kenny, street smart and suspicious, didn't trust gift horses. He'd manipulated McCormick into working for him, counting on Conn's fear of being abandoned to keep him under his thumb. But Rory, who believed he was the center of the universe, that everything should fall into line to benefit him, might see Ian as no less than what he deserved, a sign that the universe rewarded his initiative.

They pulled into a bland office park. Buildings clustered around parking lots, the names of various companies over the entrances. A staffing agency, accounting, design, medical supplies and testing.

"Where are we going?" Ian asked as he climbed out of the truck.

"Prospective client in building four," Rory said. He grabbed a leather satchel from behind the driver's seat. For a moment Ian saw the dull gleam of the barrel of a shotgun before Rory tucked a blanket over it.

Riva had said he carried a gun while he ran the route, because he collected the proceeds from the vending machines. Today he was driving his truck. HENNEMAN CANDY AND VENDING was emblazoned on the side, so maybe he'd still be targeted? Ian watched him walk, searching for the sign of a gun at his waist or ankle. If he was carrying a concealed weapon, it was small, maybe even the Sig Ian himself favored and had tucked into his waistband.

Definitely armed. Definitely dangerous.

"Synergy Staffing," Ian read as they walked down the hall. "Did you call them or did they call you?"

"They called me," Rory said. He opened the glass door to the reception area. "After you."

A young woman in a black pantsuit and a lavender blouse took Rory's name, then murmured into a phone. "Mike will be right with you. Can I get you coffee or a soda?"

"No, thank you," Rory said. Ian also declined. They seated themselves in the reception area, along with two other individuals Ian assumed were people looking for temporary work.

"Mr. Henneman?"

Ian barely stopped himself from doing a double take. Mike was Micah Sewell, Ian's contact in Chicago. What the *hell* was going on?

Rory stood and offered his hand. "It's Rory, please. This is Ian Fallon. He's shadowing me for the day."

"Right this way," Mike/Micah said. He led them to a small conference room furnished with a round table, four chairs, and the kind of inspirational art Ian often saw in corporate settings. Ian sat down and took out his Moleskine.

A couple of minutes into the presentation, Ian had to admit that Rory knew his business. He ran through a decent patter highlighting the advantages of onsite vending: improved efficiency due to fewer breaks to get food or snacks, improved employee morale, selections tailored to align with insurance incentives to make healthy choices. The materials were slick, glossy, and customized for Synergy, down to the projected gross and the profit-sharing split between Synergy and Henneman Candy.

"What would it take to get you to sign on the dotted line today?" Rory finished. He knew his sales and marketing too.

"This looks really good, Rory," Micah said. He was

studying the cost/benefit sheet with an absorption Ian had to admire. "I can't sign before the management team meets. I'm going to present this, along with two other proposals, to the team, and we'll get back to you."

Rory's smile never wavered. "There's some flexibility in those numbers," he said easily. "I'll work harder to get your business, and deliver a higher-quality product."

"I can't give you any inside information," Micah said earnestly. "But I can tell you we surveyed our employees to find out what they wanted in the machines. Your proposal falls right in line with what they wanted, and your profit-sharing plan is very fair."

Rory relaxed slightly. "Good. If you have any questions, call or email any time. We pride ourselves on our customer service, and that starts before we sign the contract."

"Great," Micah said. "Thanks so much for coming by."

"You okay?" Rory said as they left the building.

"Yeah. Fine. I wasn't expecting it to be so intense," Ian said. Might as well go with the truth. "You're really laying it all on the line, every time you go to a meeting. It's like applying for a job, over and over and over."

"Every interaction is like applying for a job, over and over," Rory said. "No safety net, no nothing. Do the job, better than anyone else out there, or lose the contract. There's nothing like knowing you eat what you kill. Still want to leave your cube?"

"More than ever," Ian said. His phone rang. Jo. "Do you mind if I take this?"

"Not at all," Rory said. "I've got some calls to make."

CHAPTER SIXTEEN

"Hi," he said, forgoing his usual brusque *Hawthorn* for a civilian's greeting.

"Can you talk?"

"Thanks for calling back. I can't talk in depth right now, but I took a look at that variance analysis, and I think you've got a problem with the data," he replied. "Tell me again what your subset parameters were?"

"Geek," Jo said with feeling. "Dorchester says everyone he's talked to thinks you're at Mayo, getting some kind of specialized testing done. I buzzed McCormick. He confirmed what Dorchester's hearing, and says nothing's shaking the web right now. If rumors were flying he might not know what they are, but he'd definitely see signs."

Ian turned the corner. "I've got maybe a minute," he said, keeping his voice low.

"How's it going?"

"Fine. It's fine. I'm running a route with Henneman

right now. Sewell was there. I'm guessing CPD's setting up a long-haul sting, trying to get Henneman for money laundering."

"Not good. Too many cooks in the kitchen," Jo mused. "That's not our turf. You should back off."

No way was that happening, because Riva answered to no one's jurisdiction, and she wasn't leaving this undone. Which meant he wasn't leaving her. "I can't," he said. "I told Riva we'd get him."

"She can take her deal to the local cops."

"A deal with them doesn't help Isaiah or her mother."

"What's her mother got to do with this? Don't answer that. Riva can do whatever she wants," Jo said, with what Ian knew was admirable patience for her, "but that doesn't affect how we police Lancaster. Rory Henneman is Chicago's problem, not ours."

"Jo, her father's a vicious sociopath. As nearly as I can tell he's manipulated her and her mother for years, playing them off each other."

"That's her excuse for what she did?" Jo asked. Probing idly, testing for weakness almost second nature.

"Not hers. She's never made an excuse."

"Hmm." Jo hated excuses, so this was a point in Riva's favor.

"Riva wants this done, now, to help Isaiah and her mother, and who knows if any arrests Chicago makes will trickle down to Lancaster? I've got a plan," he said. "The plan is to make Henneman think I'm the perfect inside guy with the city."

"I thought Riva was going to get what we needed."

"That's plan B."

"Why isn't it plan A?"

"Because this is the better option."

"No," Jo said, like she was talking to a five-year-old trying to put a square peg in a round hole, "it's not a better option. *You've* got to build trust. *She's* already inside."

He didn't say anything, because from a protocol standpoint, Jo was right. But Ian couldn't bring himself to send Riva into danger again, not now that he knew her father was of the sociopath flavor of humanity.

"Any other shitty, career-killing decisions you want to talk over?" she asked.

"I've been to more urban gardens in the last two days than I have in my entire life up to now."

"How many?"

"Three."

"What's going on with Riva?"

This was Jo. He wouldn't lie to her, but he also wouldn't tell her something she'd have to answer questions about under oath. His silence was enough.

"Dammit, Ian. You're going to lose that promotion, and possibly your badge."

What was he supposed to say to that? She was right. He was going to let down his family and the department. But when he gut-checked the situation, the person he wasn't letting down was himself. "No, I won't."

"Yes, you will," she countered. Jo wasn't gentle. She had, on occasion, slapped him on the back of the head hard enough to rattle his teeth, and the teasing Ian endured after Riva spent an evening buying drugs while wearing the very jacket he'd worn to the club last night ranked right up there with the worst of his plebe year at the Naval Academy. "Isn't there another way for you to get her out of your system? Someone who looks like her?"

"I don't want a substitute for her."

"Have you seen her since the trial?"

She'd switched into automatic interrogation mode. "No."

"Talked to her."

"No."

"Called her? Driven by her house? Searched her in a database?"

"No, no, and no. I just . . . never forgot her." He heard fabric rustle as Jo switched positions. "What the hell? Are you still in bed?"

"I took a surveillance shift for McCormick last night. What is it about her?"

How did he explain the electric spark of recognition happening on a cellular level? Best not to try with Jo, who was even less romantic and sentimental than he was. "Back then, she was mad at me, but she was even more mad at herself. She was ashamed of what she'd done. Now, I'm seeing behind the scenes. She's trying to be a good person. A citizen. A contributing member of the community." Speaking the words out loud made him stop and think. Riva's job wasn't just a job, and she wasn't doing this just for Isaiah. There was so much more than that. Riva wasn't just trying to make amends for not telling him about her father seven years ago. She was trying to atone.

"Well, fuck," Jo said. "You aren't just trying to sleep with her. You like her."

He froze for a split second. "Yeah," he said finally. "I do."

Jo's snort was eloquent. "What is it with this unit? Matt falls for an informant, McCormick's quitting to do security for a pop star, and you're . . . I don't even know what you're doing. Do you?"

"No."

"As long as we're clear on that. Don't do anything I wouldn't do."

There was an odd note to her voice. Before Ian could ask about it, she hung up.

Ian walked back to the truck and got in. Time to up the ante on getting a look at that laptop. "Hey, I was thinking. You want me to take a look at your data and see if there's anything you could optimize to increase your profit? That's my job. You're helping me out, maybe I could help you out too."

It was a risk, questioning Rory's competence like that.

"It's not rocket science," Rory said. "I know my profit margins. But why the hell not? Come to the gym with me tonight. Let's see what you're made of. We'll take it from there."

"Sounds great," Ian said easily. He spotted a coffee shop on the corner. "Hey, can you drop me here? That call was for a work thing I need to look into. I'll get a cab back."

"No problem. Call Riva. She can come get you."

Ian walked into the coffee shop and dialed Micah's number. "It's Hawthorn."

"Fuck, you almost gave me a heart attack when you walked through the door with Henneman," Micah said.

"A little warning would have been nice," Ian shot

back. "There's too many cooks in this kitchen, and somebody's going to get burned."

"We threw it together at the last minute. My captain's into this now. He hates the idea of some small-town PD getting a bust this big."

"He can have the bust," Ian said, mentally adding *as long as he doesn't fuck it up.* "I'm here to make sure my own house gets clean. What's the story?"

"A friend of mine owns the staffing agency. She agreed to let me mock up business cards and conduct some meetings there. He's got the contract; there aren't any other bidders. We're building a case, company by company, to get evidence for money laundering. We've also started surveillance on his warehouse and house, to see who comes and goes from those locations after hours. Maybe he's letting the cartels use the warehouse to store shipments. Any other places we should keep an eye on?"

"He goes to a gym," Ian said.

"Name?"

"Sweet Science."

Ian heard clicking and tapping. "Shit. I'm already getting blowback about the OT."

"I'll keep an eye on that for you," Ian said. "I'm going with him tonight. You won't get information from most of the guys in a boxing club. They're tight."

"Damn, this looks pretty serious. You a fighter?"

"On occasion," Ian said.

"It doesn't seem like your thing."

Ian thought about Matt Dorchester's battered knuckles, about the upper body strength and speed you developed from working the speed bag, about the long hours training for three-minute rounds. He thought about the sheer terror he felt every time he stepped in the ring. "I'm full of surprises," he said.

He didn't call Riva to come get him. Instead, he used Uber to get a ride back to the house. Her truck was parked on the street, so he felt pretty confident she was home, even though she'd ignored his texts. Midafternoon sunshine poured through the trees and dappled the foyer when he let himself through the back door. The kitchen counters were immaculate; the only sign Riva had been at work was the fridge, jammed with storage containers filled with food he couldn't identify.

The rest of the house was eerily quiet. He stepped softly through the dining room, then across the foyer to the front parlor. Empty. He climbed the stairs and stopped in front of her closed door. He lifted his hand to the knob, then set his shoulders and turned for his own bedroom door.

Inside, he toed out of his boots and looked at the bathroom door. It was open, and so was the door to Riva's adjoining room. She was curled up on her side, sound asleep, a soft throw covering her bare legs, a book tipped over onto its spine. One finger held her page. Jo's questions flashed him back to the second time he'd met Riva.

Six years earlier . . .

Ian was waiting in a pretrial room at the courthouse when Riva opened the door and walked in, attention focused on the county attorney. "You'll be giving your testimony from another room, to protect your anonymity," the attorney was saying.

"I understand." Her voice was quiet, even as she

resolutely didn't look at him. "Thanks for explaining everything."

"Wait here until the bailiff comes to get you."

Riva sat on one of the wooden benches running the length of the wall. Ian didn't miss the fact that she'd seated herself as far away from him as she could. She wore a simple skirt and blouse and low heels, and her hair was pulled back in a ponytail that spread between her shoulder blades like the variegated wingspan of a bird of prey.

The terms of her agreement stipulated that until the trial was over, she had to tell the department and the county attorney any time she moved or changed jobs. So Ian knew she'd left the university's housing for an apartment in the student district and that she was no longer employed as a work-study student with the business department but at a natural foods co-op downtown. But that was all.

"Hi, Riva."

She glanced at him. Impossible that such a short look could hold so much anger and self-loathing. "Officer Hawthorn."

He didn't correct her. Most civilians wouldn't know that three chevrons on his upper arm meant he'd been promoted to sergeant. Riva wouldn't care.

"How've you been?"

"Fine."

She was prettier than she'd been at eighteen, her face more angular, more reserved. She'd gained weight, too, lost the coltish look and some of the makeup. But it didn't look like life had been kind to her. There was a new reserve in her face, a new wisdom, paid for, as it always was, with pain.

Pain he'd caused her. His heart ached a little.

"Why aren't you in a suit?"

Maybe she'd thought through the impossibility of their situation, come to terms with it. Forgiven him. He seized the chance to come and sit near her, leaving a respectable amount of distance between them. "I work in a uniform, so that's what I wear to court."

"You weren't in a uniform back then."

"I was undercover. We have a hard time finding cops who look young enough to pass for college kids."

"You fooled me." She stroked the side of her mouth, indicating the place where Ian knew pain had creased his skin. He knew his face was forbidding, almost hard. "These made me think you were a grad student, though."

She was different inside too. Willing to meet his gaze, even if the challenge still lurked behind her eyes. "Another fifteen or twenty minutes you would have figured out something was going on. And then you would have told me to fuck off."

"Not exactly. Another fifteen or twenty minutes and I would have told you my roommate wasn't home." Her words were flat, unemotional, like she'd made peace with them but didn't like the terms. "I would have taken you back to my room. Asked you about all that philosophy hoping you'd think I was smart enough for you, hoping you'd kiss me. Or more. Because that's the kind of girl I was then."

His heart stopped beating and his brain jerked into overdrive. There was a new darkness to Riva, not just a soberness, a teenage girl all grown up, but a true darkness. She'd figured something out, all right. She'd figured out that he was a jerk and an asshole and had no business letting things go as far as they had. Even as

*the thoughts formed in his mind, he knew he was miss-
ing something important, but before he could ask, she
spoke.*

"Was it just a cover?"

*Did she mean the philosophy textbooks or the ten-
sion simmering between them? Wrong question. Don't
go there. "Which part?"*

*She gazed at him, unflinching, and he got a glimpse
of the woman she'd become in a few more years. A
woman he'd like to know. A woman who, because of
their past, would have nothing to do with him. "The
books you carried."*

*"Those were my textbooks from college. I majored
in philosophy."*

She raised a disbelieving eyebrow.

*The cancer diagnosis had made him very philosoph-
ical. "I don't seem like the kind of guy who's concerned
with life's big questions?"*

*That got him a very small smile, barely a curve of
her lips. He'd seen so few on her face. This one went
straight to his heart like a fist to the chest. "I don't know
what kind of guy you are."*

Do you want to?

*The words trembled on the tip of his tongue. She was
twenty. Well past the age of consent, able to vote, not able
to drink legally. He was twenty-seven, with a promising
career ahead of him, and the case wasn't over. She would
always be a former CI. It wasn't illegal. Stupid, absolutely. Immoral, possibly. Wrong. It might never be right.*

*"Look, Riva, you have to forgive yourself for the
mistakes in your past."*

"I do. I've paid the price for my mistake, if not my

debt to society, and am now so squeaky clean now unicorns could eat off my reputation."

It was his turn to huff out a laugh. Two minutes of conversation and already things felt different. His brain jumped ahead to a year from now, maybe two, when the dust had settled, and she'd had a little more time.

"I just can't forgive myself for wanting you."

His breath stopped. Maybe it was a good thing she'd dropped off his radar the day after he'd loaned her his coat, because he only wanted her more.

And she wanted nothing to do with him.

"Riva Henneman?" The bailiff's bulky body filled up most of the doorway. "Sorry, Sergeant. They're ready for her."

He cleared his throat. "Ms. Henneman."

She leaned forward to collect her purse from the floor. On the way back up, she whispered, "We both know that part wasn't a cover either."

His heart stopped in his chest. "Good-bye, Sergeant," she said, distantly polite.

Then she walked through the door and out of his life again.

He watched her sleep, knowing he'd do everything in his power to make himself the target, to steal Rory's attention and interest, so Riva could get free. It was the only chance she'd have to move on from her past.

Would she ever be able to forgive herself for giving in to her father's manipulative demands? She was obviously carrying around guilt over her parents' relationship, which wasn't her burden to bear. She was obviously ashamed of what she'd done and trying to set that right.

And tangled up in all of that was the thrumming, dangerous desire they never seemed to set aside.

He padded silently into the room and closed the bathroom door, then stretched out on the bed beside her, tucking his arm under his ear as he did. She made a little grumbling noise, turned her head to look over her shoulder. Her eyelids fluttered open. He saw the exact moment she remembered who she was, who he was, why they were in bed together.

"I didn't hear you come in," she said. Her voice was sleep rough, and lacked the vibrating tension brought on by fear and suspicion.

"I tried to be quiet," he said.

"I didn't wake up when you got on the bed, either."

Her gaze was soft, not vulnerable or defenseless, not quiet. But not guarded, or worse, sharpening in attack. Given their history and her responses to him, this was important and made him go all soft inside. A different kind of protective, like curl-up-and-purr protective. "Why did you wake up?"

"I smelled chocolate," she said.

A grin spread across his face. "That truck is full of chocolate."

She made a small noise, acknowledging his statement, then shifted so she was facing him. His heart started to pound. He hadn't felt like this since he was a kid, when lying down with a girl was new, fresh, thrilling. They weren't quite touching, but the possibility was there, hanging in the air like the scent of candy in the warehouse and truck. Soft, sweet, so potent he could taste it.

They should talk about the morning, his conversation with her father, seeing Micah at the sales call, his conversation with Jo. They should talk about the night. But he didn't want to talk. He wanted to slice this moment out of time and soak in the image of Riva's face, her thick eyelashes, her dreamy gaze, her sleep-swollen lips, the crease from the pillowcase on one cheek.

"You're getting a little scruffy," she said. She reached up and gently brushed her fingertips over his stubble.

It was the first time Riva had touched him out of the simple desire to do so, a desire not driven by fear or sex, but simply because she wanted to feel the texture of his body against hers. Not wanting to break the spell, he didn't respond. He lay there, breathing shallowly and evenly as she trailed her fingertips over his jaw to the spot on his throat where his beard gave way to skin. Her touch was still light, exploratory, as it lingered on his pulse. Her gaze went abstract for a second, then focused on his eyes.

"Fast," she noted.

Because he was lit up like a concert stage, lights and smoke and thrumming electricity. Still, he kept quiet. Letting her set the pace.

Turns out, letting Riva have her way with him was incredibly sexy. He'd never been so aware of his heartbeat sending blood south to pool in his cock, and then of his erection, thickening and lifting to throb against his zipper. His legs felt heavy, his fingers and palms tingling with the urge to touch her, stroke her hair, brush his thumb over her cheek. They were close enough for her breath to drift over his jaw. Each newly sensitized place was connected to the other, making him aware of his body in a new way, a vessel alive with pleasure, possibility, not a dumb, brute beast to alternately ignore or push to new limits of endurance.

In some dim corner of his mind he realized he was enjoying his body. Nothing more, nothing less. Experiencing sensations, not cataloging them against a list of symptoms, hating his body for its betrayal, or treating it like a patrol car the department would drive into the ground.

Maybe Riva wasn't the only one getting used to his body.

Her index finger dipped into the hollow between his collarbones, then snagged in his shirt placket, not quite pulling, not quite tugging, just holding curled into the fabric while she looked into his eyes. He didn't move to close the distance between them, just waited, forcing his breath to even, forcing his body to relax.

She lifted her chin and kissed him, a brush of lips, warm, smooth, a hint of some spice she'd used in the recipes and sampled. Glancing, just enough contact to set off the nerves under the skin, make them tingle for more. But he didn't move, didn't even follow her to return the kiss. He simply watched her explore him, herself, what they could make together.

Outside the window, birds chirped and sang. The breeze sent the shadows of leaves dancing across the floor. Riva drew her leg up, bumping her knee into his thigh, then stopping. The moment was too charmed to risk. It wouldn't shatter into pieces; it was too tenuous for that. It would drift away like the song heard faintly through the windows from a passing car, gone before they could finish it, much less name it. So he left his forearm on his hip, his hand resting on his thigh, and let Riva unfasten the first button on his shirt, then the next, then the next, her gaze never leaving his.

He was, he realized, achingly hard and bent at a painful angle in his shorts. No moving, no adjusting; his only option was to lie there and wait for whatever was coming. Maybe sex, maybe another kiss, maybe just this, but for the first time he was okay with taking it. There was a certain recklessness to holding back, to taking what came rather than trying to control the outcome. When Riva was calling the shots, this was beyond reckless.

She unbuttoned his shirt to his navel, then pulled his shirt free from his pants, tucking the top layer between his elbow and his hip. Moving a little to let her do that eased some of the pressure on his cock, which was a good thing, because she set her fingertips to the muscles between his ribs. She rubbed her thumb over his abdominal wall, the pressure firm enough to remind him that she worked with her hands and also to remind him exactly how close her hand was to his cock.

A delicate pink flush bloomed on her cheeks. She angled herself forward and kissed him again, this time with pressure to urge his lips open so her tongue could dart in and touch his.

A low rough sound. Him, giving voice to the longing he'd held back for so long it almost hurt. Then she kissed him again, hot and slick alternating with a hint of sharp teeth. Then he lost track of time again, dropping deep and dark into sensation. Mourning doves cooing. The slick sound of their mouths. Riva's tongue tracing his lower lip, then her open mouth against the corner of his, as if she were rubbing her lips against the stubble. He couldn't think. Her hand tightened on his hipbone, holding him steady while she scooted forward. Her knee nudged against his until he got the message and made room for her leg between his. Her skirt rode up to the top of her leg, allowing her thigh and hip bone to press solidly against his erection; through the gauzy cotton dress her tight little nipples brushed his chest with each inhale. It was maddening to be half-dressed, Riva's fingers against his jaw, her index finger dipping into his mouth to touch his tongue between kisses.

He nipped the tip of her finger, a suggestion she remove it. Words trembled on the tip of his tongue. He wanted to check in with her, make sure she was okay with what was happening. He was learning, slowly, too slowly for the situation they were in, but he'd do what he could with what he had. He'd keep his mouth shut.

She traced his lower lip, wet with saliva. "You're still holding back." She lifted his hand from his thigh and dropped it on her hip. "That goes there." Her fingers flexed over his, forcing pressure. "Don't hold back."

Tempting. So tempting, spurring him to curve his fingers into the sweet swell of her hip and shimmy just enough to seat his cock against her mound. With his other hand he locked his forearm around her shoulders, pulling her close. Lip to lip, hip to hip, and the temperature in the room shot up until the breeze no longer felt cold but necessary to keep them from spontaneously combusting.

Her arm wrapped around his waist and pulled, rolling them so he was on top. He had to be crushing her into the soft duvet but couldn't stop himself from tightening his grip and flat-out grinding against her body. In a flurry of hands and hips she urged him to his elbows, then reached down to wriggle her skirt up and her panties down to midthigh.

"Touch me."

He collapsed forward, burying his face in her hair as

he took his weight on his left elbow, notched his cock against her hipbone in the hope that the pressure would take the edge off, and slid his fingers over her mound.

She was slick. Hot. Swollen. One of her hands fisted in the back of his shirt; the other gripped his nape. Her body stiffened as he explored, drawing up to part her folds, ghosting over her clit, then dipping back down to circle the opening to her body. Fine tremors ran through her body, the muscles of her inner thighs quivering until he circled her clit once, watching, paying attention to her responses, then settling into a slow rhythm, fingertip to one side of her clit, stroking, stroking.

The bud swelled under his touch. She arched under him, a movement he ruthlessly controlled through simple physics: he rolled more of his weight onto her, pressing her into the bed.

"More," she whimpered. "Faster."

"No," he growled back. He was so close to her ear he barely had to use his voice. "Like this."

She went inward, eyelids drooping, then closing under the onslaught of sensation. It was unfathomable, miraculous, that such a tiny area could devastate a woman so thoroughly. A deep flush bloomed on her cheekbones. Ian fisted his hand in her hair, hovered his mouth over hers, pushed his pelvis against her hip, and didn't vary his touch by so much as a millimeter.

Flush on her collarbone. Her entire body went rigid. He sealed his mouth over hers, inhaling her sharp cries as she came until his entire body was reverberating with her release. Slowly, as slowly as he'd brought her to the peak, the tension ebbed from her body until she was soft and lax under him.

Her eyes opened. The expression in there—soft,

dreamy, satisfied woman—nearly stopped his heart. Without breaking eye contact she reached for his hand, drew it up her body to her lips, and licked her moisture from his fingertips.

Lightning bolt directly to his cock. He bent his head and helped her, until all that was left was his tongue rubbing against hers, hot and demanding, as her fingers trailed down his chest to his belt. He reached down and helped her kick her panties to the side of the bed, then trailed his fingers back up her leg to the sweet heat at the top of her thighs. This was real, every dream he'd never allowed to the surface of his mind. His cock ached, each brush of her fingers through his jeans intensifying the desire. He wouldn't last two minutes like this.

No matter. This wasn't the end.

The garage door *thunk*ed into motion. Riva's hand stopped in the act of plucking his belt free from the buckle. "That's Dad," she murmured.

For a brief, incredulous moment he stared down into her face, trying to make sense of the words. Then he rested his forehead on hers. "Damn. Damn, damn, damn."

"We can," she started.

He shook his head. "No."

"Why not?"

It was hard to put into words, so he settled for blunt. "Because I want you to know this isn't just about sex. It's about pleasure. And patience." He took a deep breath. "Because I want to look forward to this, think about it, anticipate how you'll feel when I slide into you."

One corner of her mouth lifted, and her eyes gleamed. Her gaze locked with his as she fastened his belt. A minute. All he needed was a minute, her slender fingers wrapped around his cock, her tongue teasing his, and he'd go off.

"What was your story?" She plucked her panties from the duvet, slid them up her legs, then lifted her hips to pull them on.

"What?" he asked, distracted by the flex of the muscles in her legs, the neatly trimmed curls disappearing behind cotton bikinis.

She clambered off the bed and stood by the bathroom door. "Better?"

"Yeah." He pushed back to his knees, rubbed his palms over his face, and tried to string together a coherent thought.

"I meant, why are you home without Dad?"

"I got a call from work. I'm working."

"Got it." She nodded at his zipper, straining from the pressure of his cock behind it. "Is there any chance you'll come home from boxing with that?"

He looked at her. "Do you want me to come home from boxing with this?"

Her gaze widened ever so slightly, a secondary flush blooming on her cheeks again. Then she lifted her chin. "Bring it on, *Ian*."

CHAPTER SEVENTEEN

Riva couldn't look away from Ian. He was kneeling on her bed, hands loose on his thighs, seemingly relaxed, but Riva wasn't fooled. He was as tense as he'd ever been during all those nights they'd spent together, watching her get information and buy drugs.

On one hand, this was no different: Ian was running an undercover operation with her as the bait. On the other hand, everything was different. The way he walked, talked, how incredibly intimate things had become. How very, very quickly that had happened. Seven years ago she'd wanted Officer Hawthorn with a teenage girl's impetuous, immature desire, but he'd never been just a man. In her mind, he'd never been anything more than the closed-off cop she knew.

Now he was Ian, a man who couldn't use chopsticks to save his life, with some seriously unexpected dancing skills and a knife technique that left him in real danger of slicing off his finger while making a stir-fry. This was terrifying. Either way, he frightened her almost more than words could say. Either way, she felt safe with him. Protected.

But this couldn't translate into a relationship in Lancaster. He was still a cop. She was still his former informant. They'd never get past that.

"I'll give you a minute," she said and closed the bedroom door.

In the bathroom she turned on the water in her sink, then stared into the mirror. Her lips and chin were reddened and scraped, and the orgasmic flush still bloomed on her collarbones. She wet down a facecloth and scrubbed it over her face and neck, turning all of her skin bright pink.

Her dad wanted to take Ian to Sweet Science. There had to be a reason for that; he wasn't known for making friends or socializing. Why take Ian to the club? With her dad, it could be any reason. On a good day he might want to show off his neighborhood or his boxers, entertain the out-of-town visitor. On a bad day he might want to humiliate him by seeing him get in the ring with a stronger, faster fighter.

On a really bad day, anything could happen.

Ian's best defense against her father would be to tell him he was a cop; any injury to a police officer would bring down a swift, brutal response. But that would lead her father back to the undercover agent who had infiltrated the corrupt cops in Lancaster, threatening them and the case.

The only way out now was through, all the way to the other side.

Riva splashed cool water on her face until the stinging subsided, then shut off the water and patted her skin dry. She had a plan, and she needed to set it in motion before Ian got his body under control and came downstairs.

She hurried down the stairs, using the newel-post to swing herself around and trot back to the kitchen. "Hey!" Hopefully desperate came off as cheerful. The right positive attitude could sometimes stop the slide into fuming cruelty. "How was your day?"

"Good," her father said.

Riva went up on tiptoe and kissed his cheek. "Ian said he learned a lot running the route."

"He's got potential, that guy," her dad said. He opened the fridge and peered at the wall of Tupperware boxes Riva had stacked on the shelves. "Do we have any beer?"

"Of course," she said. "Let me get it for you. I've got things organized in there."

He watched her shift boxes and find the bottled beer at the back of the top shelf. "I'm glad you're helping with your mom. I'm really worried about her."

"I am, too," Riva said with total sincerity. She got the bottle opener from the drawer, popped the top off, and handed him the bottle. "It seems worse than it has before."

"She's got no initiative to help herself. I suggested the fundraiser because I thought it would help her meet people, get involved in something besides the damn dog. Instead, it's made it worse."

"Maybe she'll get some confidence when the luncheon goes off without a hitch." Riva sent up a silent prayer it did go off without a hitch. "She's got so much to offer. I hate to see her like this."

Her father shrugged. "She never had our go-get-'em attitude."

Her mother was truly Rory's victim, prey he played with when it amused him but didn't finish off, just in case he got bored elsewhere. Riva needed to find out where he kept that laptop. Rory was too smart to mix his legal and illegal activities. He'd keep a separate machine somewhere else, and the club was as logical a place as any.

"Ian mentioned you were taking him to the boxing club tonight," she said, keeping her tone casual. "Mind if I come along?"

Rory's gaze narrowed fractionally. "Why the sudden interest in boxing?"

"Because you're interested in it."

"Tell me the truth, Riva." His voice was whip hard. "Is it my fighters, or Ian?"

In the blink of an eye he went from friendly to terrifying back to the jovial father role. Sweat broke out at her nape and her heart rate shot through the roof, sending a dizzying rush of blood to her face. "Dad," she said, like she was embarrassed. "He's just . . . He's a guy I know."

"Because if you're serious about coming into the business, the man you're marrying matters. It's too risky for you to be with someone who might get curious about how you're making your money."

And there was the father she remembered, the one who wanted her all to himself, isolated her mother from family and friends, then played her and Riva against each other until they trusted no one, not even themselves. Only him.

"It's not like that."

"He might be okay," Rory conceded. "Let me test

him, see what he's made of, if he's loyal. See if he's good enough for my baby."

In other words, let me choose your boyfriend. Let me take over every single element of your life, your work, your home, your bed. The situation was threatening to hit a screaming pitch of crazy Riva hadn't experienced since the day Ian had put handcuffs on her. "Just . . . Dad, it's not like that . . . Shh, he's coming. Can I go with you, Dad? Please?"

"Sure," he said. "Why not?"

"Why not what?" Ian walked into the kitchen, rolling up his cuffs. Riva caught a glimpse of hair-roughened wrists and his no-nonsense watch, and felt her body melt a little.

"Why not bring Riva to the club with us? Beer?"

"Sure," Ian said. When she opened the fridge he gave Riva a hard glare and one firm headshake. She smiled bemusedly, as if she didn't understand his crystal-clear meaning, then handed him a beer. He wrapped his fingers around her wrist and leaned so close he didn't even have to use his voice. "Back out. Now."

"No."

"Riva. That's an order."

"Why?" She got right in his face.

"Because I don't want you to see what could happen in the ring."

Her gaze flickered. He took the beer from her and twisted the top off. "Back out. I've got this."

"Let her come," her father said unexpectedly. "She says she can handle it. Let's find out."

It was a neat piece of manipulation. Riva watched Ian's face darken as he realized that her father had

been watching their interaction with interest, searching for the cracks, the place to drive the wedge. Riva
crossed the kitchen floor to lean against the same counter as her father, who turned his attention on Ian. "You
got some gym clothes?" When Ian nodded, he added,
"Come on, kids. I'll show you the real South Side of
Chicago."

The setting sun drenched the sky in glorious red-gold
swaths while her dad took Ian on a run of his old childhood haunts. They stopped for Chicago-style pizza at a
Lou Malnati's, then drove to the club. Ian cornered her
beside her dad's car while her dad wandered off to say
hello to a trainer leaving the club.

"We have one rule, Riva. One rule. That rule is you
do what I tell you to do when it comes to safety."

"That works both ways," she shot back. "I don't want
you off somewhere alone. Dad's getting stranger."

Ian's forehead wrinkled. "This is strange for him?
He's getting more friendly. Letting his guard down."

"That could mean he's thinking about whether or not
to take you under his wing. It could mean he's about to
destroy you. I can tell you from extensive personal experience, he's at his nicest right before he does something awful."

This didn't have the effect she wanted. She'd hoped
Ian would reconsider this incredibly dangerous plan
and supervise from a distance while she got what they
needed: his hidden laptop. Instead, Ian's gaze narrowed.
He shifted his weight, looked at the horizon, his body
language as casual as if he was buying a candy bar at a
gas station. "He's being pretty nice to you right now
too."

He was. The only person he was tormenting was her mother. "Which means my plan is working."

"Nevertheless, you'll step off and fade into the background. I've got this."

"I like this thing where you're just Ian," she said, and his lips flattened together. "You go do your macho thing. I'll be in the office, trying to hack into his partitioned hard drive."

She snatched her jacket from the back seat, then slammed the car door so hard it would have rocked her truck, but her dad drove a Mercedes too well engineered to register a slamming door. Ian grabbed for her, then changed the motion into something less threatening when her dad joined them.

"The building used to house an auto repair and body work shop." They crossed the parking lot, Riva pulling on her denim jacket as they walked, Ian wearing the bright-eyed office-drone expression she was beginning to hate. "Back in the day it was an after-hours chop shop, stripping stolen cars for parts. Bernie bought it for cheap when the owners got arrested."

The building made no pretense at being a suburban gym. The big windows were painted black; the grimy exterior glass reflected only the light from the gas station across the street. Over the door hung a weather-beaten wooden sign: SWEET SCIENCE. Her dad opened the door. Ian politely stepped to the side to let Riva precede him. She shoved her hands in her pockets and walked in.

The space wasn't huge. The first thing she saw was the red-roped ring, spotlit in the back corner of the room. A fighter in protective gear and another, older man wearing mitts on his hands circled slowly in the ring, the boxer dancing on the balls of his feet, the older man calling out commands.

"Smells like a gym," Ian commented.

Riva gave a tentative sniff, then wrinkled her nose. The air in the room, big as it was, smelled like fresh sweat layered over the ranker stench of an unwashed sock forgotten for weeks. She caught hints of other smells, rubber mats, chalk, the unique scent of industrial food handed in a bag through a window. "Someone had cheap tacos for dinner," she said, resisting the urge to fan the air in front of her nose.

Her father gave Ian a little smile, one she recognized. It was his *it's your turn to be on the inside* smile. Them against her, boys against the girl. A couple of other women sat on the benches along the wall, one flipping through a magazine, the other watching her boyfriend hit a heavy bag.

She didn't know anything about boxing. Didn't care to. Her father's interest in the sport was recent, after she'd dropped out of college. But she trailed after Ian and her dad as they strolled between the heavy bags hanging from the ceiling along one side of the ring and the speed bags in neat rows kitty-corner. Newspaper clippings and autographed photos of typical boxing poses—menacing guys with gloves lifted in sparring stance—hung on the walls, interspersed with posters promoting upcoming fights. A rack of weights, medicine balls, kettle bells, and jump ropes lined one mirrored wall.

Ian looked around. "Looks like the real deal," he said. "Not one of those big box gyms running kickboxing classes."

"This place has history on the South Side. Lots of history."

A guy, shirtless and running sweat, worked the rope with methodical concentration, not even sparing them a glance. "How do you pick your boxers?" Ian asked.

"Killer instinct." He cut Ian a look that was part challenge, part mockery. "Lots of guys come in here wanting to look like boxers. They want the muscles, the one-two punches, the swagger. They don't want to do the work, because they don't have the killer instinct. Winners have it. Losers don't. Hey, Trev."

As if given permission, the guy stopped midjump, the rope slapping to the floor. "Mr. H.," he said, coming over to shake her dad's hand.

"How's it going?"

"Finished my warm-up. I'm just staying loose while they spar." He threw a glance at the ring.

"I'd like you to meet my daughter, Riva," her father said.

"Miss," Trev said with a respectful nod.

"And her colleague Ian."

Ian got a handshake, and that look guys gave each other, the sizing-up look. "Trev's in training for a fight next month. Ian's a fighter, too," Rory said.

The look on Trev's face was almost comical. "Not a fighter," Ian said. "I train for the exercise."

"Ever been in the ring with a real boxer?"

"Just the guys at my gym," Ian said.

Rory nodded at the ring, where the trainer and the other boxer were still circling. "—exhale . . . eyes on me . . . stay balanced, you're too far left—" The steady stream of instructions came as the trainer held the mitts up for the boxer to hit.

"How much longer, Jimmy?"

"One more round, Mr. H.," the trainer called back.

"They've got a few more minutes. He's sparring today."

"I'm not going to be much help," Ian said.

"It's an easy day," Rory said.

"You got gear I can borrow?"

"No problem. Get warmed up," Rory said. "Locker room's through there."

Ian picked up his bag and strode into the locker room. Riva took a seat along the wall. When Ian emerged he wore a loose pair of basketball shorts and a tank top with the sleeve holes extended. The complex weave of muscle and bone forming his ribs and torso flexed as he walked to the ring and ditched his bag by one corner.

Her father was watching him too. "You look pretty good for a bureaucrat."

"Just staying in shape," Ian said.

He reached for Trev's discarded jump rope and started warming up. Riva tried not to be too obvious about watching, but as a minute passed and Ian's footwork grew more complex, she couldn't stop watching. He slipped into a completely different headspace, mental focus on something she couldn't see and wasn't sure she wanted to if she could. His shoulders, arms, and wrists tensed and flicked with each revolution of the rope, too fast for the eye to catch in individual motions.

Watching him encapsulated everything wrong about her relationship with Ian. As a purely physical body, he went beyond attractive into dead sexy, all muscle and bone, exuding strength and power and a discipline she found almost unbearable. Unlike Trev or the other boxer in the ring, he wasn't shirtless, showing off his muscles. She couldn't shake the intuition that the T-shirt hid something he didn't want her father or Trev to see.

"Maybe that's part of your fantasy," she muttered to herself. "You want him to be smart and interesting and not just another muscle-bound jock cop lifting weights so he can take down the bad guys."

Smart? Check. Philosophy degree.

Interesting? Check. He cooked. He boxed. He wasn't some one-dimensional cop.

Except for the fact that everything Ian did sharpened his focus on righting the kind of wrongs her family committed, she committed. All she could have with him was this chance to destroy her father. Maybe, just maybe, if he didn't discover the truth, they could part as friends. She wouldn't have to fear seeing him walk through Oasis's front door, but could greet him with a smile. Even if he was always forbidden, her secret would be safe.

She needed to get access to her father's laptop. "Mind if I take a look around, Dad?"

He waved at her rather than responding, all of his attention focused on Ian. Riva made a quick tour of the club, peeking into the grotty bathroom reeking of urinal cakes and damp before rattling the doorknob on the office at the back of the club.

Locked. "Hey, Dad," she called. "Can I borrow your laptop to check in on things on the farm?"

"Not now, Riva," he snapped.

"All yours," Jimmy said. He tugged the mitts off his hands and held up the rope so his boxer could duck out of the ring. The back of his T-shirt clung to his spine as Ian replaced the jump rope and jogged over to the ring. Jimmy started to wrap his hands and wrists, while Rory did the same for Trev. He murmured something to Trev, then slapped him on the shoulder to send him into the ring.

Riva took advantage of the distraction to peer through the grimy glass. No laptop obviously in sight, but the brick wall held a safe. "Dammit," she muttered.

When she turned around, Ian was suited up for his round with Trev. The protective headgear gave him a hard, almost mercenary appearance, reducing his face to the deep lines on either side of his mouth, the thrust of his jaw and nose. Any softness disappeared into the ultramasculine image, all hard muscles, fast hands, dancing feet.

"Jabs only," Jimmy said. His voice was a rasp that carried through the room. "Warm up first."

Ian and Trev started circling each other, trading jabs. Ian threw the first one, landing a blow, only to rock backward when Trev's left connected with the side of his face.

"Not bad," the trainer said to Rory as they watched Ian and Trev get a feel for each other. "No chicken wings. Keeping his head up."

"What am I looking for?" Riva said.

"Watch his body," her father said, distracted. "He should look like Trev. Knees bent, staying on the balls of his feet. Glove up to protect his face. He's got good reflexes."

It was no hardship to watch Ian Hawthorn fight. When Jimmy called time, they bumped gloves and backed off a few steps. Ian's gaze was narrowed, assessing Trev, who was about Ian's height but carrying more muscle.

"Go," Jimmy said.

The first flurry of punches came faster than Riva could catalog them. All she saw was Ian's left up, parrying Trev's punches while his right powered straight from his shoulder at Trev's ribs. When the two men separated, blood trickled from a cut over Ian's eye. Breathing hard, he rolled his head on his neck, feinted right, and bulled into Trev's body.

This time, when they separated, Trev was working his jaw and eying Ian with a new, cautious respect. "Whoa there, brother," he said. "Mr. H. said to go easy on you."

"You can step it up a notch or two," Ian said.

Trev shot Rory a look. Riva felt Rory shrug, then smile. "You asked for it."

Two blinks later, Ian was on the ropes above her, taking punches to his ribs for what seemed like forever but had to be only a few seconds before he evaded Trev and backed into the center of the ring again.

"Nice slip move," Jimmy said. "You sure this guy isn't on the amateur circuit?"

"I'm sure," Rory said.

They boxed two more rounds. Before the final round, Trev leaned down to catch something Rory murmured in his ear. Trev asked a question, and Rory shook his head, brief but firm. Trev nodded, then went back to the ring. This time, his punches came full speed and full strength at Ian, who was quickly propelled into the rope. His gloved hands came up to protect his face while he landed the occasional punch, finally driving Trev back. Ian threw one fast cross at Trev, who slipped to the side and roundhouse clocked Ian on the side of the head. He went down to the mat and didn't get up.

Understanding flashed like a lightning strike: Trev wouldn't hesitate to kill Ian if her father gave him the nod. That quick little headshake was the only thing holding him back. Ian wouldn't stop in his quest to get the evidence they needed to arrest her father and root out the corruption in the Lancaster Police Department. The deeper into this they got, the more danger they faced.

Trev glanced at Rory, eyes questioning. A snakelife flicker of smile, then nothing but concerned attention.

"Oh my God," Riva murmured. She started to boost herself into the ring, but her father stopped her. "He's fine. Let Jimmy do it."

Ian was already sitting up, holding up a glove to show Trev he was okay. Jimmy pulled off the headgear and cradled Ian's jaw in his hands, obviously checking the state of his pupils.

"I'm fine," Ian said around the mouth guard.

"You're pretty tough," Jimmy said. "You just went three rounds with a two-time Chicago Golden Gloves champ."

"He's an idiot," Riva said under her breath.

"He's tough." Her dad wasn't looking at her when he spoke. He was watching Ian. "Just the way I like them."

CHAPTER EIGHTEEN

Riva sat in the back seat of her father's car, all her senses on high alert. The car smelled like freshly oiled leather and copper pennies, a scent that slowly crept into the air as blood dripped from cuts over Ian's eye and cheek-bone into his shirt. His breath hitched every so often, like he was regulating it into smoothness but couldn't quite maintain the rhythm when they went over a bump or he shifted sideways with a turn. He wasn't holding his ribs, and his hands were loose on his thighs, but even in the car's darkened interior she could see the tension in the back of his neck.

His willingness to take the beating astonished her. It was the vulnerability she'd accused him of running from, a level of commitment to getting the job done she'd never anticipated him to be capable of.

Her father had talk radio on, the host in full rant about something or other; she couldn't quite make out the words, only the tone. It meant they didn't have to talk, leaving her mind free to wander.

Where was he keeping that laptop?

Why would Ian let himself get beaten up like that?

How could he possibly take it? It went beyond the call of duty for a police officer, into something visceral and deep in Ian's soul.

She watched the houses slip by, windows dark, doors closed, maybe a porch light on or a night light gleaming in an upstairs room. Resolution crystalized inside her. One way or another, she was getting to the bottom of Ian Hawthorn. Tonight.

Her father took the stairs two at a time, whistling the whole way. Ian and Riva followed more slowly, Ian wincing with every step until he stood at the bathroom sink, washing his hands before probing at the cut over his eye. Riva found a first-aid kit decorated with *Sesame Street* characters under the sink and marveled at her mother's lingering hope that she'd bring home grandchildren. She jammed her fists on her hips and tried to tone her look down from a glare to an assessment. He'd taken enough hits already tonight. The cut over his eyebrow had stopped actively bleeding. The one on his cheek trickled into his stubble when she pulled the cotton pad away, and his left eye was developing a very nice shiner.

"You're an idiot. Sit down and let me do that."

He shut off the water and eased down on the toilet lid. She popped open the lid on the first-aid kit.

"I heard you the first time," Ian said.

He kept his voice low, so Riva did as well. "You had to know he'd arrange to give you a beating."

"It's a male-bonding ritual."

She couldn't imagine the father she'd seen talking to Ian watching his son get beat up in a boxing ring, but she'd proven herself to be no judge of men. Or fathers. A suspicion formed in her mind. "You knew how good Trev was."

"I did some research."

"You did some research. Golden Gloves? And you still got in the ring?"

"I needed a way to prove myself to your father." He stuck his finger into his mouth and probed around his teeth. The finger came out tinged with bloody saliva. "This option presented itself."

He sounded a little tired. A little lonely. It made her feel something she hadn't felt toward Ian before: tenderness. To cover the emotion she doused a gauze pad with hydrogen peroxide and tried to decide which cut to tend first. She tipped his face back and pressed the gauze to the cut over his eye. He winced, then winced again and reached for his ribs.

"Let's have a look at that."

He reached for the hem of his sweat-soaked T-shirt, then hissed in pain. Riva helped him get it over his head, then exhaled slowly. Bruises were blooming on his ribs, more on his left side than his right. "Are your ribs broken?"

"No." He probed tentatively at his side. "Probably not. There's nothing useful they can do to fix them, anyway."

"Like I said. Stone-cold idiot."

She'd turned on the recessed lighting over the shower, not the brighter makeup bulbs over the sinks, leaving the room bathed in a soft glow. He was looking up at her, his hazel eyes soft, vulnerable with the kind of fragility that came only after taking a big hit, literal or metaphorical. "I never said I was smart."

"You didn't need to say it. Hold that there." She dampened a facecloth with warm water and started to clean up the dried blood on his cheek and chin. With his head tipped back the light fell on his torso, a messy collage of spreading bruises and scars. "Why on earth would you let him do that to you?" she asked.

The air in the room froze like it had been plunged into dry ice. "See the scars on my chest? One's an appendectomy scar. I had it out when I was sixteen. The other's a port scar."

For the first time, Ian's eyes were focused slightly to the right of her own, on something she couldn't see. Was this some anatomy element she'd never heard of? "What's a port?"

"It's a medical device. A plastic disc that's inserted under the skin and attached to a catheter that threads into one of the large veins in your neck. It makes drawing blood and giving medicine easier during a long-term treatment situation."

Riva dabbed at the blood crusted in his stubble under his ear. "What kind of long-term treatment situation?"

"There are a number of conditions where people need medications delivered over a long period of time. In my case, it was cancer."

The word slithered into the room, a low, sibilant threat that curled up in the corner. It was the kind of word that never went away. It became part of a person, defining, like a job or a degree or a conviction. Some labels were sought—Ivy League graduate, investment banker, cop— while others—criminal, for example—you chose, one way or another. Fate handed you others—cancer survivor. When someone wrote Ian Hawthorn's obituary, using words like "police officer," maybe "husband and father," they'd include "cancer survivor."

"I didn't know you had cancer." She tried not to feel hurt.

"I was diagnosed just before I turned twenty-one. I finished treatment at twenty-two."

Ian gave his ages very precisely. Riva turned back to the sink and rinsed out the cloth, then started cleaning space between his eyebrow and the cut. "Is this some kind of dance with death? Cancer didn't kill you so you're going to see if Trev can?"

"No." He lifted the gauze from the cut on his forehead, examined it, then put it back. "I'm very aware of how much I want to live."

"So why do it? Why get in the ring?"

"I'm not going to die in there."

"You know that killer instinct Dad was talking about? Trev's got it. He only stopped because Dad called time."

He looked at her, the emptiness gone from his eyes. "You think he's that dangerous?"

She gritted her teeth against screaming in frustration. "I may not be an expert on the drug trade, but I'm an expert on my dad, his moods, his patterns, the way he uses people. He's got the same freaky edge he's had in the past when he was on the verge of something big. If your information is correct, he's under a lot of pressure to find new markets for the heroin. He's crossing lines he's never crossed before—in deep with the police department, on the hook for selling pretty big shipments, which means holding the territory he's got, expanding into new. He'll do whatever it takes to make this work.

If it were me, I'd think twice before I got back in the ring with Trev. His eyes were freaking me out." She shivered a little.

"You're right," he said, unexpectedly. "It was a stupid move."

"Did it hurt?"

"Knowing a beating's coming doesn't make it any less painful." He lifted the gauze from his forehead, looked at the blood staining it, and tossed the wad in the trashcan.

"That's not what I meant."

She'd clutched at his shoulders while he went down on her, dug her nails into his lower back through the most intense session of making out she'd ever experienced. But she couldn't bring herself to touch his scar without his permission.

He looked at her hovering fingers. "You can touch it."

She recognized that look, that tone, from the first time they had sex. Shoulders braced, lips tense. He'd given permission because he was proving something to himself, and he was angry. Maybe he saw the scar as a symbol of weakness. Of shame. "That's okay. Thanks, though."

He flicked her a glance, a little suspicious, a little surprised. Whatever. They had history, years of it, individual and shared, that brought them to this middle-of-the-night moment, in the silence of her sociopath father's house bought with illegally gained proceeds. With every passing day the complex tangle of emotions Ian raised in her unknotted a little more. He became less her downfall, less her enemy, less her worst nightmare, leaving behind just Ian. Just a man.

Tipping his head back obviously strained his ribs. She

was feeling less pissy about the whole thing, so she sat on her heels to clean the blood from his jaw and throat. Ian's breath eased from him in a soft, low sound when he finally relaxed. His eyes closed, his hands lax on his thighs, he sat still and let her tend to him.

Long minutes passed as she alternately cleaned away the dried blood and rinsed the cloth. By the time she finished, his head drooped on his neck ever so slightly. Coming down off the adrenaline rush, she supposed. Overcome by an infinite, raw tenderness, she lifted her face and kissed the bruised corner of his mouth. When she pulled back, his eyes were half-open.

"Is this what we've come to? You throwing me a pity fuck?"

One corner of her mouth lifted. "I wish this were about pity. That's what I'm supposed to feel, right? Big bad tough cop is actually literally and metaphorically wounded." She did it again, feeling the hot, swelling skin bristling with stubble under her lips. "Sorry. Not about pity. All this blood and bruising and damaged, naked chest is turning me on."

The man looking out from Ian's eyes when she pulled back sent a spike of sheer lust through her core. This was under Ian's intellectual, carefully controlled, analytical exterior. He'd layered acceptable veneers over the raw power and rage driving him. Right now, the truth of him was very close to the surface.

"I know," she said, like he'd spoken. "Just when you thought this couldn't get any more messed up." She kissed him again, same spot, this time open mouthed, so she could taste the sweat and faint trace of blood on his skin. Her muscles and bones were softening, drawing in around her hot core.

He was holding himself very still, all but vibrating with the effort of keeping the façades in place. "Be very, very careful what you do next."

In that moment, she loved him just a little for trying to protect her from herself, from him. She looked at him, at the cut above his eyebrow, at the purple-blue skin around his eye, at the puffy corner of his mouth. Saw him for the first time, up close, like a lover. Let herself really look at him, at the crow's feet, at the sharp, savage lines of his bones that had taken the impact and given back proud bruises as badges of pride and honor. His lashes were ridiculously thick, wasted on a man. She let herself see him, the real him, the feral creature who *lived*, lived through cancer, lived as hard and ferociously as he could. At the bruises on his torso, darker than his black eye, fist sized, spreading as she watched.

She could handle this. Handle him.

Gaze locked on his, she reached out and pressed her fingertips into the bruise.

His breath caught in a sharp hiss at the same time his hands clamped to her jaw and crammed his mouth to hers. The impact sent fresh blood seeping from the cut inside his mouth, because he tasted coppery, sweet, penny bright. His hands smelled of sweat, and boxing gloves, and the hydrogen-peroxide-soaked gauze still pinched between his fingers.

The kiss was raw and fierce and possessive, nothing held back, no questions asked, no concern for whether or not Riva could keep up with him. She gave him back as good as she got, her tongue warring with his until he'd conquered her mouth, until their teeth clacked together and her own lips felt bruised. Inside she screamed with elation. This was the truth of Ian Hawthorn, the man so complex he made puzzle boxes seem rudimentary. Cop. Philosopher. Wicked dancer. Cancer survivor.

Man, her body roared. *Man, all man*.

It was the truth of them. Dark, and deep, and intimate in a way very few people could understand. To truly know all of Ian you had do the job with him. To truly know her, you had to have sat in the unmarked patrol car with her while she did deal after deal.

Only one person had been in that car with her. Ian.

The insight disappeared into a smearing of open mouths that was less a kiss and more of a shove. Wild with desire, she curved her hand around his ribs, squeezing ever so slightly. "Fuck," he growled. In one smooth movement he stood up, hoisted her right off her knees, and backed her into the counter. The strain of the movement opened the cut over his eye, sending a fresh trickle of blood over his brow bone. Another unsubtle lift with his arm and push with his powerful thigh, and she sat on the edge of the counter with Ian between her knees. One hand braced on the mirror behind her, he leaned forward and pulled her snug against his pelvis.

The loose shorts did nothing to confine his erection. Riva gasped, then wound her legs around his hips, hands slipping over sweaty muscles in search of a safe spot to hold on. It was one thing to gently probe. It was another entirely to use them as leverage for what promised to be a very fast, very powerful fuck. "Your ribs," she said.

"Forget about my ribs," he growled. "I have."

Full steam ahead. He curled his fingers into the hem of her floaty little dress and pulled until she shifted her weight to release the fabric from under her butt. This was the Ian she'd always imagined, actually here. Raw and in person. He wasn't thinking about who she'd been, what she'd done, who he was. He just wanted her, with a raw, untroubled desire.

"Get these off. C'mon," he rasped. Yanking, pulling, until her panties strained at midthigh and she had to lean back and pull her knees up so he could yank them over one boot. He pushed her thigh open with his palm and brushed his thumb over her sex, setting her muscles quivering. He made her wait until he parted the soft folds and stroked slick heat up to her clit.

"Is this from earlier?"

"No," she whispered. His thumb rubbed firmly against the swollen nub, drawing her muscles tight with anticipation. When she opened her eyes she saw him watching his hand between her spread legs. Holding her open. Touching her.

He glanced up at her, then at his face in the mirror behind her, then back at her. "So hot," he murmured, his voice a low, vibrating threat. "Who's more fucked up? You, for liking this, or me?"

Her toes curled inside her boots, and her nipples peaked. Dizzy with longing, she inhaled blood and sweat and skin overlaid with the growing scent of her desire. She reached back and braced her hand against the mirror to lift her hips into his touch. The movement strained her dress over her breasts. Ian locked his free hand in the top of the dress and yanked, jerking her with the movement. A few stitches popped, but nothing else happened.

Fingers trembling, Riva started unfastening the small buttons running down the front of her dress. "Faster," Ian said.

"Fuck it." She closed her fist on the other side. "Pull."

He did, and the next few buttons flew into the air,

pinging off the tiled walls, floor, the mirror. She shimmied when he used his battered, abraded hands to work her bra straps off her shoulders and pull the cups down, baring her breasts. He cupped one breast, brushing his thumb over the nipple, baring his teeth with a hiss when she shivered. She shoved at the elastic waist of his shorts, watched his cock bob free when they dropped to his ankles.

"Now," she demanded.

He reached for his shaving kit, tore a condom off the strip inside. Wanting to see both of them, she turned to look over her shoulder. Her hair was tousled and wild around flushed cheeks, wide, avaricious eyes, swollen mouth, wrecked dress. Ian's body was the picture of dangerous masculinity, muscles, blood, bruises, raw knuckles as he smoothed the condom down his shaft. He pushed her hips level on the counter, wrapped his other hand around his cock, and without any further preamble started pushing into her.

Raw, sensitized nerves went on high alert, sending thin, hot wires of sensation pulsing to the very edges of her skin. "Oh, God," she said.

"Shh," he said. "Be quiet."

Being ordered to hush shouldn't be hot. It was. She braced her hand against the mirror and looked up at him. His face was a study in intensity, muscle popping in his jaw. She tried to imagine how she felt around him, after the slow tease earlier, after the adrenaline rush of boxing. Hot, slick, tight. He leaned one hand on the mirror and closed the other around her hip, used his hips to widen her legs, and sank the final inch inside her.

She couldn't breathe. Her heart pounded up into her throat, tightening it. Her legs trembled, and she wrapped her arm under his, clawing her fingers into his shoulder to stay upright as her vision swam.

"Breathe, Riva." To punctuate his command he thrust once, hard, shocking the air right out of her and forcing an involuntary inhale. Her vision cleared, bringing her back into her body in just enough time to feel his cock pulse once inside her, strong enough she thought it was over.

He bent his head, gritted his teeth hard enough she could hear them grind, and exhaled with a long, slow hiss. "I move, this ends. You do it."

She squirmed, trying to figure out how to make this work. It was awkward, giving her no leverage to rise and fall on his cock. "We should move this to the bed."

"I'll bleed on your sheets."

"Your bed?" She tried to lift herself a little higher, searching for the traditional feel of a woman on top.

His head jerked up. "No. Like this. Know why? Because feeling you work for it is turning me right the fuck on. *Move*."

They were so very, very, very fucked up. Trying to find a way to make this work, she shimmied and writhed and wriggled, clutching his hard length, his shoulders, his hips until, frustrated, she slapped a hand against the mirror and arched into his body. The movement sent his cock gliding over the sweet spot inside her and forced a little cry from her throat.

"Shh," he said again. Sweat dripped from his forehead to her collarbone. "Come on. Again."

She held him close and fought for it, the combination of stretch and fight and slick friction inexorably building the searing hot coil of pleasure low in her sex. Her head dropped back to *thunk* against the mirror. He loomed over her, gathering her close. "Don't, don't," she begged.

"Shh." This time the sound was low and filthy, placating her in a domineering way that pushed her dial up to eleven. He pulled out and thrust into her, slow and hard.

She went rigid. "Again, again, oh please, again."

A low laugh. Sweaty blood trickled between her breasts, but she didn't care, because release shimmered just out of her reach. Heedless of injuries, her own precarious position, she climbed his body, clamped her knees to his hips, and rode him just as hard. Each measured stroke ended with a thud against her clit. She turned her head and stared over her shoulder. "Look. Look at us."

It was *betterhotterfiercer* than she'd ever imagined, unreal and dominating her senses. The sight of his powerful hips flexing between her legs magnified the pleasure. She saw it before she felt it, the blood flush blooming on her cheeks, throat, collarbones. Then the certainty of orgasm froze her.

"There you go. There you go," he growled.

Sharp, hot pulses clenched her sex around him. Ian never faltered, thrusting through the heart of each gripping pulse, covering her mouth with his as she came, their sweet, bruised lips sealed together as he shuddered deep inside her.

They were as close as two people could possibly be. She knew it couldn't last.

CHAPTER NINETEEN

Ian had survived months of chemo and radiation that had basically killed him from the inside out. He'd been as weak as a human being could be, carrying a hundred and twenty pounds on his six foot frame, hunched over and shuffling to the bathroom, praying he got there before he threw up, or worse. He'd been weak. He'd been bald. He'd been as close to death as a person could be. He'd thought he could never be that vulnerable again.

He was wrong.

His legs were quivering more than a little jumping rope and footwork in the ring could account for. Riva's thighs trembled against his hips and the elbow bent beside her head to support her weight shook. He slid one arm up her back, taking most of her weight. "I've got you," he said.

She sat upright, her legs falling away from his hips as she did. The movement helped his cock slip from inside her. She winced a little and used both hands to boost herself off the high counter. "Thanks."

Ian looked in the mirror. With the adrenaline rush fading, they were a wreck. His reflection told the story of who he was in this precise moment: a cancer survivor now in great physical shape who'd taken one hell of a beating, then had sex. He worked the condom off his flagging erection, dropped it in the toilet, flushed, then closed the lid.

A crooked smile danced on Riva's mouth. "Thanks," she said again, and sat down. Hard. Her fingers were trembling as she went to work on her bootlaces. Her panties, a pale pink bikini, were still looped around her left ankle. Her dress was beyond repair, several buttonholes torn, buttons missing almost to her waist.

"Sorry about your dress."

"It's fine," she said.

He needed a shower, but his heart was still racing and his vision kept going soft around the edges. Riva had managed to get her boots off, tossing her socks and panties by the door to her bedroom. She scrubbed her hands over her face, then smoothed her wild, thick hair back, her gaze focused on some distant point outside the bathroom, maybe even outside this world.

Ian made an executive decision. "Shower," he said.

"I'll take one in the morning," she said.

"I need you in there with me."

"Why?"

"Because I'm still a little unsteady on my feet."

Her gaze snapped into sharp focus, flicking over his face and torso. "Do I need to take you to the ER?"

"It's not that bad. I don't want to pass out in your shower and hit my head."

"You've got sixty pounds on me. I'm not going to be able to keep you upright if you do pass out." But the words came through her dress as she lifted it over her head.

God. This woman. All in, no matter what.

He reached out and gently squeezed the curvy muscles in her biceps and shoulders. "You look pretty strong to me," he said.

A hint of darkness flashed in her eyes, but she just reached past him and turned on the water in the shower stall. In moments steam billowed into the air over his head. "In you go," she said.

The glass door closed behind them, sealing them in what felt like a hidden grotto, the greens and blues of the tile sleek with water. Ian let out his breath and stepped under the showerhead, then winced as the water rushed into his cuts and all his bruises throbbed. Blood-tinged water flowed into the drain.

Leaning against the opposite wall, Riva slicked back her hair, then let the waterfall rush over her shoulders. "You okay?"

"Never better," Ian said.

Riva gave a delicate snort. "I will never, ever understand men."

"It's just pain," he said. "Pain is manageable. Controllable, even. You learn to go with it, let it be what it is. Fighting it only makes it worse."

"Which of the philosophers said that?"

"All of the ones worth reading," he replied. "It's a universal truth."

"Like death and taxes?"

"Like death and taxes."

She didn't say anything. She didn't move, either, not

to reach for the soap or the shampoo or her razor, sitting in the little niche where she could rest her foot and shave easily. Ian, who could outwait the most reticent of criminals, started talking.

"I'd wanted to go to one of the service academies since junior high, when a West Point graduate came back to speak to the school. My brother, Jamie, joined the navy because he wasn't interested in college, and by twenty, he's a SEAL. Anything Jamie can do, I can do better, so I went into the Naval Academy. I'd graduate, accept my commission, then go through BUD/S. Basic Underwater Demolition/SEAL training, be an officer and a SEAL." He looked at her over his shoulder. "I'm competitive."

"Driven," she said.

"Spring of my junior year I'm a little tired, but nobody at the Naval Academy gets enough sleep. I go to the infirmary, and long story short, my white blood cell count came back off the charts. I was worried I had some kind of infection and I'd have to wait a year. Then we got the diagnosis."

He looked at her.

"I went through treatment but graduated late and was boarded. It means I have my degree, but no commission. No career in the navy. No SEAL teams. My dad was a cop. So I joined the LPD instead. I went from having a future to being a miracle."

He thought back to those early days, how eager and excited most of the other recruits were, how the sheer devastating fury over what he'd lost settled low in his belly. Like a cancer, in fact.

She was watching him, face calm, seemingly unaware of her nudity, or his. "I can imagine how you felt about being a miracle."

He glanced at her, long buried rage warring with unwilling amusement. "You don't have to imagine it. I showed you, every night we spent in the front seat of my car. I was so goddamn angry. I had it under control, but you . . . you pushed my buttons. This is getting pretty close to how I felt then."

"I've always been poking you." She wiggled her fingers at him, long, slender, callused, dripping with water. "Tonight I did it with my fingers, not just my attitude."

He kept both elbows braced on the wall and talked to the floor. "A pretty common thing that happens after a kid or young adult is diagnosed with cancer is we start doing crazy stuff. Blackout drinking. Drugs. One-night stands with strangers we only barely remember. You take a male under the age of twenty-five and give him a life-threatening prognosis, and odds are good he's going to do some crazy shit."

"I assume that's where you picked up your mad dancing skills."

"Yeah," he said, without relish.

"Is that when you started boxing?"

The case was bringing up everything he hated and feared in his past: doubting his body, his inability to control what was happening to him. Ian knew himself too well to blow all of this off; he didn't de-escalate situations. He met them, mastered them. He'd keep ramping up and up and up until somebody got hurt. Or arrested. Or both.

But Riva met him there, in all the ways he could lose control, and didn't flinch. "Yeah. I needed a way to work out the anger. Jamie learned hand-to-hand combat in the navy. He started teaching me techniques that went way beyond what Dad had taught us both, but we both realized pretty fast we'd hurt each other if we kept up. So he got me started at a boxing club. He knew I needed to fight something."

"I'd like to meet him some day." She blushed, looked away.

"Maybe you will," Ian said, because why not? In this shower, anything could happen. "I don't mind being my father's son. I don't mind being in my brother's shadow, just LPD to a Navy SEAL. I never have, because they never thought of it that way. But disappointing them? That was worse than the cancer. And then . . . then I met you."

"Arrested me."

"Yeah."

"Handcuffed me to a table in an interrogation room for over an hour."

"Yeah."

"Gave me the choice of being an informant or going to jail."

"You're not going to forget that, are you?"

She wouldn't meet his eyes. "It's a difficult thing to forget."

"I can't apologize."

"I didn't ask you to." For a few moments the only sound in the room was his occasional caught breath and the water pattering against the tile. "I think you do mind being just LPD to a Navy SEAL," she said. "You don't like failing, but no one does. You really don't like it when things don't go according to your plans."

He shot her a glare.

"Do you think you're somehow different from the rest of us? More special? Godlike in your ability to control the outcome of everything you touch? Everyone's got disappointments. Regrets. Dreams they didn't achieve. Welcome to being human."

Her words stung, because they'd hit home. Hard. "I know that."

"Intellectually, sure. In your heart? In your soul? Nope. Not even close."

"You know, no one else talks to me like you do," he said conversationally. "Not Jamie. Not Jo."

She turned her face to his and grinned. "What, no one else calls you on your bullshit?" Her eyes gleamed. "Well then. You need me, and not just for this."

A thrumming silence hung between them. He couldn't look away. A pale flush bloomed under her freckles before she broke eye contact. He couldn't think about what it would mean to need Riva, so instead he thought about how much he'd loved the Naval Academy, the discipline, the devotion required to become a SEAL. He let the memories of the day they'd packed up his room at the Naval Academy, how he'd held back the tears until they were in the car. How he'd sobbed, his parents in the front seat with nothing to say, bigger worries on their mind. He let himself think about what Jamie knew, did, saw, his service, his experiences, and felt a wave of anger and regret and sadness roll over him. "Yeah, all right, I fucking regret it, and I fucking hate the cancer for taking that chance from me. It's gone, and instead I got to be a miracle."

"Did you ever let yourself feel that regret?"

He huffed out a bitter laugh. "No. Somehow with the cancer and the chemo and the chance I might die, we kind of forgot about it."

"You never forgot."

"You're fucking ruthless, you know that?"

"How do you like me now?" she said. Her tone was light, but her eyes locked on his.

"Is this payback? For before?"

"You keep saying you're not that twenty-five-year-old kid. I'm not eighteen, either. This isn't payback. This is just me."

"Damn," he said.

"You liked me better when I kept my mouth shut and did what I was told, didn't you?"

"You never kept your mouth shut and did what you were told," he said. "I like you now. Not better. I couldn't let myself like you, then."

"But you did. Let yourself like me."

"I did," he admitted. "But it's a slippery slope from liking to abuse of power and authority and we were ass over elbows down it from the moment we made eye contact in the coffee shop."

She looked at him, a nymph in the grotto, chestnut hair and shocking blue eyes, pale skin. Nipples and wet curls and pink-painted toenails. "I regret what I said, about you not knowing what it was like to have to choose between a life you didn't want and death."

"You didn't know about my cancer."

"Or that it cost you a chance at your dream."

"Or that."

"Still. I'm sorry for what you lost."

He shrugged. "I think back on those nights and I remember three things. How badly I wanted you, and how sick that made me feel. How terrified you were when you thought I was going to assault you. And how scared I was for you."

"Scared?"

"CIs die. I was sending you into a dangerous situation, over and over again. I was terrified, every single time."

Like he was now. But not for the reason he thought he'd be frightened. He'd thought telling Riva about his cancer would make him feel vulnerable. But that didn't feel like a risk at all. No, what frightened him the most was that they were currently cocooned in a shower at the home of a sociopath. They were on Rory's territory, and anything could happen.

He had to get Riva out of this nightmare. Then maybe they could figure out what came next.

Exhaustion hit him like one of Trev's punches, fast, sneaky, potent. He got clean more slowly than usual, hampered by his sore ribs and the cuts on his face. Riva was outside the shower and dry, attired in a towel wrapped around her torso, when he shut off the water. He sat down on the toilet and let her close the worst cut with a big butterfly bandage. When he followed her into her bedroom, she said, "Do you think this is a good idea?"

"We're past good and bad. We're into what keeps us safe. Right now I want us all but handcuffed together."

"That'd be new," Riva quipped, but she didn't protest, just pulled her nightie over her head and crawled into bed. Ian tried to settle on his side without sucking in air through his clenched teeth. He failed, and fell asleep waiting for the painkillers to kick in.

The next morning he woke up with Riva burrowed into his side. The windows were still open, the spring air both damp and chilly. He was fine, but despite pulling the duvet up to her ear, Riva had apparently gotten cold overnight and turned without thinking into the nearest heat source: him.

Moving very, very carefully, he turned his head to look at her. She was sound asleep, face adorably slack where it was crammed up against his shoulder, her leg hitched over his thigh, pressing her warm sex into his hip. Her hair was a tangled mess, burnished red against the white pillowcase by the rising sun pouring in through the window.

All this time she'd been the vulnerable one, under his control, afraid of what he could do to her life, her reputation, her freedom. Now it was his turn. He'd trusted her with his deepest truth, the fact of his life he told almost no one. She'd taken it with just the right balance of dispassionate acceptance. With Riva, it didn't define him. She'd been through too much to care about remission or recurrence rates. *Who are you now?* she asked. *What are you doing? Are you more alive?*

He was, he found, fine with Riva holding that detail of his life, one he shared with so few. He didn't just trust her with this operation. He trusted her with himself.

Swiveling his head on his neck hadn't hurt anything, so he risked trying to shift out from underneath her. Pain shot through his ribs at the same time Riva made a snuffling noise. He froze, muscles jerking into rigidity, and waited for the pain to subside.

It did, but with a residual throbbing that told him he'd better not make any quick, abrupt movements for a couple of weeks. Gingerly he touched at his forehead and looked around. The butterfly bandage had held, the sheets still unmarked.

Staying in bed until Riva woke up sounded fantastic.

Unfortunately, he'd taken enough hits in the ring to know that what sounded like the worst idea—moving—was actually the best idea. He tugged his pillow from under his head and tucked it under Riva's. She burrowed into it as he eased off the mattress, then pulled the extra blanket off the quilt stand and tossed it over her for good measure.

In the bathroom he examined himself dispassionately. Black eye, bruised cheek, swollen lip, cut over forehead. Ribs blooming with bruises like his mother's peonies, bright and big and colorful. No big deal. He'd felt worse. He hitch-walked to his bedroom and pulled on a long-sleeved T-shirt and a pair of running shorts. He wouldn't be running, but a walk would be a good idea and would get him clear of the house to make a phone call. He peered out his bedroom window, which overlooked the garage. Rory's car was gone. Presumably Stephanie was still asleep, with Sugar, who was in as much danger as the rest of them. Rory's malevolence threatened everyone within reach.

He let himself out the front door and started walking. A couple of blocks later he could walk without wincing, which was key for any conversation with Jo. She'd pick up on the slightest hint of pain or weakness.

"Are you dead?"

"No."

"Are you near death?"

"No."

"Then why are you calling me at this obscene hour?"

"Jo, it's after seven. Did you do another shift for McCormick?"

"Something like that." Sheets rustled, a pause, probably Jo looking at her phone. "Ugh, you're right."

"Make coffee and call me back."

She hung up on him. Ian kept walking. His muscles were loosening up with movement, so he added a few tentative shoulder rolls, then arm swings, testing his ribs. He'd turned for Henneman's house by the time Jo called back.

"It takes you twenty-five minutes to make coffee?"

"Sometimes. What's going on?"

He brought her up to speed, covering the conversation with Rory, glossing over the boxing injuries.

"You're hurt," she said. "I can hear it in your breathing."

"I'm fine. Bruised, not broken."

"You're an idiot."

"Riva said the same thing."

"I liked that girl seven years ago, and I like her more now."

"She says Rory's wound up, ready to do something big. What are you hearing there?"

"McCormick says there's signs of something big happening, but he doesn't know what. Could be an expansion effort, could be something else. He's meeting with a couple of Kenny's lieutenants later today."

"Let me know as soon as you know," Ian said.

"Obviously. How are things otherwise?"

"Fine," he said. "We're picking up the ingredients for her mom's party later today, then getting ready for it. A cleaning crew is coming through this morning."

"It all sounds very ladies who lunch," Jo said. "Tea and cucumber sandwiches and ten thousand dollar checks. Pinkies up, bitches."

"Part of it is," Ian said. "But Riva's part isn't. She's trying to get her mother out. I thought this was about

Isaiah, but she's actually trying to find a way to help her mother."

"Her mother's a grown woman. She can help herself."

"She's been living with a sociopath for over thirty years. I'm not sure she can operate a light switch."

"True." Jo was silent for a moment. Ian heard the sound of a spoon against china, which didn't make any sense. Jo took her coffee black, and made it in a coffeepot her dad used to own, then poured it directly into a big insulated mug. He couldn't remember the last time he'd seen her drink it from a mug, much less a china cup. Before he could ask, she said, "So what's your plan? How long do you think you can stay after this lunch thing?"

"I don't know. A day, maybe two at the most. If Rory hasn't taken the bait by then, I come home, stay in touch through Ian Fallon's email account, and hope he comes sniffing around."

"Any other options?"

"No."

"If I remember correctly, Ms. Henneman said she'd go into business with him." He heard Jo swallow, then mutter, "Damn, that's good."

"Not an option, Jo."

"It's a very good option, Ian. If Chicago can't get this guy, we can. She's done it before."

"With midgrade dealers, with small stakes, with us supervising her every move. No. That's not an option."

"You may not like it, but it may be our only option. She came to us. If we don't help her, what's to stop her from going to the FBI and making a deal with them?"

The thought sent a bolt of fear up his spine. "Me."

Jo laughed.

"I don't want her in the middle of this, Jo. It's not her job to bring down a major drug pipeline."

"It isn't," Jo agreed with an even tone that set Ian's nerves on edge. "It's her family. She's trying to help her mother and to do that, she has to turn in her father. Don't make this harder for her than it has to be."

"I don't want to make it harder," he snapped, then flinched as his ribs twinged. "I want to make it easier for her."

"Your girl doesn't do easy," Jo said. "Think about it. She could have called in a really expensive lawyer, plead down, gotten off with probation. She didn't. She dealt with us, week after week, rather than slink off and pretend it never happened. Then she dropped out of school and started farming. Remember how God punished Adam for the original sin? He punished him with farming. Cops probably hadn't been invented back then or God would have made Adam a cop."

He heard the clink of silver against china again. "Gone upscale?"

"What?"

"You're drinking your coffee out of a cup. Since when do you use a cup, not a travel mug?"

"The women's magazines all say I should pamper myself."

"Since when do you read women's magazines?"

"It's all over the covers in the checkout lanes."

"Since when do you shop for groceries?" Jo ate better than most cops, but takeout salads were still takeout.

"Stop trying to distract me. I'm curious. Ask her about it."

He'd just found a tentative peace with Riva. He wasn't

about to risk it by asking her to defend her choices made so long ago. "Ask her yourself the next time you see her."

"I will. You don't think I will?"

Fuck. He knew Jo would. "Call me as soon as you hear anything from McCormick."

CHAPTER TWENTY

Her nose woke her up, rich earthy scents winding deep into her brain as she drifted from sleep to wakefulness. The lilac bush in bloom under her window, the scent of the dew on freshly mown grass, the dark layers of mulch laid over all the flower beds and around the trees, cool, crisp morning air that held the promise of warmth.

It was Riva's favorite way to wake up, called out of sleep by nature's smells and sounds, anchoring her consciousness to the life she'd built with her own two hands. The day she woke up and resented what she smelled was the day she put the farm up for sale. But under the scents carried in by the morning breeze was something more primitive, wired to her back brain: the scent of Ian's soap and skin coming from the pillow under her head.

She had a vague memory of turning to him in the middle of the night, blindly seeking the heat his body gave off, and another memory of him tucking a pillow under her head before he eased out of bed. Indulging in a great big yawn, she smoothed her hair back from her face. A stretch made her body hum with residual pleasure, a low, vibrating resonance that softened her joints.

Oh, she was home, asleep in her own bed, which smelled deliciously, sinfully of Ian Hawthorn, which meant what she thought were memories of the last few days were only a dream, an awful dream. Somehow, she couldn't remember exactly how, they'd gotten past their history and were together.

Then she opened her eyes. Guest room. Fireplace, still with the fire unlit. The door to the bathroom was open, the light off; no sounds came from Ian's bedroom.

Wrong dream.

Memory steamrolled her pleasant fantasy, spiking her adrenaline and sending her scrambling out of bed. Where was he? With his ribs as battered as they were she doubted he'd gone for a run. He could be with her dad, doing God only knew what in an effort to worm his way into her dad's confidence. He could be downstairs, reading the paper and drinking coffee. Only one way to find out.

She dressed quickly in clothes suited for a day of work—jeans, a blue V-neck T-shirt, and her Converse sneakers—and trotted down the stairs. The front rooms were empty, silent, dust hanging in the still air. The light was on over the stove in the kitchen, but otherwise, no signs of life or movement. No half-empty coffeepot, no dishes in the sink. He'd basically vanished.

A foot thudded against the back porch, making Riva jump. Ian crossed the veranda and opened the back door. He wore loose shorts and a faded T-shirt advertising a 10K cancer fundraising race back in 2012.

"You went running?" she asked, incredulous.

"Walking. Slowly walking," he said as he closed the door behind him. "Movement's good for sore muscles. Where's your dad?"

"Who knows?"

"Text him and find out if he's at the warehouse today or not. We're going out to pick up the ingredients for the party, right?"

"Yes," Riva said absently as she pulled her phone from her back pocket. *Hi! Are you at the warehouse or on a route today?*

"What else is on the schedule?"

"Um, the rental company is bringing over the chairs and tables today. The forecast is perfect, so we'll set up in the backyard, then cover everything with drop cloths."

"How long until your mom wakes up?"

"I'll get her up after we get back from the grocery run," Riva said. "There's no point in her being awake and fretting over the china or the centerpieces."

"I want to search the house and the warehouse again. I haven't been able to search the third floor because she's been sleeping so much. His laptop has to be here."

"We don't know that," Riva said. "He has breakfast most mornings at a coffee shop about a mile from here. Maybe the owner keeps it there for him."

Ian shook his head. "He wouldn't let it out of his immediate control for the same reason he wouldn't keep it at the boxing gym. It would have to be a place that's safe, secured, where he's confident no one else will get their hands on it. Would he back his data up to the cloud?"

"I can't see him doing that," Riva said. "He wouldn't run the risk of an accidental hack."

"House or warehouse." His words were decisive and blunt. There would be no talking about what happened last night, much less about their emotions. For all she knew, he didn't have any emotions, much less feelings for her. They couldn't act on them anyway. "I'll start down here."

"I need to get organized," she said. "Are you up to lifting and carrying today?"

He nodded, his face already distant.

"What's up?" she asked, keeping her voice low.

He closed the distance between then and bent to murmur in her ear. "Jo says there's something big going down in Lancaster. Soon. She's going to call me as soon as she's got details."

"Okay," she said. She started a pot of coffee while Ian laboriously climbed the stairs to the second floor and returned a minute later wearing a pair of black latex gloves.

While she examined recipes and blocked out the timing to prepare, assemble, and then make different components, backing into the schedule from the moment when everyone sat down to lunch, Ian methodically went through the first and second floors of their house. He pulled up rugs, tested floorboards, removed light switch plates, shook out pillows, and looked in every single pot, pan, and drawer in the kitchen. In the office just off the kitchen, he lifted pictures off the wall and ran his hand over it.

"What are you doing?" she asked.

"Looking for seams," he said.

The whole scene had a surreal feel, windows open to the fresh spring day while a black-gloved, beat-up cop methodically took apart her family home. "Want more coffee?"

"Yes, please."

By the time he reappeared, she had a schedule blocked out down to the minute and a to-do list that covered the front and back of a single sheet of paper.

"Nothing?" she asked.

He'd changed while he was upstairs, and now wore jeans, boots, and a button-down shirt. "Not yet." He stripped off the gloves and tucked them in his jeans pocket. "The third floor makes sense. Your mother's not going to have any idea what he's doing while he's on the laptop."

"I need to pick up the ingredients," she said.

"I'll search the rest of the house when we get back."

She looked at her phone. "Dad says he's running a route today." She handed him the sheet of paper. "That's what we're doing today."

He did a double take. "Okay. Let's get moving. I want to search the warehouse while he's out."

It was funny how easily she and Ian settled into that most mundane of tasks, running errands. They stopped at the upscale party supply shop and picked up the place cards and menu cards, then went to the florist. She'd half suspected Ian would brood in the truck, but to her surprise, he stayed by her side the whole time, carrying bags and boxes of floral arrangements without complaint.

"Thanks," she said after he secured the florist's boxes in the truck's bed.

"For what?" he said, surprised.

"For helping," she said quietly. "With everything."

She had so much more to say, but the day had taken on a surreal quality, fresh green leaves dancing in the sunshine and soft breeze while she ran errands with Ian for a garden party and Ian plotted how to root out drugs and corruption and keep them safe.

"You're welcome," he said, just as quietly.

She was once again left with the feeling that everything about them was too big, too explosive, too charged to fit into a day-to-day life. They had baggage, history, friction, and then something like this happened, the kaleidoscope shifted and the fragments were just colored beads, bit of glass, nothing more. They were just Ian and Riva, running errands. Like normal people. Like a couple. Like a normal couple.

He looked at her to-do list. "All we have left is to pick up the ingredients from Urban Canopy and Growing Home," he said. "And hit the warehouse."

"Let's do the warehouse first," she said. "I don't want to leave the ingredients out in the hot sun."

"Fair enough."

"Stop here."

Riva's truck wasn't visible through the office window or door. The site was quiet, no one coming or going. She peered out the windshield, then at Ian, who was doing some cop-radar-listening thing. "Why?"

"I don't want to just rock up to the door and find him there."

"Why not?"

"We have no reason to be there."

"Sure we do."

"We do?"

"I want candy for the party tomorrow," Riva said. "I'm making dirt cakes for dessert."

"You're making what?" Ian asked.

"Dirt cakes. They're a refrigerated pudding cake. You use crumbled cookies as the 'dirt' and get gummy worms and fake flowers for decorations."

He gaped at her. "Really?"

"No. But I told Dad it was a way to promote Henneman Candy and Vending. A boost for business. That kind of thing. He believed that. I already texted and asked if I could grab some packages of cookies and gummy worms."

"Nice," he said. "What are you going to do tomorrow when you serve those chocolate bomb cake things?"

"I'll tell him I got worried about being too cute, or the worms didn't go with the napkins, or I couldn't find any unglazed flower pots. You can't make them in glazed pots."

Ian didn't seem interested in this detail. "What if he's got the laptop with him?"

"We still need to do the search. You never know what we might find."

They pulled up to the gate. Riva keyed in the code and drove through the gate when it opened. She parked in front of the building and looked around.

"What?" Ian asked.

"Dad's car isn't here."

"So?"

"He said he's running a route. If that's the case, he'd leave his car here."

"Maybe he changed his mind," Ian said. "Do the drivers ever come back for something they forgot?"

She shook her head. "Unless there's some special request, they usually just fill the machine with what they've got."

"Still. I don't want to be here any longer than I have to."

They quickly searched the warehouse to make sure they were alone, then Ian went to work again, this time pulling at the carpet to make sure it didn't roll back.

They stood in the warehouse and looked at the wall-to-wall shelving holding hundreds of boxes.

"High or low?" Ian said.

"Low," she replied.

He grabbed a couple of boxes of snack-package Oreos and the gummy worms. Keeping an ear cocked for movement in the office, she pushed over the rolling ladder and went to work, shaking boxes to gauge their weight, riffling through packages of candy. They worked quickly, thoroughly, and found nothing at all.

Ian appeared unfazed. "Had to be done," he said.

She stripped off her gloves and rubbed her eyes. "Let's get going. The rental delivery people will be there around four."

She felt like she was racing the clock in every way possible, her mother's luncheon, getting her dad's laptop, and her time with Ian. They made stops at Growing Home and Urban Canopy for the luncheon ingredients, then pulled up alongside the house just as the delivery truck was backing into the driveway. "Can you unload the perishables?" she asked. "If you run out of room up here, there's a fridge in the basement. I'll deal with it later."

"I've got it," Ian said.

She directed the rental company in setting up the tables and chairs, counted the linens and drop cloths to protect the furniture, signed for everything, and then headed into the house. The truck started with a rumble, and she sent them off with a wave. In the kitchen Ian had unloaded everything, neatly sorting things into their projected uses.

"Why doesn't this surprise me?" She set the linens on the table next to the place cards and menus.

He surveyed the piles. "You're going to have to sort it eventually. Might as well do it when you're unloading it. What next?"

"I'll go upstairs and see what Mom's doing," she said. "I don't think she's been out of bed all day, and that's not like her."

His eyebrows rose. "I'll wait in my room and head up when you get her downstairs."

She climbed the steps to the second floor, then walked through the unused spare room to what looked like a closet door, opened it, and climbed the steps to the third-floor master suite. Her mother and the architect had worked out a way to remove the original walls sectioning the space into two rooms and a bath in between; now the small landing at the top of the stairs opened on her parents' bedroom to her left which flowed into a sitting area cuddled around a deep window seat that overlooked the backyard. The bath and closet were discreetly tucked away to her right.

Her mother was sitting in the window seat, a hazelnut cashmere throw draped over her lap. Her blond hair hung lank around her face. Riva crossed the gleaming maple hardwood floor and sat down at the opposite end of the window seat.

"Hi, Mom," she said. "I didn't know you were up."

"My head hurt." A faded smile, a pause. "Is everything coming together?"

"We're on schedule." She reached for her mother's hand, chafed the limp, cold fingers between her own. Her hand was far too cold for someone sitting in the sunshine under a wool blanket. "How are you feeling?"

Another pause. "Fine."

"Mom." Her voice was a little sharper. She turned her

mother, as unresisting as a small child, away from the sunlight and peered into her eyes. The pupils didn't move, even though she was facing the darker room. "Did you take something today?"

"Your father gave me some pills before he left. He said I should take them if I wanted to be his good girl."

Warning bells went off in Riva's head. "Where does he keep the pills, Mom?"

Her mother lifted a hand in the direction of the bathroom. Riva hurried through the door and flung open drawers and doors to the vanity. She counted over a dozen bottles rattling in the second drawer, with more in the third. Riva stared at the bottles, too many for her to hold in her hands. How on earth had he gotten a doctor to prescribe all of these for her mother?

Then she sprinted back down the stairs and found Ian on the landing to the third floor. "What's going on?"

"Come look in the drawers in the bathroom. There's enough medication in there to drop a herd of elephants!" She clutched her hair in her hands. "He's been *drugging her.* He's gotten her addicted to Percocet and Oxy-Contin! How could I have done this? How could I leave her here for so long?"

Ian grabbed her shoulders and turned her to face him. "Riva. You've been on a plane, right?"

She stared at him, so solid and true and real. "What? Of course I have."

"Remember the safety check? If the cabin loses oxygen, you put on your own mask before helping your child or anyone else. Remember."

His warm, firm hands helped her focus. The little yellow margarine cups, the stretchy elastic bands, the smiling cabin attendants. "Yes. I remember."

"You were putting on your own mask. That's all. We're here now. We're going to fix it now. We will end this. I swear to you, we will end this."

She stared at him, torn between fear and despair and a wild hope because he kept saying *we*. *We're here now. We'll fix this, end this. We.*

They were a *we*.

"Go sit with your mom and keep an eye out for your dad," Ian said urgently. His heart soared at the delight in Riva's eyes when he said "we," but first he had to get them all as far away from Rory as possible. "He could be home any minute."

They took the stairs in a rush, Riva hurrying over to her mother while Ian turned and strode to the bathroom. Riva was right. The drawers in the vanity contained several thousand dollars' worth of antipsychotics and painkillers. The OxyContin alone was worth over a thousand bucks on the street. Unfortunately, neither the vanity nor the wardrobe nor the shelves and drawers cunningly tucked into the eaves and window seat nor the mattress and box spring nor the nightstands contained Rory's laptop or any other incriminating notebooks, index cards, tablets. Nothing.

Ian stripped off his gloves and shoved them in his back pocket. His search had turned up nothing more interesting than a stash of porn tucked behind Rory's nightstand, a finding he would not be sharing with Riva, who, while he searched, had gently enticed her mother down the stairs with tempting offers of coffee and biscotti.

His phone vibrated in his pocket. *Dad's on his way upstairs.*

He hustled down the narrow stairwell and crossed the floor to look out the windows at the street below. Rory walked into the little library.

"Hey, Rory," Ian said, striving for friendly. "I was just enjoying the view."

"It's a really prime piece of real estate," Rory said easily. "Have fun today?"

Ian took a chance. "Yeah," he said, allowing just a hint of reluctance to creep into his tone. "To be honest, it's not all I thought it would be."

"Really? You're ready to go back to the IT department?"

"No way," Ian said. Determined, this time. "I still want to be my own boss, but I want something a little more exciting than farm-fresh fruits and vegetables."

Rory looked Ian right in the eye for a long minute. "Exciting."

"You know." Ian huffed like he was irritated with himself. "I'm tired of being a good guy all the time. All the same guys competing for all the same promotions or projects. It's all so . . . boring. I don't give a shit if I get the next promotion, because it's all the same bullshit anyway. Once I started boxing, started reading up on the street fighters, met some guys, my horizons expanded, you know what I'm saying?"

He made like he'd said too much. "Look, I'm not saying Trev's like that. But in Lancaster, there's all kinds of interesting deals being made at the boxing gyms, with the guys the boxers know. Trev's pretty serious. He wouldn't get into that. But they're talking about the kind of business, and money, that's not playing for forty K a year and benefits."

"Lancaster's been a possible expansion zone for me for a while."

Adrenaline dumped into Ian's bloodstream. Yes. Finally. This was it.

"I'm looking for someone to work for me. I'd hoped that someone could be Riva, but she's proved . . . not up to the task."

"In the vending machine business," Ian said, sounding dubious. "That's . . . interesting."

"That's only one part of the business." Rory's eyes were heavy lidded. "I'm looking for the right guy to run that expansion, and a couple of other sideline jobs."

Ian perked right up at that. "A chance to go into business with you? Let's talk."

Rory smiled, almost fondly. "Now?"

Was he laying it on too thick? Too obvious? That was the trouble with sociopaths. They were impossible to read. "I've got nothing better to do."

"What about Riva and the party?"

He put a little mocking into his half laugh. Rory wouldn't want a potential business partner to be more devoted to Riva than him. He'd love to see Ian ditch Riva for him. "She's got it under control."

"Let's go."

They drove through the spring sunlight, the golden glow to the world almost unreal. Rory didn't say much, and Ian found the silence a little unnerving. Unsettling. His radar was going off like crazy, something was wrong, something was very, very wrong, but he didn't know what. He was trained to stay with that feeling, deal with it, and do his job.

He got a text and hit the button on his phone to read it.

From Jo: *Get out of there.*

"Everything ok?" Rory said.

"Fine. I just need to call a coworker about a problem they can't fix without me. Look, it's really not a good time right now," he said when Jo picked up.

She kept her voice down. "According to McCormick, Kenny said their Chicago connection was taking a dog to get neutered. That's code for getting rid of a rival, or a snitch. Get out, Ian. Get out now."

It felt hinky, as Jo liked to say. The bones at the base of his skull were vibrating. He wasn't in any danger, and if he backed out now, Rory wouldn't let him in again. Which left Riva vulnerable to her father's devastating form of manipulation and cruelty. He had his chance, right now, and he wasn't going to throw it away and hope for a better one to show up at some random moment in the future.

He went for a hint of impatience. "I'm on my way to a really important meeting. I don't have my computer with me. I'll look at this when I get home."

He hung up on Jo's hissed *goddammit, Ian.* "Database issues," he said. "I swear to God no one can run the nightly file imports without me."

"They're going to have to learn," Rory said genially.

Was he going to take Ian to some warehouse and shoot him in the head? Ian knew the streets they were driving. They were headed straight to Sweet Science. No big deal. When they got to the gym, they walked through the front door. Micah knelt on the floor of the boxing ring, hands secured behind his back with a zip tie. Trev stood over him, his face blank as the cabinet fronts in Rory's kitchen.

Ian slowed his step. Jo and McCormick had it wrong. Ian's cover wasn't blown. Micah's was.

"Isn't that the guy from that meeting we went to a couple of days ago?"

"The HR guy?" Rory ducked under the ropes. Ian followed him in, hoping he seemed eager, intentionally staying close to do what he could to deflect attention from Micah. "It is, and it isn't. He's actually a cop."

Micah wasn't looking at him. He stared straight at the floor, head down. Ian let out a low whistle. "No way. Um, I don't want to tell you how to run your business, but isn't assaulting a cop a pretty risky thing to do? Like, they don't stop searching until they find you?"

"I'm not going to assault him," Rory said, still smiling genially. "You're going to do it."

Just like that, the spot where his skull met his spinal cord started to hum. That was the trick, the evil, the danger. Because no one knew where he was. Jo wouldn't stop with the phone calls, but it would take time for her to get in touch with the right people at the CPD, and even then, they'd be searching for a Lancaster cop. If they didn't know about Micah, she might not get them moving in time to stop whatever was going to happen.

Whatever Ian was going to have to do.

Get out of this. Get out now, call 911, get an immediate, coordinated response that would be like the fist of God landing on this building. He held up his hands and started backing away, trying to stay in character. "Look, I know I said I was interested in going into business together, but this is way out of my league."

A click. Trev held a gun to the base of Micah's skull. Micah flinched. "Whoa, whoa!" Ian shouted.

"Did you think this was going to be like kids playing cops and robbers?" Rory laughed, an evil delight in his eyes. "You either get in the ring and deal with him, or Trev blows his brains out. Then he'll blow yours out."

"Why me? I'm not going to tell anyone. I promise," Ian babbled, staying in character.

Rory gave him the shark's grin. "Remember what I said about killer instinct? Let's see if you've got it."

Beat him up or he dies. The command was so crazy it took Ian a moment to process it. Rory was ordering him to beat Micah with his bare hands. It was the product of an insane mind, a brutal death for Micah. Landing a single punch would permanently scar Ian to his soul. He'd boxed at the gym. He'd participated in the department's tournament. But that was with gloves, against men and women he knew were trained to fight, and in the ring by choice. Micah, if he remembered correctly, had never even played contact sports in high school. He was a state champion gymnast.

Micah looked up at Ian, a desperate challenge in his eyes. Ian climbed in the ring, and nodded at the zip tie. "Cut those off him."

"What?"

"The plastic thing," he said, trying hard not to sound like a cop, gesturing at the restraints. He threw a quick glance at the front windows. Not a single scrape in the paint covering the glass. No one would have any idea what was going on in here. "Cut it off him. He gets a chance."

"Fine," Rory said, lifting a finger toward Trev, "but if you lose to him, you both die. I guarantee the Chicago

Police Department gave him some hand-to-hand-combat training."

Trev leaned over and used a bowie knife to cut the zip tie off Micah's wrists. Micah rubbed them, rolled his shoulders back and forward, trying to regain circulation. Ian stepped into the ring. "Gloves?"

"Bare knuckles," Rory said. "Get to it."

Micah was no idiot. His gaze flickered all over Ian's body, studying stance and hips and shoulders, raised hands. He'd know a little bit about punching—every guy did—but Ian was most concerned about showing him how to block.

"Come on, you stupid motherfucker," Micah said. "If I'm going down, you're going down with me."

Ian almost smiled. Instead he hit him, feinting with his left before landing a sharp jab with his right. He pulled the punch as much as he dared, but Rory and Trev would both know a real punch from a pulled one. Micah's head snapped to the side and he staggered a couple of steps. Blood streamed from the cut Ian's knuckles opened over his left eye. He touched his face, then looked at Ian, incredulous.

Then he turned and barreled right at Ian. It was an all-out brawl, rolling on the ground, grunting and cursing, Ian howling at punches Micah landed, theatrically swinging his fists and landing in spots that wouldn't do much damage. Micah's shoulder rather than his face, his hip rather than his kidney. But every time they drew back, panting, Micah was bleeding from a new spot, a cut lip, his nose. Try as he might, Ian hadn't been able to avoid landing body blows, gut, ribs, low back. The line between a real fight and a partially faked one still meant two out of three hits landed. They landed softer, or they landed in less sensitive places, but they still landed.

Micah bulled in close again. Ian aimed for his chest but Micah pulled back reflexively at the last second and Ian's fist caught him right in the chin. His head snapped back with a sickening crack and he slumped to the floor, unconscious. His breathing started to gurgle. Ian used his foot to turn his head to the side so he wouldn't choke on his own blood.

"I need a minute," he said to Rory, not having to fake his rough breathing. He looked at Trev. "Get me some water."

Trev looked at Rory. Rory waited a beat, then nodded.

Ian swiped at the sweat and blood on his face. "You've seen enough."

"So has he," Rory said. "He'll remember your face, and mine. Kill him."

"Fine, but not like this," Ian said. "I'm sore and I'm fucking tired after the beating your boy gave me yesterday. I'm not going to punch him to death in here. There's no way you'll get the DNA out of the ring. Don't you watch *CSI*?"

Rory laughed. Trev came back with a bottle of water and chucked it at Ian. "What are you proposing?"

"Give me the gun and I'll drive him somewhere and finish him."

Rory used another one of those minimalist hand gestures to indicate Trev should climb into the ring. "With the money I'm going to make on this deal, I can buy another boxing ring. Kill him. You, watch."

CHAPTER TWENTY-ONE

The air froze in Ian's lungs. Trev was in the ring, lifting his arm to aim the Glock at Micah's unconscious body. A beat of silence followed, interrupted by a harsh, metallic thunking sound.

An unmistakable *shutk-chutk*, metallic, weighty, powerful.

A singular noise, not a buzz or a whine or a thud, but mechanical, insistent, and dangerous.

The most recognizable sound in the modern world. Rory and Trev turned to look for the person holding the shotgun.

Ian didn't.

In the space between one racing heartbeat and the next, Ian knew everything he needed to know about anything, ever, for the rest of his life. Riva was here. She'd come to the club, taken the gun from behind the driver's seat of her father's truck, walked into the club, and cocked it. He didn't know how she knew to come here, and he didn't care. All he knew was that his soul, wounded and half alive for so long, soared with joy.

In the split second when Rory and Trev looked for the significant sound, Ian moved without thinking. Fuck boxing. He went straight for the hand-to-hand-combat moves he'd learned from Jamie. He spun low and fast, leg extended, and delivered one hard kick to the side of Trev's knee. The joint gave a sickening crunch. Mouth open in a soundless wail, Trev collapsed and reached for his knee. Ian punched Trev's wrist. He dropped the gun. Ian grabbed it and lunged to his feet, then swung the butt of the Glock at Trev's skull. He dropped to a limp sprawl, unconscious before he face-planted into the mat.

Ian put himself between Micah, terrifyingly silent and still, and Rory. "Police. Get down on the ground."

Rory laughed. "What?"

"Lieutenant Ian Hawthorn, Lancaster Police Department. Get down on the ground."

Casual and calm, Rory turned away from Ian and looked straight at his daughter. "Riva. What's this all about?"

Riva's hands were steady on the shotgun, aimed directly at her father. "You heard him."

"He's got no authority here."

"Then I'm making a citizen's arrest," Riva said.

"For what? I've done nothing wrong. He's the one who beat up that cop. Not me."

He was walking toward Riva, his face that smiling, sane mask that frightened Ian more than any hopped-up, screaming, incomprehensible junkie. At least you knew what the junkie was thinking.

"Stop where you are, Henneman."

Rory ignored him and continued walking toward Riva. "Did you know he was a cop?"

"No," Ian said. He flicked a glance at Trev. Still out for the count. Unfortunately, so was Micah. He could use a Chicago cop right now. "She didn't know anything. I lied to her."

Riva's stance never wavered. "Shut up, Ian. Of course I knew. Dad, stop where you are right now, or I swear to fucking God, if he doesn't shoot you, I will."

"You wouldn't kill your own father. I'd know if you had that kind of backbone, you betraying little bitch."

She had nowhere else to go. Ian could see the shotgun was locked and loaded, shell in the chamber, safety off. "Riva, put the gun down."

"Just so we're clear, if I do pull the trigger, it's because I wanted to. Not because you made me."

Riva's tone was matter-of-fact and bone-certain, drawing strength from deep inside her. Rory hesitated before taking the next step, but not from fear. He wanted Riva to think about it, to understand what she was going to have to do, to anticipate it, dread it. You could think through a lifetime of consequences in a single moment. Ian knew that, because the moment after *it's cancer* held the life he would never have, the navy, the SEALs. He'd been living in that moment for over a decade.

No more. Not for him, and not for Riva.

"Stop. Now."

Rory turned to see Ian aiming at him. "You going to blow my brains out in front of her?" His voice was congenial.

"I'd rather make sure you rot away in a prison cell," Ian said, "but if you take one more step toward her, you're a dead man."

Rory's knee flexed, lifting his foot off the floor. Ian's finger was sliding to the trigger when a loud bang blew the front door open. In a matter of seconds the room filled with Chicago police officers, some in uniform, some wearing windbreakers with CPD on the back, all of them shouting as they pointed guns at Ian, at Riva, and at Rory Henneman, who'd ducked for cover when the battering ram tore the door right off its hinges.

"I'm a police officer! I'm a police officer!" Ian said loudly. Even as he spoke he raised his hands over his head. He knew it wouldn't matter. Protocol in this situation said to get everyone disarmed and restrained, then sort things out later.

"Jesus Christ," one of the guys behind Ian said. He heard a low moan from Micah. "Who did this to you?"

The cop by Ian took one look at his bloody knuckles, the bruises on his face and body, then his eyes went blank. Hard. "You did this?"

"I'm a lieutenant with the Lancaster Police Department. It was that or shoot him," Ian said.

"He's telling the truth" came weakly from Micah.

"Drop it!" an officer shouted at Riva. Gun drawn, extended, wild around the eyes in a way Ian didn't like.

She looked frantically at Ian. "It's okay," he said, calm and controlled, because the last thing they needed was for the situation to escalate. It was a miracle her hand hadn't convulsed and pulled the trigger when all hell broke loose. "Riva. It'll be okay. Put it down."

She flipped on the safety and bent over to set the shotgun on the floor, going straight to her knees from there. The officer shoved her forward. She barely broke her fall with her hands.

"Lighten the fuck up," Ian snapped just as he got

shoved to his knees as well. A uniformed officer cuffed him, then hauled him to his feet and walked him over to where Riva was getting cuffed.

"Sit."

"This is different," Riva said.

She sat cross-legged on the floor, her hands cuffed behind her back, which was as uncomfortable as she remembered. Next to her, Ian sat in a similar pose, his gaze focused on the team of EMTs around Micah.

"Not the being-cuffed part. You being cuffed with me. It's not much fun, is it?"

"I've been cuffed before," he said.

"When?"

"It's part of the training at the academy."

"Oh. I thought maybe you were a little kinky."

The look on his face was priceless. "You're joking at a time like this?"

"I must be in shock." It was a reasonable guess. Sixty seconds earlier she'd been two steps away from shooting her father with his own Remington 870 Express. She couldn't make sense of the chaos in the club—EMTs trotting in with bags and a gurney, a woman in a CPD windbreaker, gun and badge on her belt, pointed and directed while talking on her cell phone, looking at Riva, then Ian, then Rory and Trev. "In hindsight, you were very gentle with me seven years ago."

Ian was watching with a much more alert gaze as they lifted Micah onto the gurney and covered him with a blanket. "Different circumstances. One of their own is going to end up in the hospital."

"Is that going to get you in trouble?"

"I hope I'll get a chance to explain before I disappear

into a back room with the three biggest guys here," Ian said. "How did you know to come find me?"

"Sorenson called. You know how she's always level and laidback and a little sarcastic?"

"Yeah."

"She was ice. Short sentences, mostly commands. I was in my truck and driving before I really understood what she'd said."

Ian's cover has been blown. He's with your dad, and your dad's going to kill him if you don't find him. Think, Riva. Where did they go?

Sweet Science.

She'd known in her bones before her brain even caught up, steering not to the warehouse but to the gym. It had taken her two seconds. They weren't at home. Her father wouldn't jeopardize the business. So they were at the club.

"She called the Chicago police but had a hard time getting through to someone who would actually mobilize on the situation. So I told her about meeting Micah, and maybe he was in danger? I lied about that part, but I know cops well enough to know they'll move heaven and earth to save one of their own. She had me on her cell and the CPD on another phone," Riva said.

"She was probably at home. She wouldn't want to alert our department to the situation, in case that blew our internal case." He paused. "What made you get the gun out of your father's truck?"

"I'm tired of this bullshit." She surprised herself with her matter-of-fact tone, but she was done, down to the very marrow of her bones. "I am so fucking tired of this bullshit. I wasn't thinking clearly. Maybe I would have . . . I don't know. I wouldn't have . . . maybe. He makes me *crazy*."

"Riva," Ian said gently. "You weren't crazy. You were frosty."

"I was *terrified*. He's had my mom, he's had Sugar. Now he had you. That was the final straw. All I could think about was getting to you. But I'll take frosty. It sounds better than scared shitless. All I could think was that I was getting you away from him, and then all of us were going home. You, me, Sugar, and my mom."

She stifled a giggle. It wasn't easy, because the sound started deep in her belly, ricocheting around her throat on its way up. But if she started laughing, she wouldn't stop. She'd held her father at gunpoint. She'd saved Ian. And Micah, and her mom, and Sugar. The day had reached a pitch of crazy so supersonic she was surprised it hadn't left contrails in the atmosphere.

The urge to laugh subsided, although she suspected something would work its way out eventually. But she was safe. Her father was under arrest. She was safe. She'd done it.

"The sound of a shotgun being cocked," Ian said.

"I hoped you'd know it was me holding the gun," Riva replied.

"I did," Ian said. "I didn't even have to look. Deep down, I knew you'd have my back."

But knowing she'd have his back didn't mean she'd have a future with him, and they both knew it.

A tall woman with dark brown hair pulled back in a ponytail and a cell phone to her ear approached Ian. "Lieutenant Morales, CPD. Who are you?"

"I'm Lieutenant Ian Hawthorn of the Lancaster Police Department," he said patiently.

"You got any ID?"

Riva looked over at him. He was wearing the cargo pants and running shoes he'd worn all day. "My ID is tailored to my cover," Ian said, less patiently. "Call Captain Eli Swarthmore. He'll verify my identity."

"I've got a Detective Joanna Sorenson on the phone. Any identifying marks?" she said, her gaze flicking professionally over Ian's chest.

Jo must have given the right answers, because the woman lifted her chin to get the attention of a nearby cop. "Uncuff him. He's one of us. My captain will be calling your captain about this, Detective," she said into the phone. "Hell, your chief might get a call from ours. You better have a good reason for beating the hell out of my officer."

"It was beat him up or kill him," Ian snapped. "I pulled my punches best I could."

"He did," Micah called weakly as the EMTs started wheeling him toward the door. "Lieutenant, he tried. This could have been worse."

Morales didn't look convinced. "What the fuck is the Lancaster Police Department doing running an undercover operation on CPD's turf?"

"We've been investigating a group of corrupt cops using their influence and inside knowledge to take over the drug trade in Lancaster. My associate had a way to get the evidence we needed to indict the cops and get Rory too."

"And you are?"

"I'm Riva Henneman."

The woman's gaze sharpened. "Henneman? Any relation to Rory Henneman?"

"My father."

"What the hell was going on?"

Ian succinctly laid out the framework of the case. "I was trying to get inside," Ian said. "Yesterday he had me fight the other guy in the ring. Trev. This was supposed to be proof of my willingness to play ball."

"Did you get the evidence?"

"No." Ian blew out his breath, then laced his hands behind his head. He must be glowing with adrenaline, because the movement didn't even hurt. "Fuck. We didn't get anything. He's got a laptop somewhere. I've seen it, but it's not on him now."

Rory gave him a vicious smile.

"It's got to be here," Riva said. "It has to. It's not at home, and it's not in his office."

"Fucking tear that office apart," Ian said.

"We already are," Morales said grimly.

A low whistle came from the office, then one of the CPD officers came out of the gym's office with a laptop in his hand. "I found this, Lieutenant," he called. "He had a little hidey-hole under the filing cabinet. And . . . there's about twenty kilos of heroin and a couple hundred grand in the same space."

"That's not my laptop," Rory said distantly. "I don't own this building, and I don't know anything about what goes on in the office. I just sponsor a boxer who works out here."

They opened the lid. "Password protected," Morales said. "Great."

"May I?" Riva said. Her heart was pounding, trying to crawl out of her throat.

"No way, LT," one of the other cops said. "She could erase the drive."

"You trust her?" Morales said to Ian.

"With my life," Ian said.

Morales unfastened Riva's cuffs and folded them away. Riva took the laptop and set it on the boxing ring floor. Ian lifted the ropes out of her way. She looked at the password box, then at her father.

For a moment, all Riva noticed was what she wasn't thinking or feeling. She wasn't thinking about how easy it would be to type in the wrong password, erase the data, say she'd been wrong. She wasn't thinking that maybe, just maybe, if she did this thing for him, her dad would love her then, choose her, say she'd done well. This wasn't a fork in the road, a place where she made the choice that changed her life forever. She'd done that years ago, when Ian had asked her if she wanted a lawyer present, and she'd said no.

She set her fingers on the keyboard and entered *icantremember*.

The little icon jiggled. She blinked.

Rory laughed, the sound mean, mocking, dismissive.

She tried again, this time entering *ican'tremember*.

The lock screen disappeared. "It's 'I can't remember'," she said. "The first time I didn't enter the apostrophe. He thinks it's clever, when someone asks him what his password is, to say 'I can't remember'."

"You little bitch."

Ian moved so fast all she saw was bunched muscles and a flurry of movement, then Rory was hauled off the floor and slammed back against the wall. "You lost. You hear me? You lost the most valuable thing in the world, your daughter's love, trust, respect, using her to set up your little satellite operation in Lancaster. She was just a kid, your own flesh and blood, and you hid behind her."

"She was a worthless girl. Just like her mother."

Ian fisted his hands in Rory's shirt, yanked him forward, and slammed him into the wall. Rory's head thudded against the bricks, then his eyes rolled back in their sockets and he slumped in Ian's hold. None too gently, Ian let him slide down the wall to the floor. Everyone in the immediate vicinity turned to look at him.

"He slipped," Ian said curtly.

No one said anything. They were avoiding looking at Riva, still standing in front of her father's laptop.

"He's got a partitioned drive," a cop wearing black gloves said. "It's password protected."

"Try the same one," Riva said. Her lips felt numb, bloodless.

"I'm in. Spreadsheets up the fucking ass . . . Man, I love criminals who keep detailed records," he said after a moment. "It's all here. Records of intake from . . . Jesus, there's half the known list here. Bank accounts, offshore accounts, details about deliveries. God*damn*. This is the fucking jackpot."

"He's a businessman," Riva said. "Accounts for every penny."

Her head was clanging, her voice coming from a long way away, like outside the building, or maybe outside the state. She was watching Ian look at her, watching emotion flick over his face, almost too quick to catch. Now they had the proof. Her father was a large-scale drug distributor. There was no way he could be with her and advance the career that had meant everything to him since his diagnosis.

It was over.

He wouldn't look at her, instead watching the EMTs wheel Micah out.

Morales yelled, "Statement time, Hawthorn. Are you going first or is Ms. Henneman?"

For the first time in her relationship with Ian, she would make things easy for him, not harder. "At least this part's familiar," she said, mustering a smile. "Mind if I go first? I have to go home. I need to tell my mother what's happened."

"Sure," he said. "I'll make arrangements for you. What are you going to do?"

"I'm going to call the committee chairs and cancel the luncheon. Then I'm going to pack my mom's suitcase and take her and Sugar back to Lancaster with me. She needs to start over from scratch." She gave a small, humorless laugh. "She might need time in a treatment facility. I don't know. Maybe the farm will heal her. It healed me."

"This isn't over, Riva."

"I know. Interviews and depositions and trial preparation and trial, and this time the media will be all over it. But things can only get better from here, thanks to you," she said. "Come back to Oasis anytime."

"Thanks," he said, his attention focused on his ringing cell phone. "That's my captain. I have to go. I'll see you soon."

He wouldn't, and they both knew it.

CHAPTER TWENTY-TWO

Riva eased into the porch swing and tucked her feet underneath her, the better to watch the glorious May sunset. She'd had a long day on the farm, starting at sunrise with work in the fields and greenhouses, a hasty lunch with her mother, and was taking a short break before starting an afternoon session with the kids from the ESCC. Her mother was throwing a tiny pink cat-shaped toy for Sugar, who'd taken to farm life with a delight they both needed. Watching Sugar's pink bow bob up and down in the long grass as she chased birds and insects made them laugh. The bow was grimy now, Sugar's once-pristine fur matted and tangled. Her mother said she'd never seen her happier.

She checked her cell phone for missed calls, messages, and emails. It had taken a couple of days, but the *Lancaster Star Trib* had tracked down the connection between the arrests of nearly a dozen crooked cops to her father's arrest in Chicago. After that news outlets in both cities circled her like sharks on fresh chum, trying to get in touch with her, the local press going so far as to do stories on the road outside her farm. She'd ordered them off the property to protect her mother, canceled a week's worth of sessions with the ESCC kids, but the stories still aired. The next day a young uniformed police officer knocked on her door and introduced himself, then sat in his parked cruiser just beside the farm's sign, keeping the reporters at bay. She suspected Ian's hand in that.

A quick scan through her recent calls indicated another one from Kelly. She owed her a call, and not just because Kelly had called every other day for over a week. Her best friend was due an explanation.

"Hey, oh my God, how are you?" Kelly said without preamble. "Are you okay? Is your mom okay?"

"She's through the worst of the withdrawal symptoms," Riva said, remembering the restlessness, the tremors, the total loss of appetite. "She was pretty anxious, and we took lots of long walks. I think being on the farm really helped."

"The farm, and being with you," Kelly said staunchly. "It's been a tough couple of weeks. What do you need?"

Riva blinked back tears as she watched the goats munch on their evening ration of hay. She could see Kelly's house now, the wooden blocks and soft toys on the living room floor, Wyatt cruising the furniture, babbling the whole way. "I'm fine. We're both fine," she said staunchly. "But thanks for the offer. I'm just calling to give you the whole story."

"I want to hear it," Kelly said. "I'm just going to blow bubbles for Wyatt while you talk."

Without thinking, she started at the beginning and went through until that terrible moment at Sweet Science. Hearing Kelly's soft, slow puffs of air, imagining the iridescent bubbles floating to the sky and Wyatt's little giggles made it so much easier to tell the tale.

"Ian's a cop."

"Yes."

"He arrested you seven years ago."

"Yes."

"Wow," Kelly said, an understatement if Riva had ever heard one. "But you didn't go to jail."

"I was never officially charged. I helped him, and the arrest never happened."

"That's why you dropped out. Disappeared."

"Yes. Through his eyes I saw what I'd become, and I was so ashamed. The only thing worse than being a teenage drug dealer was being a teenage drug dealer because I thought it would make my daddy love me."

"Oh, honey," Kelly said.

"It's no big deal," Riva lied. "I haven't talked to him since I left Chicago. It's not like television. When something like this goes down, it's a fire drill for days, maybe weeks, and he was involved in both the Chicago and Lancaster situations. I gave my statement, packed up Mom and Sugar, and came home. It was just the heat of the moment," she said firmly. Like she could talk herself into believing that.

"Honey, I know heat of the moment, and I saw you two at Lit. That wasn't heat of the moment. If it was heat of the moment it would have faded, not grown stronger."

Riva tucked a faded chintz pillow under her head and lay down on the swing. The beadboard over her head needed a new coat of paint, she noted in the back of her brain as she remembered Ian's "fantasies." Helping her. Asking her out. "Do people change?"

"You did."

Riva didn't say anything. It was true. She had changed. She'd started the moment Ian arrested her and was still changing. She wouldn't have been strong enough to face down her father if Ian hadn't bared his soul to her.

Ian did bare his soul, scars and all, to her.

"Look at this from his point of view. He's had all the power, all the authority. But maybe he's afraid you won't want him. Maybe he's waiting for you to come to him."

She remembered his face when he told her about his cancer diagnosis, his shattered dreams. Maybe he hadn't come to see her because he was afraid she would see him as damaged goods.

"You can't think he doesn't want you. Unless . . . was he pretending to like you?"

"No." Quiet and sure. "No, that was real. But it might cost him a promotion."

"Look, I can't even begin to understand what you've been through and I have no idea what cops can or can't do when it comes to informants. But if nothing else, you should talk to him. Either you two will find a way to start again, or you can move on."

"I can't move on from him, Kel. He's a part of me."

As soon as the words left her mouth, she knew them to be true. Ian was a part of her, knew her at her worst and at her best. He was the other half of her soul.

"Then you'd better talk to him."

"What a terrifying thought," she said with a shaky laugh. "Go find Ian Hawthorn and talk to him. I've spent

years looking over my shoulder in coffee shops and restaurants and farmers' markets, hoping I wouldn't see
him. I only went into the precinct because they'd arrested Isaiah."

"Time to stop running, my dear," Kelly said fondly.
"If nothing else, you'll face this head on and put it behind
you."

"I have to go, Kel. Mom and I are making dinner
together. Turns out she's actually a pretty good cook."

"Like mother, like daughter. Grant and I are talking
about taking a long weekend to drive down to visit this
farm of yours."

"Wyatt can help me feed the chickens," she said.

"You can put all of us to work," Kelly said comfort-
ably. "I'm glad you called me when you came home. I've
missed you."

"I've missed you, too," Riva said.

The call disconnected. She laid her phone on her abdomen and set the porch swing rocking with her foot.
Just outside the porch roofline the sky was darkening to
twilight blue.

She had changed. Ian had too. Could she let down her
guard that last little bit and trust him with her heart?

For the first time in the long days since he'd driven back
from Chicago in a rental car, Ian wasn't walking into
the Block with his calendar full of meetings with HR,
Internal Affairs, and the top brass as they went over . . .
and over . . . and over what had happened in Chicago.
For fun, sometimes they switched to what had happened
in Lancaster, documenting the corruption case, taking
statements, compiling evidence. Ian had driven through
the night to be there for the arrests, carried out in

coordinated early morning raids all over the city, arresting most of the cops at home or just coming off their night shifts. McCormick had taken the honor of putting the cuffs on Kenny, while Ian watched. Kenny had clammed up immediately, but they had months of evidence against him, both from McCormick's work and from Rory Henneman's meticulous records.

Long days sandwiched between early mornings and late nights, all of it fueled by caffeine and takeout food. He found himself daydreaming about dinner at Oasis, fresh vegetables infused with the rich earth of Riva's farm, the calm atmosphere of the dining room. He had every right to track her down. She was, once again, the star witness in a case he'd built. But he made himself wait. Sent Matt Dorchester, who for all he looked like a champion boxer had gone to town on his face, had a great demeanor with witnesses, to go over her statements. Sent a rookie cop to keep the reporters off her property. She had to come to him. For the first time in their crazy relationship, she had to seek him out, for him.

Today his first appointment was with Dorchester, Conn McCormick, and Captain Swarthmore as they prepared for an in-depth interview with a reporter from the *Star Trib*.

"All three of you will have to be there," Swarthmore announced. "A photographer's coming too."

The one person who deserved a big chunk of the credit wouldn't get it. Riva had risked everything to bring down her father. The least Ian could do was to assign protection outside the farm, to keep the media swarm at bay.

"Wow, sir, I feel a migraine coming on," Dorchester

said. Ian snorted. Dorchester's aversion to publicity was well-known in the department.

Swarthmore glared at him. "Don't start with me. I remember what happened after the jewelry-store heist. We practically had to threaten to fail your probationary period to get you in front of the cameras. Man the fuck up."

"A terrible migraine," Dorchester said, unrepentant. "The bright lights of the cameras will make it worse."

"Shut it. You, stand still." McCormick stopped backing away, hands up, a hilarious look for a six-foot-six inch mountain of muscle. "Come on."

"Sir," McCormick said desperately. "I put in my papers yesterday."

"You better get used to bright lights," Dorchester said, studying his fingernails. "You're going to be paparazzi fodder every time you leave Lancaster with Cady."

"That's different," McCormick said stubbornly.

Swarthmore rubbed his forehead with his thumb and blew out his breath. "I have cops who would sell their mothers for time in front of the camera and a bust this big on their records. You three act like you brought me a big steaming pile of dog shit, not a multijurisdictional operation that ended more successfully than anyone dreamed."

Dorchester shrugged and opened his mouth. Swarthmore pointed a finger at him. "Let me guess. You're just doing your job."

Dorchester tilted his head at Ian and McCormick. "The LT brought down the connection to the cartel, and he's up for promotion. McCormick did the undercover work to take down Kenny. They deserve the press."

"Thanks," McCormick and Ian muttered in unison.

Swarthmore wheeled on Ian. "You're a Hawthorn. You'll take this. You'll stand in front of the cameras, in uniform, and be the face of the department for this."

With a typical case, Ian had no trouble dealing with the press. He'd watched his dad do it long enough to be familiar with the drill and could spew stock phrases promoting teamwork and community involvement in his sleep. But through all the questioning, Riva had explained their relationship only in terms of her previous work as a CI.

The privacy couldn't last. Someone, either the ADA or the disgraced cops' defense attorneys, would ask a pointed-enough question, one neither of them could duck without an outright lie. Until then, he would protect her privacy as long as he could. But he had to tell Swarthmore.

"Give us a minute."

McCormick and Dorchester left with a speed Ian would have found funny under any other circumstances.

"What?" Swarthmore said, resigned. "What now?"

"You don't want me to be the public face of this operation."

"Ian," Swarthmore said, already shaking his head. "Don't say it."

He had to say it. For his own peace of mind, for his soul. He had to claim what he'd been unable to claim for so long. He had to claim Riva, everything she'd been, everything she was to him now. "I had a relationship with Riva Henneman while we were in Chicago."

Swarthmore folded his arms and looked at his shoes. "You said it."

Silence. There was nothing else to say.

"What kind of relationship?"

"Physical," Ian said bluntly. "And emotional. I'm in love with her."

That brought Swarthmore's head up. Ian imagined the expression on his face mirrored his captain's; the words blindsided him. But it was true. He'd been falling in love with her for years, ever since he walked through Kaffiend's front door that ill-fated night and she'd looked up at him.

A month. I'll give her a month to come find me. If she doesn't, I'll track her down.

"Fuck me sideways." Swarthmore rubbed his temples, like he was getting Dorchester's "migraine," but the words were without heat. "I told you that could kill your career. What happened to your ambition?"

Ian shrugged. "I'm still ambitious. I just want something more than a career."

Swarthmore grunted. "Her?"

"Her." Maybe claiming Riva as his, now and forever, would cost him the captaincy. Maybe it would cost him his career. He found he didn't care. Jamie would be leaving the navy in a few years. He and his brother would make a formidable team: a former cop and a former SEAL with connections in the business world through Jamie's friend Keenan and the entertainment world through Conn McCormick? They could *own* that market. Eve would help them write the business plan. Until they got their feet under them, he could run the company out of Riva's spare room . . . if she'd let him.

A week after the paper runs the story, I go after her.

Swarthmore leaned against his desk and studied Ian. "I've postponed putting in my papers. When the shit hit the fan, the chief and your dad asked me to stay until the worst of this blew over. I want to be sure the clean-up's done right. You know, some people are arguing that you're the best choice for the job because you'll do whatever it takes to keep this place clean. That happened on my watch."

"We're all responsible," Ian pointed out. "McCormick's the one who linked it all back to Kenny."

Swarthmore tapped his desk. "The buck stops here, kiddo."

"Dad would say it stops with him." He searched his soul for the relentless grind that had once driven his every word, action, deed, and found it humming away in neutral. "Retire when you're ready. If the brass offers me your office, I'll take it. If not, that's fine." Ian took his internal temperature and discovered he actually meant it. He could take the captaincy or leave it. He was, he found, willing to wait for it. "Ever since the diagnosis, I've been trying to make up for what cancer cost me. The navy. A chance at a SEAL team. The kind of blind confidence every twenty-one-year-old kid has in his body, himself. The definition of crazy is doing the same thing and expecting different results. I was crazy. I was the best cop I could be, the best sergeant, the best lieutenant. It was never enough. But she's enough. She's more than enough."

"It's probably love then," Swarthmore said morosely, like he was delivering the worst possible news, like he was sending Ian to the scene of a highway wreck between a livestock truck and a toxic waste tanker.

All Ian knew was that he wanted Riva right now, and forever. He just had to find the right way to tell her.

"Fine, Jesus, *fine*," Swarthmore said. "Tell those two

jokers who report to you they'd better be here at one, in uniform, or they'll answer to me."

"Yes, sir," Ian said. "Anything else?"

"There better not be anything else. Why? You have somewhere to be?"

"I have an appointment with my oncologist to get my bloodwork done."

Relief lightened Swarthmore's expression. "About damn time. Get out of here. Take a couple of days off while you're at it. You look like recycled shit."

An image of Oasis Farm drifted into his mind. The soft folds of hills scored with carefully nurtured furrows, the pond at the bottom, the bright, fresh green color of the branches arching over the gravel road to the gate. All he wanted to do was sprawl out on Riva's porch swing and listen to the birds, the chickens, the breeze in the trees.

Today. I find her today.

But first, he was going to get the damn bloodwork done.

Goal clear in his mind, he strode through the bullpen and shoved open the door to the reception area. A woman stood in front of the reception window. Automatically he registered details, a summer-weight denim wrap skirt, a tank top, and flip-flops, with red-brown-bronze hair tumbled around her shoulders as she spoke to the desk officer through the bulletproof glass. His heart kicked hard when her words registered.

". . . Ian Hawthorn available?"

"Riva," he said. *Riva, Riva, Riva. Here to see him. Saying his name.*

She spun, blinked. "Oh. You're here." Her gaze flicked

to his keys in his hand. "But you're leaving," she said, backpedaling. "I'll come back later."

Nancy, his oncologist's receptionist, had said they'd fit him in anytime. He'd take her at her word. "Now's good. Now's great," he said, thinking fast. Not his office, where she might feel scrutinized. "Let's step outside. It's a nice day."

The parking lot was fairly quiet, a few civilians coming and going with paperwork in hand. Riva caught her hair in one hand and looked at him. Rather than blurting out *you came you came to me*, he fell back on routine. "What can I do for you?"

"Nothing." She gave a little huff of a laugh, then looked at him sidelong. "I . . . I wanted to tell you something. You know how you said you used to dream about saving me? Rescuing me?"

He flushed but kept looking at her. "I remember," he said.

She tucked her hair behind her ear and peered up at him. "I wanted to tell you . . . you already did. The day you arrested me was the day I started to find myself. I literally owe you my life because you couldn't have saved me any more completely than if you'd dragged me from a burning building or pulled me from a wrecked car." She took a deep breath. "That's all. I'm not asking for forever. I just wanted you to know that. You've already saved me."

He looked around, at the fluffy white clouds drifting through an expanse of blue, at the new leaves dancing in the breeze, and felt his heart expand to fill the sky. "Riva, you saved yourself. You were so brave despite being thrust into situations that panic trained undercover cops. You did everything I asked of you, never complained, never backed down, never tried to justify your actions or make excuses. I should have asked. And," he said, warming to his task, "I never should have listened to you that day I came to Oasis. When you told me to leave and I did, you thought I cared more about who you were, what you'd done than I did about who you could be. I let you think you couldn't be someone different, that seven years of growing and learning and working your ass off to make something real and strong and connected didn't matter. That no matter what, I couldn't like you, much less love you."

"Ian, I really don't think—"

"Riva, I'm trying to apologize here." He took a deep breath. "The thing is, I've been head over heels for you since the day I saw you at Kaffiend. Seeing you before trial only made it worse, and it was game over when I saw you with those kids at Oasis. I've been in love with you for the last seven years."

"Ian. I love you too."

"You don't owe me anything, by the way. After the way you came through that door at Sweet Science? Trev would have shot me and Micah right there. You saved my life. We're even. Wait . . . what?"

She smiled up at him, obviously amused and touched by his declaration. "Shut up for five seconds so I can tell you I love you."

His heart stopped, flipped a slow loop in his chest, then started beating again. "I thought that's what you said."

"That's what I said."

"Are you sure?"

"I'm sure."

He searched her gaze and found mirrored there the

certainty he felt deep in his heart. The past was the past, and their future, while uncertain, would hold only the kind of love that made the bad times bearable and the good times the best. "Again, with my name," he whispered. Because that would never get old.

Amusement flashed in her eyes, but she humored him. "Ian. I love you."

"Then I can do this." He cupped her jaw in both hands and leaned down to kiss her, soft and sweet, lingering a little longer than was perhaps appropriate for the civilian parking lot in front of the Block, but he'd waited so long. The simple contact felt so good, so right.

"Am I keeping you from something?" she murmured when he bent his forehead to hers. "I know you're on duty. I just had to . . ."

"I was on my way to find you. After one stop," he said. "My oncologist's office. I haven't gotten a checkup in over two years. I've been avoiding it."

Her strong fingers wrapped around his wrist and stroked his pulse. "Ah," she said. "Been busy?"

"Yup."

"Don't see the point?"

"A little of that."

"Afraid of getting bad news?"

"A little of that too." He squinted at her sideways. "Maybe a lot of that. But that's where I was going. My oncologist's office, to get the blood drawn. Then to Oasis."

She reached up and stroked her thumb across the heated skin before he captured her hand, kissed her wrist, then linked their fingers together. "Want some company?"

This time his heart lodged in his throat, making his voice a little thick when he answered. "That'd be great."

"My motives aren't entirely pure," she said. "The ESCC kids are coming later today. I want to tell them my story. Can you be there?"

He knew what she was offering, and asking. He wouldn't be anywhere else. "Absolutely."

She bent her head and let it rest on his chest. He wove his fingers into her hair, glinting red and russet and a hint of gold in the sunlight, then kissed the top of her head. "Always," he promised, in no more than a whisper. "Always."

Her fingers tightened on his hip. He felt more than heard her response.

Always.

CHAPTER TWENTY-THREE

Ian reversed into a spot at the end of the line of cars in Eye Candy's parking lot and shifted into park. Late afternoon sunlight slanted through the trees lining the lot, dappling the cars backed into the spots nearest the door. You could always tell when a bunch of cops and military types got together. They all reversed into parking spaces to make for quick departures. "Dorchester's here already," he said.

Riva followed his glance to a rugged Jeep and recognized the car as the one driven by the detective who reviewed her statement out at Oasis. "So I know one person," she said.

"Hey." Ian reached across the truck's console and clasped her hand. "Don't be nervous. They're all really nice."

"Let's run through it again."

They'd been on a few proper dates, one of Cady's impromptu concerts, the movies, a couple of quiet dinners, taking it slow so she could get used to the idea of being seen with him. But this was a big step into his world, meeting his brother for the first time. Despite her nerves, she was determined to put her best foot forward. "You've seen pictures of Jamie. He'll be easy to pick out because he just flew in from Virginia Beach and he'll probably still be in uniform."

She nodded. "He's dating Charlie Stannard. She used to play pro basketball and now she's the girls' coach at the high school."

"Right. Jamie's got his two SEAL buddies here. Keenan Parker—"

"He's with Field Energy—"

"And Jack Powell, who's working as a contractor in the Middle East. Keenan's dating Jack's sister."

"Rose," she said, obviously gaining confidence. "Jack's girlfriend is Erin. She's a librarian at Lancaster College."

"Used to be. Jamie says she quit. Jack and Erin came back to catch up with Jamie and pick up some more of Erin's stuff for their place in Istanbul. You know Eve."

"And Matt. He was really nice when he came out to Oasis to go over my statement."

"And Conn McCormick, and Cady."

"Who is actually Queen Maud of the Maud Squad." She drew a deep breath. "Everyone here is either famous or a hero. I wish Eve had taken me up on my offer to cater this party. I'd feel much more comfortable in the kitchen."

"You're a hero," Ian said. "My hero. This is actually a club meeting of People Who Have Tried to Say No to Eve Webber and Failed."

Riva gave a shaky laugh, then startled when a suit-clad figure strode up to Ian's window and rapped a knuckle on the window.

Ian rolled his window down. "Hello, Caleb," he said, resigned.

"Hello, Ian."

Caleb sounded far more chipper than Ian did. Based on his loosened tie, he'd probably just dismantled a rookie cop's testimony and left the kid humiliated on the stand. "What are you doing here?" Ian said.

Caleb rested a forearm on the roof of the truck and leaned in the window. "Nice to see you too. Eve invited me. Lions lying down with lambs, swords into plough-shares and all that," the man said. His gaze flicked to Riva. Ian had no doubt Caleb knew exactly who Riva was, and everything about their past history he could pick up from his web of connections in politics, community organizations, and the legal community, but Riva didn't know Caleb.

"Riva, this is Caleb Webber, one of the city's fore-most defense attorneys."

"You managed to do that without choking, Ian. A pleasure to meet you, Ms. Henneman," Caleb said formally. "You're doing great work for the ESCC. Eve's been talking up Oasis. I'm going to get out there for dinner one night soon."

Riva's eyebrows lifted. "You're Eve's brother. It's nice to finally meet you," she said.

"Don't rush to judgment," Ian said, unable to help himself.

Caleb smiled a wide, easy smile. "Ian and I go way back," he said. "High school, and then he nearly got my sister killed by putting an undercover cop in her bar without her knowledge or consent."

"That seems unlikely," Riva said, frowning.

"It's true, except for nearly getting her killed," Ian added, managing to sound bored.

In the side mirror he saw Jo strolling toward his car. She rapped twice on the rear window and said, "Move along, counselor, or I'll run you in for loitering."

Still leaning on Ian's open window, he cast his inscrutable gaze on Jo. "Detective Sorenson. Always a pleasure."

Jo made a shooing gesture with her hand. Caleb held up one big basketball-sized palm and turned his attention back to Riva. "Do you have a minute? Eve and I have been meaning to talk to you about the ESCC's next dinner dance fundraiser. We'd like to showcase what the kids are learning at Oasis, if they're up for the challenge."

Ian felt Riva's breathing halt for just a moment. After just a few weeks with Riva, he knew what that kind of platform could do for Lancaster's fledging urban garden programs. "They're ready." She unbuckled her seat belt. "Do you have a date? The season will determine what we serve."

"Eve's in charge of all of that." Caleb tilted his head toward the door. "Let's talk."

She smiled at Ian. "See you inside?"

Ian leaned over and gave her a quick kiss. Riva slid out of the truck, smoothed down her skirt, and followed Caleb to the door he courteously opened for her, into Eye Candy. Just like that, she was walking into the building as a partner.

"Every time I think he's just a smart-mouthed asshole, he goes and proves me wrong," Ian said.

Jo was still standing by his door, one hand on her service weapon, the other on her hip. "He's a man of contradictions."

Ian stepped out of the truck. "You don't like him," he said as he closed the door and clicked the locks.

"Not liking him hasn't stopped me from sleeping with him."

Ian tripped over the parking curb in front of his truck. "What?" he said, steadying himself on the hood of Dorchester's Jeep. "What did you say?"

"You heard me."

"No, I didn't, because you said you were sleeping with Caleb Webber. Eve's brother? The defense attorney? That guy?"

"See? You did hear me."

"Since when?"

"Since around the time Matt wrapped up the case with Eve."

"That was eight months ago!" He stared at her. Jo had always played her cards close to her chest, but this was insane. "You're dating Caleb?"

"Did I say I was dating him?"

The penny dropped. No way would Joanna Sorenson, third generation LPD, fall for a defense attorney. He started to laugh. "He's your booty call. Jesus. Oh, to be a fly on the wall when that negotiation happened."

She threw him a glare. He sobered up. "Congratulations?"

"Asshole."

"Jo, seriously, I'm speechless."

"That's kind of the deal. No talking."

Ian turned a bark of laughter into a cough. "So, what's the problem?"

"He wants to start talking."

"Don't tell me anything more."

"Pervert," Jo said, freezing him with a look. "Not that kind of talking. Like, on a date. He wants to date me."

"Wow. And I thought dating a CI was bad. Dating the attorney who regularly wins the department's Most Hated award . . . that's worse."

"I'm not going to do it."

Ian sobered instantly. "Of course you're not going to do it."

"Except he says he'll cut me off if I don't."

"Jo, what part of *don't tell me anything more* didn't you understand?" Unable to resist asking, he said, "What did you say to that?"

"I said we'll continue exactly as we are," Jo said, so sweetly all the hair stood up on the back of Ian's neck. She saved that tone of voice for really special occasions, like when she was about to demolish a cop demonstrating terminal stupidity or make an intractable witness cry. "I'd like to see him try to stop."

"Irresistible force, meet immovable object," Ian said, laughing.

They walked through the door, past the big wooden bar where Matt Dorchester had mixed cocktails and protected Eve Webber, down the hallway to the brick-paved courtyard Eve had opened late last fall. White fairy lights dangled from the cast-iron railings, and soft music played from the speakers set into the corners. Ivy growing around the fencing provided a measure of privacy. Everyone else was there, Keenan and Rose, Jack and Erin, Jamie—fresh off the plane and still in his cammies—and Charlie. Jack finished up a story that made the women laugh and Keenan raise his voice in protest, only to be drowned out by Jamie's "That's exactly how it happened!" Jo was steadfastly not looking at Caleb, who was deep in conversation with Riva and Eve. Natalie was behind the smaller outdoor bar, teaching Chris, Cady's manager, to make mojitos while Cady took a picture while offering commentary from the other side of the bar.

McCormick walked over to Ian and handed him a beer. "Posting to social media," McCormick said at Ian's elbow. "I don't like that everyone and his uncle knows where she is all the time, but it's part of the game these days."

"You're not going to be bored," Dorchester said. "When do you leave town?"

"Cady's got an album ready to pitch to her management at the label," he said. "We fly out next week."

"Good luck," Dorchester said seriously. He held out his hand and Conn shook it. "Have fun."

"I'm on it," Conn said.

Riva gave Caleb an excited nod and a huge smile, then broke away. "Ian," she called, hurrying around the tables to Ian's side. "Ian!"

He'd never get tired of hearing his name on her lips or seeing her all but vibrating with excitement and happiness. "Good news?" he asked.

"Very good. The board wants to really personalize the annual fundraising campaign. Eve's getting more involved, and she's got tons of ideas to show off the various programs. It's an amazing opportunity for the kids, for the farm, for the urban garden movement."

Her eyes were gleaming, and she was looking around the patio not like a suspect or a criminal but like a person who belonged exactly where she was. He pulled her close and kissed the top of her head. "Congratulations. Let's get you a drink and start introducing you."

"I'm ready," she said. "Ian. I'm really ready."

"Me, too." He kissed her again, this time on the lips, soft and sweet and without a care for who was watching or what they thought. Maybe he'd be a cop. Maybe he'd run a global security company. He'd always be Riva's.

Always.